The endgame track

THE ENDGAME TRACK

Copyright © 2026 by Brittany Wilson

All rights reserved. No part of this book may be reproduced in any form or by any electronic or mechanical means, including information storage and retrieval systems, without written permission from the author, except for the use of brief quotations in a book review.

This novel is entirely a work of fiction. The names, characters, organizations, businesses, places, events, and incidents portrayed in it are either the work of the author's imagination or used fictitiously. Any resemblance to actual persons, living or dead, events or localities is entirely coincidental.

The Endgame Track is a steamy romance with strong language and mature themes. It is the third book in The Hookup Type series. For a full list of content warnings, please visit the author's website.

Proofreading by Sadie @DotTheIEdit

Character Art by Nina @croquith

Cover Illustration by Layla @designwithlayla

ISBN-13 (paperback): 979-8-9882216-6-1

ISBN-13 (eBook): 979-8-9882216-7-8

*To anyone who has lost themselves once or twice.
Trust that you'll find your way back, and believe that it can get even better.*

Prologue

MACI

July 2018

When I was at Bowling Green State University, my room-mate Katie and I would binge-watch TV shows with fabulous characters living in New York City.

My apartment must have been in a different New York City.

I was sweating my ass off in a backless dress and heels, praying I didn't melt into the unpolished wood floor. My air conditioning wasn't working, my neighbors were having a rager downstairs, and I was tired of the pizza smell that floated in from the tiny family-owned restaurant below.

It was magical, chasing my dreams. This had to be the part I laughed at when I finally landed my university job and could afford to live in a place where I couldn't touch all four walls at the same time.

My phone buzzed on top of my dresser, and a wave of relief washed over my sweaty forehead. For a moment, I thought I had lost my phone among the piles of clothes on my bed. My friend Jared was probably waiting downstairs, and I was running late.

I propped it up against the mirror to answer the video call. "Hey! I'm almost ready—"

"Hey."

I froze at the sound of Jaxon's voice, ignoring the shock factor that came with hearing my boyfriend instead of the guy who was minutes away from picking me up.

"Did you just get home?" I asked, hoping he hadn't heard past "Hey!"

"Yeah." He let out a hefty sigh and confirmed my hope. "The traffic today was horrible."

I rolled my eyes. "Well, it's Friday."

He exhaled loudly through his nose, adjusting his tone before he spoke again. "What are you up to?"

Heat rose to my cheeks as I secured the clasp on the watch that Jaxon sent me for Christmas. "I'm getting ready to head out in like five. Jared invited me to that mixer tonight since Spencer can't go. It's for his job, but the drink tickets and rooftop bar were pretty convincing."

While the drinks and the event's setting helped, Jared hardly needed to convince me. I was desperate to do something that didn't involve the crowded halls of NYU or a classroom. I had been working like crazy alongside a handful of professors, all while keeping up with a year-long Master's program that the university paid for as long as I was enrolled in my internship.

It would all be worth it. I'd have the credentials necessary to start applying for university positions, and I could move out of New York. I had no problems with the state, but once my internship ended, there was nothing for me here. Jared and Spencer were moving back to the Midwest, where my best friend Katie and her boyfriend Connor currently lived.

Jaxon was in California, and I was ready for this long-distance bullshit to be over.

"Yeah, Jared mentioned he was going to ask you," Jaxon said, staring at his work phone. "I didn't realize it was tonight." He placed it down on his bed and stared into the screen. "So, I've only got five minutes, huh?"

His tone was playful, but it snapped a line in me that was already strained. "Well, you said you'd call an hour ago, so yeah, five minutes is all I have. Four now, actually."

"Jared's never on time," he murmured. "Don't do that."

"I'm not doing anything. Just repeating what you told me this morning," I said dryly.

Jaxon looked off to the side. "I asked Helen to tell you this morning—"

"Yes, and when I spoke to Helen for the third time this week, I asked her to remind you about the time change," I snapped, searching for Jared's headlights on the street so I wouldn't have to have this conversation.

"Mace, I forget sometimes. I'm sorry."

"We've been working with these time zones for over a year, Jaxon." The uncomfortable pressure started to build in my chest. There was only one person in my life who got the time zone excuse, and that was my brother Chase, who was living in Europe with his husband, Trey. "A text works too, you know. I didn't realize texting worked differently in California than it does in New York."

Jaxon pulled off his shirt and turned around to throw it in the hamper. "I'll just call you tomorrow."

"Yeah, that's fine, Jax," I said through a breathy laugh. "Just walk away like you always do whenever we have this fight."

The muscles in his back tensed, and I hated how much I wanted to reach through the screen and run my fingers down it. When he peered back at me with a hardened green gaze, I knew it was his turn to snap.

"What other fight is there?" he prompted angrily, his voice getting louder. "I tell you a time I think I'll be done, and when I don't call, you get pissed. Or you tell me the next time you're gonna fly out here, and when you cancel because of a class or a seminar, I get pissed. It's the same shit."

I scoffed. "Yes, because I'm the only one who can travel for us to work."

"I can't take the time." He leaned his hands against the mattress. "You know that."

"Yes, you can't take the time to come see me," I said with a sarcastic grin. "You've made that *incredibly* clear."

"You're the one who makes it sound like that. Not me. That's not what I said."

"You don't have to say it, Jaxon. I know your work has to come before me right now, and that's okay."

"Clearly, it isn't. You tell me it's okay, and then we end up having the same conversation over and over again." His eyes wandered off to the side, and he took a deep breath. "You told me you were coming here next weekend."

"And I have to cover a class," I explained calmly. "It's my professor's section and—"

"It's always something."

"So you don't have to move around opportunities, but I do?"

As the words left my mouth, my stomach sank. Before answering the phone, I was excited for tonight. Yet here I was, refilling my cup with a different kind of stress that I was tired of emptying.

"I can't move around the fact that my dad is stepping down," he stated.

Another fire lit inside me, but I chose to walk around it. I didn't need to be reminded why Jaxon was living on the West Coast.

"Look," I said, taking a deep breath before I continued. "In a few months, when you're back in Charlotte working to open the East Coast branch—"

Jaxon's jaw ticked, and I had my answer. He swallowed, unable to look back at the screen.

"That's where this is coming from, isn't it?" The tears returned to their homes in the corners of my eyes. I kept them there, refusing to let them out. "You're not coming back in a few months."

"My dad is moving back to Charlotte," he said, unbothered by his admission. "I'm not sure how long he'll be there, and I have to run things out here until he decides. He's earned that."

I closed my eyes in an attempt to regain my composure. "Why didn't you tell me?"

"Because I knew it would make you upset. And with what little time I get to talk to you, I didn't want to spend it fighting." He dragged his hands down his face, and when he looked up, I noticed the bags under his eyes and the glossy tint that appeared when he was thinking through something. "I'm *tired*, baby. I'm tired of fighting with you through a phone screen."

"I know. I'm tired, too," I agreed weakly. "Maybe I can ask Peter to cover for me next weekend. I can fly out there, and we can talk about this in person."

"I love you, Mace."

My heart sank. "I love you, too."

"But I—" His voice grew raspy, and I braced myself for what was coming next. "Baby, I just don't know if it's enough anymore."

"You don't mean that," I argued. "You can't call me baby and expect me to think you mean it."

"I do." His green eyes met mine, as if both of us needed convincing instead of just me. "Look at how last year went. We saw each other, what, seven times? The seventh time was a fluke. Is this really what you want for the next few years? The fighting, the back and forth, and a boyfriend who doesn't have time?"

"Jax, I know it's been hard, but—" I couldn't take it anymore. The tears won, and I bit my lip to keep from falling apart. "Jaxon, I love you."

"And I love you. But if you come out here, there's no way I'll be able to end this." He let out a shaky breath. "I won't be able to do it, and we can't keep going like this."

I closed my eyes. "Sounds like you've already made up your mind."

"I don't see how anything is going to change, Maci." I tried not to recoil at the sound of my full name instead of "Mace" or any other term of endearment. It sounded like a death sentence. "I'm sorry, but this is for the best."

There were a few exchanges that went exactly as portrayed in the movies. I begged him not to do this, and he assured me we were making the right decision. He told me he loved me and that he wanted to stay in touch. I told him we could get through this, and that tons of people had gotten through the long-distance part of their relationship. He told me he couldn't keep me waiting for a life he couldn't plan.

I gave him reasons to keep going, and he gave me reasons why we couldn't try. This wasn't the part I laughed at, and when Jared picked me up ten minutes past when he said he would, he saw right through my tear-stained expression and parked the car.

"Do you need a song?" he offered, his blue eyes softening behind his long blond locks. Last week, I had teased him about becoming a boy band member. He told me how Spencer loved to have something to grab at night, and that shut me up immediately.

I shook my head, unable to speak in case I had a complete breakdown in his passenger seat.

"It's impossible to be sad while listening to this song," he assured me, turning up the music. He started down the street as "Unwritten" by Natasha Bedingfield blared through his speakers.

We sang as loud as we could, and it wasn't until I got about halfway through the chorus that my voice cracked, and I had to stare out the window so Jared wouldn't see me cry.

Like the true friend he was, he squeezed my hand before grasping my shoulder. He didn't ask questions, and he didn't give me shit. He let me have a few sobs before he said, "J can be an idiot sometimes, Mace. But remember"—he shot me a comforting smile—"endgame."

I played the supportive best girlfriend at Jared's work event, and when it was time to leave, we met Spencer at a bar downtown. It had been exactly four hours since my breakup with Jaxon, and my phone never felt so dry. I checked it one last time before I ordered enough shots for me to forget—one shot for every letter in the word *endgame*.

Chapter One

MACI

September 2018

"You need to get your ass here *now*," Jared whisper-yelled into the phone. "Spencer is running out of ways to distract Katie from coming downstairs."

I turned on my blinker and veered off the highway. The exit to Connor and Katie's house was under construction, and it wasn't my fault that the speed limit was still fifty even though the workers were clearly off duty.

"What do you want me to do, Jared? Roll right through the barriers and fly there? I am five minutes away," I lied, knowing I had at least ten.

"You said that fifteen minutes ago," he snapped. I laughed at his ability to keep his voice down even though his stress seeped through the speaker. "You have ten minutes. I'm serious."

As if the best-friend gods heard my silent plea, another lane opened, allowing a steady stream of cars to pass the truck holding up traffic.

"I can do ten," I said. "I'll see you soon."

Connor and Katie's house sat on a quiet street on the outskirts of Chicago. It was far enough away from the city to avoid the hectic hustle and bustle, but close enough for Katie to commute to the hospital. It was an adorable bungalow, and I hated how it was the first time I was seeing it since they bought it a few months ago.

Familiar cars lined the street, and I ignored the pull in my chest when Jaxon's gray Jeep wasn't one of them. Jared mentioned he was invited, but I knew he wouldn't show. He wasn't answering my calls or opening my text messages, so I was pretty damn confident he wasn't responding to invitations that required him in the Midwest.

Spencer pulled me into an open corner in the living room just in time for me to witness the event of the year. Connor had just finished up a speech he had practiced at least twenty-five times, and Katie was staring down at him with her hand over her mouth.

Connor peered up at her with a giant grin. "Katie, will you marry me?"

"Of course I will," Katie sobbed, barely allowing Connor to stand up before she kissed him.

I wiped away my own tears and clapped along with the rest of the crowd. Katie's parents whistled and hollered with Connor's from the couches, and Katie's cousins cheered alongside Connor's brothers. It was a beautiful montage of close friends and family, and the newly engaged couple couldn't have been happier.

"Maci!" Katie squealed, locating me in the corner. She flew right past Jared's open arms, and I burst into hysterics.

"Damn!" Jared spun around and pulled Spencer closer. "All the work we did to make sure she was here on time to see it, and *nothing*?"

Katie waved a hand in his direction before throwing her arms around my neck. I moved slowly down the list of reasons for me to cry on her shoulder, and when she hugged me tighter, I knew our silent conversation had started.

She said she was sorry to hear about Jaxon and heartbroken to learn he was still in California. She thanked me for coming all this way for this exact moment, even though she was eager to hear about the interview for the job I had right before this.

I told her I couldn't be happier for her and Connor, assuring her I wouldn't miss this for the world. She pulled away slowly, and when her eyes met mine, I smiled and nodded.

"You got the job?" Her eager question sounded more like a statement.

"I got the job," I echoed softly, not wanting to take any of her spotlight.

A fresh set of tears formed in the corners of her eyes.

"Do you know where you're going to live yet?" Spencer asked. She and Jared had leaned in closer to get within earshot of what I thought was our private conversation.

"No idea," I admitted. "Probably some fixer-upper since I'll be a fresh grad with student loans."

"Mhm," Katie hummed disapprovingly.

Jared held out his hand for me to shake. "You can be my first client." His smile slowly creased his cheeks, showing off his contagious dimples.

I eyed him playfully. "You got the business loan."

"He got the business loan!" Spencer exclaimed, sending all of us into another fit of hugs and excitement.

"I'm opening my contracting business," Jared stated proudly. "I officially have a disappointed father and student loans that I won't be using my degree to pay off."

"I'm so proud," Spencer gushed.

"I'll be a client of yours for years," I warned him. "There's no way I can afford an entire home demo right away."

Jared shrugged. "No rush. I'll consider it our five-year plan."

I loved the sound of that—a five-year plan—a fresh state, a fresh career, and a fresh start.

Soon after Jared and I exchanged an official handshake, Connor joined our small group in the corner. I struggled to fight off more emotions as I hugged my best friend's future husband.

Twenty minutes ago, I had an ache in my chest given to me by the man I was still in love with. In less than twenty-four hours, I'd be signing the official offer letter from the University of Chicago, and in a few weeks, I'd be moving to my new home.

Chapter Two

Jaxon

September 2018

There was one thing I hated about living in California. The heat never paired well with the suits and dress shirts I had to wear for work, and a room full of excited people wasn't helping.

Maybe it was me. Maybe the air wasn't thick, and the tightness in my chest came with being nervous. I was craving the touch that always calmed me down, the one that brought me back to earth when I drifted too far into my headspace.

I craved *everything* about that touch, but it wasn't mine to crave anymore. Only mine to miss.

My phone buzzed on the table, the light bright against the black tablecloth. My mom snuck a peek from the seat next to me before looking back at my dad, who was standing at the front of the room behind a Hayes Sports and Entertainment embellished podium. It was the first time my family had been together in months, and the first time my mom had been on the West Coast in years.

Dad held up his glass of champagne, doing a quick scan of the room, which was full of investors, potential sponsors, and clients. "I could not be more honored or—" He looked up at the ceiling to regain his composure.

When he looked back at me with glossy eyes, I wiped the smirk off my face. My older brother Alex and I took bets on which one of our parents would cry first. He chose Mom, and I chose Dad. Reed Hayes was about to win me fifty bucks.

Dad's suspicious glare lingered between me and Alex. "You guys took bets on this, didn't you?"

The room burst into a comfortable round of laughter.

"No!" Alex exclaimed, feeding into the crowd around us.

Dad shook his head. "Jaxon, I love you, Son. I cannot wait to see what you do with this company. We've talked about this day for a long time, and I couldn't be more proud of you." He raised his glass again. "To Jaxon Hayes, the new CEO of Hayes Sports and Entertainment!"

I clapped along with the rest of the room as it exploded into applause, cheers, and commotion. I bent down to kiss Mom on the cheek before I stood up and met Dad at the podium. He pulled me in for a hug, and I peered out into the crowd, making sure I acknowledged every table that showed up—every member of Dad's staff and every familiar face that had been greeting me in his office since I was a kid.

Finally, my eyes landed on the smaller table in the front where Alex and Bella stood proudly with their daughter, Evie. Alex held her against his chest while Bella clapped above her head. He waved her little hand in my direction, and I almost melted into the floor. She was only two months old, but I lost count of how many times she pulled on my heartstrings. I loved that little girl, and when I made eye contact with my mom, I almost lost it.

It was the moment I daydreamed about in my boring undergrad classes, just waiting to take over my dad's legacy and our family business. Tonight was everything I wanted. It was also the first night I ever lied to my mom.

There was an empty seat at the table, and the girl it was reserved for wasn't coming. I didn't have it in me to dim any more of the light that remained in my mom's eyes. I didn't have the heart to tell her that I ended it with the girl we both thought I would marry. I was still reminding myself that it was the right thing to do, but I didn't have the words for why I had to let her go in the first place.

The next day, my name replaced Dad's on his office door. My parents flew back to North Carolina, and I waited until they landed to tell them about Maci. Mom checked on me every hour to see how I was doing, while Bella sent me a rant I didn't feel like reading. Alex offered his support if I needed anything, and Dad did the same. In less than forty-eight hours, I accomplished being my family's proudest moment and their worst disappointment.

It was shameful, really, being that talented.

My phone buzzed on my desk, lighting up the darkness around me. The silence grew louder with every vibration, and I finally gave in to the messages coming through.

Connor

> Popped the question an hour ago. Hope you're good, man.

Underneath Connor's text was a picture of Katie's hand with a diamond engagement ring. I smiled weakly at the evidence of an event I was invited to a few weeks ago. I never responded to Connor's text, but I liked the image to let him know I'd seen it.

Bryson

> Will you be home next weekend?

> Or are you already at Connor's?

Bryson Kennedy. We hadn't spoken since he started his job at the financial firm in New York. He was busy, and I was busy. He was the only human on the planet who matched my schedule and the only friend I had left who needed an update. I sent him a photo of the door with my name and new title.

Jaxon

I couldn't go to Connor's.

Bryson:

My man!!!!

Fuck yeah. Next time you come to see Maci, we should meet up.

My thumbs hovered over the keypad. As I was about to start typing, I got a text from Jared. It was a giant selfie, with Jared holding the phone and everyone squeezed in behind him. Connor and Katie were at the center, with Spencer's arms wrapped around Katie's shoulders. I recognized Connor's parents, and then right beside Connor was a pair of blue eyes and a gorgeous smile.

Jared

Tell your Dad thank you for the reference! I GOT THE LOAN!

My smile grew slightly, and I texted Jared back to congratulate him. His business was finally happening. There was no one I could think of who was more deserving, and I wouldn't be there to watch it all come together.

I pulled up my text thread with Bryson and told him that Maci and I had broken up. I deactivated my social media accounts and replaced my personal pages with the business credentials Dad's PR team left me. It was like ripping off a bandage from a wound I gave myself. It was time for it to heal and scar over, with the hope that one day, I would barely be able to see it.

When Bryson texted back to ask if I would rather go to Vegas instead, I didn't respond. My messages sat unanswered in my inbox for two weeks before random ones trickled in.

Jared sent Marvel memes and updates for his shop. He sent me a link to his website and a photo of Spencer's engagement ring after he proposed.

Bryson followed up about Vegas and asked if I was attending Connor and Katie's wedding.

Connor sent a Save-the-Date for next September, followed by an invitation to the wedding a few months later. I told him I wouldn't be able to make it, and when Jared tried to say that it fell under his duty as best man to ensure I was there, I told him I'd be traveling for work.

Eventually, without me even realizing it, the texts stopped altogether.

Chapter Three

MACI

An hour after the wedding pictures ended, I walked down the aisle with Jared Foster. He threatened to make me laugh before we had to separate at the altar, and I offered to trip him with my strappy sandal. It was a totally normal interaction between two people who fought like siblings at least three times a week. I would come up with ideas for my charming two-story house on a corner lot, and Jared would deliver hateful phrases like "load-bearing wall" or "there's a gas line there, and we can't knock that wall down either."

Again, *normal* interactions.

Because I wasn't ready to cry again, I averted my gaze from Connor and took my place as maid of honor. We had just wrapped up a few hours of photos and some light pregaming on the party bus, but I knew a picture-perfect reaction was coming. Connor would watch my best friend walking down the aisle, and he would cry like it was the first time he was seeing her.

Once the rest of the wedding party was in their place, the music picked up, and the crowd stood. Katie glided flawlessly through the rows of guests, looking like a goddess in a strapless gown, flowing veil, and a sweetheart neckline that made her boobs look fantastic. I looked over my shoulder at Spencer, who wore the same adoring smile.

"If Jared doesn't let a few tears slip like Connor is doing when I walk down the aisle, I'm kicking him," Spencer murmured.

I bit my lip to keep from laughing and adjusted my posture for the vows. The ceremony was elegant and quick, and after the grand entrance of Mr. and Mrs. Jenson and a three-course dinner, I joined the rest of the bridal party at the open bar.

It wasn't until the first slow song that I remembered my date. In my defense, Derek sort of invited himself. I was prepared to ride solo and was completely caught off guard when Derek casually congratulated Katie and Connor, claiming he had noticed the wedding invitation on the fridge. Katie sank the ship before I could even evacuate.

"You should come!" she had insisted. "Once her maid of honor duties are over, Maci will be ready to drink and dance the night away."

I stared at Derek in his crisp navy dress pants and a white button-down shirt. He looked amazing, drawing the eyes of every woman around us and pulling me closer with his contagious grin. His blue eyes matched his pants, and a cloud of cologne surrounded me as he invited me onto the dance floor. I rested my hand on his broad shoulder, swaying to the steady beat of a slow country song I recognized but couldn't remember the name of. All I could focus on was my next cranberry and vodka.

"You look beautiful," Derek said.

I forced myself to meet his gaze. "Thank you."

He chuckled softly at my response, causing me to smile. "There it is."

We drifted into a comfortable silence for the rest of the song. That was my favorite part about Derek. He never asked for more and didn't expect anything beyond what I offered.

He was content with what we had, and casual company was all I could invest in right now.

My smile faltered when the next song began to play. "All My Life" by K-Ci & JoJo forced me to step away from Derek as the piano introduction overwhelmed the sound system. I was reminded of another wedding, with another man in a much darker suit.

I was reminded of *him*.

Derek didn't follow me to the bar. I mentioned having to use the restroom, but he wouldn't question that I was heading in another direction. Derek never asked questions.

A familiar voice came from behind me. "Hiding?"

I turned around and stared into the golden-brown eyes of Bryson Kennedy—an old friend, an old fling, and a reflection of a version of myself I didn't recognize anymore. He looked . . . *annoyingly* handsome. Time had made him even more attractive, accentuating his jawline and the broadness of his chest. Four years ago, I drooled over his college fuckboy appearance. Now, he was a grown man carrying the same swagger he had when we were at Bowling Green State University. He was a fuckman.

Fuckman? I'd have to run that by Katie and coin it someday.

"Who would I be hiding from? I don't have any bullets I'm dodging. Can you say the same?"

I ordered my drink, leaning my elbows on the counter as Bryson joined me at the bar. I raised a suspicious brow, prompting the smile that pulled me in the first night we met. He ordered a whiskey on the rocks and mimicked my body language, leading with his exposed forearms.

"How many women are shooting at you right now?" I asked. Half of me was joking. The other half of me experienced too many morning-afters with Bryson Kennedy.

He cocked his head. "I don't follow."

I rolled my eyes and laughed. "Just how many women have you slept with at this wedding?"

"Would've been tied with you"—he scanned the room behind him—"but he's not here."

He's not here. My stomach dropped, and the pressure in my chest continued to build. "I don't want to hear about him."

"The last I heard—"

"Bryson," I warned.

He nodded behind me, and I followed his gaze. If there was one thing Bryson hated, it was an awkward conversation. "Is that your boyfriend over there?"

I watched Derek strike up a conversation with Jared and Spencer. "Nah. He's a guy I've been seeing for a few months."

"How many months?"

"Thirteen?" I winced, hoping a sip of my drink would wash away the terrible taste in my mouth.

"Damn, girl! Is he the current Fun Dip?" A warm wave of nostalgia washed over me, and an impressed Bryson kept the current coming. "J told me about your candy thing a while ago. It's clever. I was just too cool at twenty-two to tell you that."

"Yeah," I scoffed. "You were something."

"That's why you're smiling."

I pursed my lips, racking my brain for something smart to say back. Bryson was like that fine line on a night out. You could ride the playful buzz or take one more sip and risk having a hangover.

His eyes softened. "You seem . . ."

It was nice to see I wasn't the only one without words. "So do you."

"I was going to say different."

"So do you," I repeated, a thick set of word vomit forming on my tongue. "I like to credit my difference to two fuckboys I met in college. One of them was too good at the title, and the other broke my heart. What about you?"

Bryson eyed me cautiously. "Elle."

"Jared's sister?" I exclaimed.

He couldn't hide his smirk. "I know. I thought *you* were bad at giving me shit. But that girl . . . when I moved to New York, it was over. She didn't trust me, and I didn't blame her. Maybe it's just not in my nature to settle down."

"Bryson Kennedy"—I shook my head and smiled—"has a girl that got away. I forgot you were in New York. Are you still there?"

There was an unexpected heat in his gaze that wasn't there before. He took another sip of his drink and leaned in a little closer. "For now."

We locked eyes for a moment, and all of the memories from my junior year in college flashed before me. Bryson opened his mouth to speak again, but the DJ's voice came over the loudspeaker. He was requesting couples to the dance floor, and when Jared dragged a laughing Spencer to a spot in the front, I was reminded of everything we still had to look forward to.

I stood with Bryson on the sidelines as we watched Katie and Connor dance in the middle of their friends and family. Next year we'd be celebrating Jared and Spencer, and who knew what other things would happen in between. Our lives were changing, and I was moving in a direction I felt good about.

"Yeah," I whispered, trying to hold back a tearful smile. "For now."

Chapter Four

JAXON

"IT'S HAPPENING, J! I'VE been through this before, and I don't remember shit about it!" Alex's frantic yell boomed through the speakers in my Jeep.

I stepped on the gas and merged into the far left lane. It would be a bitch to get back over in a few exits, but I couldn't deal with the slow-moving traffic.

"*Breathe*, Alex," I stressed. "I'm fifteen minutes away. Bella is going to be fine, and pretty soon Evie will be a kick-ass big sister."

"Fuck, I forgot about Evie," he murmured.

"Damn. Already no love for the firstborn."

"No, you asshole," Alex said, sounding more like himself. "Evie needs to be picked up from daycare in like two hours."

"I got it." I started the dreadful merging process off the highway, ignoring the blaring horns and honks. "Let me chill with you for about an hour and then I'll head toward your place and pick up Evie."

"You've never driven with her before."

I tried not to be offended by the hesitation in his voice. "Okay . . . does she prefer minivans over Jeeps? Not seeing the problem here."

"I do *not* drive a minivan."

"You traded in your Mustang for a third-row SUV." I laughed. "That's basically the same thing."

As I listened to Alex go on and on about the selling points of his new dad car, I made my way onto the exit ramp and down the road to the hospital. I found parking fairly quickly and took the elevator up to labor and delivery.

Alex met me in the waiting room with an update from the doctors.

"She's still got some time left until she can start pushing," he said quickly, running a nervous hand through his hair.

I patted him reassuringly on the shoulder. "I already called Mom and did the overview for you. She's on her way to the airport now with Dad."

"J, you know she shouldn't be—"

"You try telling Mom she can't meet her second grand-child." I held out my hand. "Now give me your minivan keys so I can go get my niece."

When I walked into Evie's classroom, she was sitting on a rug with six other miniature humans, all of them clapping to a song sung by a happy woman in a bright pink shirt. Even though she was completely outnumbered, she didn't look terrified at all. Bella left me alone once with Evie for an hour so she could go to a spin class, and I lasted fifteen minutes before I called my mom.

I made a mental note to remind Alex to give this teacher a hefty Christmas gift.

Evie's teacher checked my ID to make sure I matched the information from the front office before sending us on our way. I strapped Evie into her car seat, mimicking the way Alex checked the tightness of the harness and the placement of the buckle. Then, I drove five miles under the speed limit and made turns like I had fifty glass vases in my trunk.

How the fuck did parents drive with their kids in the car? Alex and Bella lived ten minutes down the road from Evie's daycare, and it was the longest car ride of my life.

I spent Evie's entire meal of cereal and strawberries in a panic as she put handfuls of tiny pieces into her mouth. She'd widen her bright blue eyes and laugh uncontrollably while I stared back at her. My options were to watch her and hope she didn't choke or look away and hope she wasn't choking.

How the fuck did parents feed their kids? Why did they make a requirement for living so hard to watch? If I were still here in the morning, she'd be getting popsicles and pudding for breakfast. Safe, dairy-free, and delicious. I saw no flaws.

"Muh, pwease." Evie smiled and banged her tiny hands on the tray table.

I smirked. "Don't look at me like that, man."

She giggled as I poured more cereal onto her tray. Right as her next handful went into her mouth, my phone rang on the counter behind me.

It was a FaceTime from Alex. He smiled into the phone before shifting the camera to Bella. She shared the same blissful expression, turning her attention from the tiny bundle in her arms to the phone screen. "Hey, Jax," she whispered.

"Hey, mama," I said in my best baby voice, turning the camera to Evie. "Hey, mama."

Evie waved as Bella said, "Are you ready to meet your new niece?" A tiny face took up the screen. "Meet Peyton. Peyton May Hayes."

"Peyton May Hayes," I echoed softly. She was beautiful—blonde hair, a tiny nose, and pouty lips.

"And her eyes look just like Evie's when she was born," Alex added.

"I love her already. Congratulations, you guys."

"Mom and Dad will land later tonight and get a cab to the house," Alex explained. "I wasn't sure if you had to get back to the office tomorrow, so don't feel like you have to stay."

Tomorrow's schedule weighed on my chest. I had two conference calls before noon and a signing at two. I had no choice but to go into the office.

"Yeah, okay." I ran a hand through my hair. "I love you, guys."

"We love you too, J. Kiss Evie for us, and I'll call you tomorrow."

I placed my phone on the counter and planted a kiss in Evie's tiny blonde curls.

"Peyton May Hayes," I said with a sigh. It would be nice to hear the name Peyton without thinking of *One Tree Hill* and red bullets.

Evie's dimples dug into her cheeks.

I smiled weakly back. "Just another blue-eyed girl tugging on my heartstrings, Evie."

Chapter Five

MACI

July 2020

Living through a pandemic taught me three things. One: People can really suck sometimes, regardless of their age. Two: Schools are essential for our country to thrive. And three: Don't schedule projects for your fixer-upper when everyone is bored and working from home.

After staring at my unfinished kitchen and disheveled living room for almost an hour, I called Katie. Thirty minutes later, we were masked up and wandering the aisles of Target, begging for any kind of distraction to appear. Things were picked over since everyone was getting home delivery and bulk pickup, but it served the purpose of getting me out of the house.

"This was so much more fun when my ankles weren't swollen," Katie whined. She waddled next to me in a pair of biker shorts and one of Connor's giant Michigan State T-shirts. She was two weeks away from her due date, and my future nephew was driving her insane.

"Hey, pretty soon we'll have a tiny human in the seat of this cart," I teased, tossing a few tubes of lip balm into our haul.

"With the way this country is going?" She scoffed before adjusting her mask. "I don't know if he'll see the inside of a store until he's two."

It sucked to agree with her, but it was true. People were told to social distance, and they lost their fucking minds. They came out into the wild and didn't know how to act right in public.

I shrugged. "We'll do deliveries instead, then. But it will have to be at your house. At this rate, I'll have a completed seating area in two years."

"You know Jared is doing everything he can."

"I'm not faulting Jared," I assured her, steering us toward the candle aisle. "He feels horrible about the timeline. I finally start making some real money, and now that I can pay him what he's worth, he can't build anything. Yesterday, he labeled all of the water lines in my house because my hardwood floor was delayed again. I'm pretty sure I have all of the bonus content from *Avengers: Endgame* memorized, and it plays in the background of all my dreams."

Katie laughed as I explained the blue tape tabs covering the pipes and how Jared claimed that having a Marvel movie on in the background made him work harder. I was halfway into my story when I caught a whiff of memories I didn't ask to reunite with.

"Someone in this godforsaken store is wearing the cologne he used to wear," I murmured, plucking a lavender candle from the shelf and smelling it. We were past the point of knowing who "he" was in conversation.

"They do say that smell is our strongest tie to memory," Katie added, getting lost in the packages of wax melts. Her nose caught his scent. "God, it's like I'm back in our apartment."

"Right?" I directed us to the baby clothes, desperately seeking a new distraction. "I wish I could say it brings back all the things I want to forget about him, but all it does is bring back the good. Like what the fuck?"

"It's okay to have good memories, you know," Katie said, attempting to shift my mood. Her pregnancy made her incredibly optimistic, heightening her hopeless romantic mindset. Suddenly, she wasn't the only nauseated woman scanning onesies. "How's Derek?"

A reminder of Derek, however, never took me by surprise. Never butterflies or a smile, just another task to talk about on my list of to-do items.

Damn. I was spending way too much time on the phone with Bryson.

"He's fine. He's coming with me to Jared and Spencer's wedding."

"Wooow," she teased. "You're scheduling him for an event that is two months away?"

"It's almost a year from the date I took him to your wedding. Well, the wedding he weaseled his way into getting invited to."

Katie rolled her eyes, her mask hiding the smirk I knew that followed. "I don't know what's more concerning. The fact that you keep dismissing Derek as someone who could be good for you, or that my wedding sparked your newfound friendship with the biggest fuckboy from your past."

Welp, that confirmed my Bryson theory. "Bryson is . . . *different*. He's grown up a lot since college."

"You mean he's doing really well for himself and justifies the way he spends his money?" she challenged with a hint of sarcasm. "When he was here last weekend, he rented out a rooftop bar downtown and invited anyone he knew within twenty miles. Spencer said Jared didn't get home until four in the morning."

"That explains the late arrival at my house on Monday." I laughed at Katie's furrowed brow. "So he's single and has a great time living the lifestyle he worked hard to get. I'm not seeing the problem."

Katie took in a sharp breath, placing a hand on her stomach. Mine practically fell out of my ass while I watched her recover from whatever pain she was feeling. I rehearsed at least fifty times in my head how I would proceed if she went into labor, and all of my prep work came up missing.

"It's not a problem," she said, returning to our normal strolling pace. "It's just my own lifestyle choices judging out loud. It's hard to relate when I'm buying baby booties and some people my age are buying shots to *get* booty."

"It's nice to see your sense of humor won't be leaving us during your transition into motherhood," I teased. "If I hadn't had to shadow my director on Monday morning, I probably would have gone to that party."

Eventually, I hoped all the small steps I took behind my director would lead to bigger ones—a more permanent place on the staff and becoming a lead professor in my department.

"With or *without* Derek," she prompted. Katie always had a way of bringing our conversation full circle.

The scent from before returned, and this time I looked over my shoulder to find the culprit. A guy with short dark hair and a crisp jawline was holding up a tiny Minnie Mouse dress and showing it to the girl next to him.

I chuckled weakly, my mind wrapped around dark green eyes and a smile that could still make me weak in the knees.

"Oh my gosh!" Katie plucked a navy fedora from the rack. "This is fucking adorable!"

There were perks to having a pregnant best friend. They were easily distracted by finding gifts on their registry that they didn't receive at their baby shower.

Chapter Six

JAXON

OCTOBER 2020

IF ONE MORE PERSON needed to be reminded that they were muted in this virtual meeting, I was going to lose it. We'd been meeting this way for almost seven months, and some people still didn't understand the microphone setting.

Working from home had its ups and downs. I enjoyed the client-facing part of the job—the meetings and travel opportunities were fun while they lasted. But when Nadeen showed up last night and I didn't have to worry about making it to the office in the morning, the travel seemed a little overrated.

Nadeen was gorgeous. Dark hair, a pretty face, and a nice set of tits made her a welcome visitor as long as she was out by nine. She was a good time at night, but I didn't host broads the morning after. So I was confused when I looked up and saw her lingering by my office door.

Nadeen smiled when I made eye contact and mouthed, "I'm going to go!"

I had a client on a call, and she was kidding herself if she thought I was going to talk back.

I let out a deep exhale when I heard the front door click shut. Nadeen was getting too comfortable here. I'd have to call Tara tomorrow night to mix it up a little. I knew the signs too well, and I was exhausted at the thought of cleaning up her emotions when I told Nadeen I didn't feel the same way about her.

Eventually, my client agreed to a five-year contract, and I sent over the paperwork. My dad would've lost his mind with the technology shift. The world had changed so much in the last year, and the thought of him editing a PDF made me chuckle.

I missed my parents. I missed being close to everyone.

This pandemic was fucking with my work/life balance *and* my family dynamic. Our mom couldn't travel, and since I couldn't leave California, Alex felt obligated to. He wanted the girls to grow up in Charlotte; he wanted to go back home. Once he placed the idea in Bella's head, she ran with it. They had showings booked and put their condo up for sale. It sold in two days over the asking price, and they headed back to the East Coast.

My phone buzzed on the desk in front of me. I expected to see Helen's name and for her to call to let me know we received the client agreement through our portal. Instead, I saw a name that sent me memes and text messages.

I saw Jared's.

I stared. After ten more seconds of going back and forth in my head, I decided to answer it. "Jared?"

There was no cocky remark about how we hadn't talked in a while or an attempt to crack a joke at how I actually answered the phone. He asked how I was doing, and when I told him I was doing well, he let me know that he and Spencer got married.

"I had a wedding last month," he said with a chuckle. "I'm sorry you had to miss it."

"Only you would get married in the middle of a pandemic," I joked, prompting us both to laugh. Suddenly, I was twenty-two again, and Jared was giving me shit from down the hall. "How is Spencer?"

"She's great, man. She works above the shop, and I love coming to work together. She's got her own thing upstairs while my team takes over the first floor. I don't know how she does any writing with all the noise, but she says she doesn't mind it."

"And your dad? He still hates you for starting a business?"

"Ehh." He scoffed. "I learned eventually that my dad is going to hate me no matter what. He has his own demons to battle."

There was a break in our conversation, and for a split second, I wished for him to bring up her name. I just wanted a glimpse of how she was doing—anything that would let me know what she was up to.

"Have you seen pictures of Connor's kid yet? He's so fucking cute."

Jared dove into all of the memories he and Spencer were making with Connor and Katie's son. He told me how much he loved being an uncle and how wild it was that Connor was responsible for keeping another human alive.

I stared at the ring of condensation settling at the bottom of my iced coffee. After two sips, I decided it wasn't hitting right. It was another item in my day-to-day that I wanted until I had it in front of me. Another example of how often I sought instant gratification.

"I read the article about you on ESPN's website," Jared said. "I almost sent you the sketch for a desk I'm working on. I planned on paying your dad back for letting me bounce ideas off his lawyer, and I figured donating a nice piece to his, well, I guess now *your* company would be the next best thing."

"You should've sent it. I would've loved to look at it," I admitted a little too eagerly. I spent so little time on social media that I had no idea they even ran that interview.

"I know you're busy. I didn't want to add another thing to your plate." He paused, and I felt a slight shift from the other end of the phone. "How's your mom?"

I swallowed, his question hitting me hard in my chest. "She's good." My voice was raspy, and I knew Jared heard right through the bullshit. "It's been tough, you know? But she's good. We will know after her next scan."

"Well, I'm thinking about you, J." He chuckled. "Not in a weird way or anything, but I miss you, man."

My smile wavered, and I ran a hand through my hair. "I miss you, too. It's been a long time."

"It has, but hey, you're where you're supposed to be. It's always been part of your endgame." He sighed heavily into the phone. "Shit. I'm gonna let you go. A customer just walked in, and he's already fifteen minutes late for our consultation."

I started pacing around my desk. "Good luck with everything! Send me that sketch when you get a chance."

"I will. Any time you want a break from Los Angeles, just know I've got a loft with your name on it. Take care of yourself."

A few hours later, I received the sketches. In two weeks, I had an original piece from Jared Foster.

Chapter Seven

MACI

FEBRUARY 2021

I NEVER UNDERSTOOD THE importance of babyproofing until I had an eager baby doing tummy time on my living room floor. He wasn't even rocking on all fours on a nice plush rug. Max Jenson was thriving at six months old on original hardwood while his aunts and uncles spent a Valentine's Day evening in so his parents could have a night out.

Watching Max was a group effort, and everyone took their roles very seriously. Jared tackled random projects around my house because he couldn't sit still. Spencer and I shared a bottle of wine and made sure Max was breathing every thirty seconds, while Bryson . . . well, he was still getting used to the fact that he'd decided to settle down in Chicago.

When Bryson came to Thanksgiving last year, he told all of us that he wanted to move out of New York. His work was shifting toward a more remote setting, and he claimed his penthouse lifestyle was growing boring. I wasn't sure how that was possible since his free time consisted of women, going out, and partying, but I had a hunch there was another emotion Bryson Kennedy would never admit to owning.

He was lonely. Coming into town for holidays and significant events reminded Bryson that a city couldn't replace the genuine connections he had with his friends.

Even though Katie cringed a tad when she realized Max would officially have an *Uncle* Bryson in his life, I thoroughly enjoyed having him across town. Without both of us realizing it, Bryson and I formed the exact opposite of what we had when we first met. We were friends who didn't sleep together, and it was the easiest relationship I'd ever had with him.

I tried not to get lost in the irony of it all.

"Can we do our toast now?" Spencer whined. Her polished pink toes tapped impatiently against the hardwood. "Jared! You said that when you're done with the cabinets, we could—"

"*And* I haven't even hung them yet, baby," Jared said, peering around the corner of the kitchen. His raised brow told everyone that he was running behind, but his boyish grin assured us that Spencer would get her way. "Let me wash my hands." His voice drifted down the hall as he headed into the bathroom. "Get me a beer, Kennedy!"

Bryson scoffed from his seat on the floor next to Max, sending the six-month-old into a fit of giggles. "I help the man part time with his business, and he thinks he can demand drinks."

I thought my heart was going to implode when I saw the smile on Bryson's face.

"Get up, Uncle Bryson," I teased, tapping him on the shoulder. "And can you bring me more wine?"

After a short and sweet Valentine's Day toast delivered by Spencer, we all settled in for a kid-approved viewing of *Hamilton.*

"Do all these motherfuckers do is sing?" Bryson asked.

I wanted to take a picture of his puzzled expression as Alexander Hamilton spoke to Eliza Schuyler for the first time, but that would've meant picking up my phone. I was trying my best to ignore how we were slowly inching closer to seven o'clock.

"Language!" Spencer scolded. Jared laughed at her lame attempt to cover Max's ears.

As Jared and Spencer engaged in a nauseating couple fight about babies, Bryson elbowed me gently in the side. "You good? I just made fun of your show, and you didn't say anything." He gestured to my phone. "Is that guy up your ass?"

Derek was out of town for work, and I couldn't have been happier with how that timing worked out. Being out of town meant absolutely no obligation from me on a holiday I'd rather spend with friends.

"Thank you for that *lovely* visual of Derek, but I'm fine." I knew by Bryson's cocky smirk that he read right through that bullshit. "Fine. I'm waiting for—"

My phone rang in front of us on the coffee table, and I practically tossed Max into Bryson's arms.

"Mace, what's up—" Jared began before I sped out of the living room.

Since it was the middle of February in Chicago, it wasn't my first choice to take a phone call on my front porch. But the space provided the privacy I needed to react accordingly. I steadied my shaking hand and took a deep breath before I answered. "Hello?"

"Maci, it's Owen. Sorry to call you on Valentine's Day."

I crossed my arms as an unforgiving breeze blew through my zip-up hoodie. "I know it's you, Owen, and you know you aren't interrupting anything." His hearty laugh filled the space on the other end of the call. "Can you just give it to me straight?"

Owen exhaled slowly, but I felt his smile through the screen. "This is the call, Maci. This is the call I told you about the first day you walked into my office."

"I got the seat." I gasped, immediately covering my mouth. "I got the seat?"

"You got the seat, kid," Owen exclaimed proudly. "Congratulations."

After an agreement I couldn't verbally commit to fast enough, Owen assured me that the official paperwork would be emailed to me by next week. I was a few signatures away from becoming a Lead Instructional Designer for The University of Chicago.

With tears in my eyes, I returned inside, where an eager audience waited for me to speak.

"I got the seat," I said, still shocked at the words as they left my mouth.

Spencer's arms reached me first, followed by Jared's unruly, high-pitched screech. "That was the call?"

I nodded over Spencer's shoulder, and his smile grew wider. "Congratulations, Mace."

Bryson approached the circle of congratulatory hugs and shifted Max to his other arm. He was fast asleep, completely unaware of everything going on around him.

"All that time you spent whining to me about how you might not get it," Bryson teased, "and you got the call."

I wiped away a lingering tear as Bryson wrapped his free arm around my shoulders. "I got the call," I echoed proudly.

About two hours later, I broke the happy news to Katie and Connor. It was clear from her glossy eyes and low new-mom tolerance for wine that she was completely out of it, but Katie threw her arms around me and hugged me until I couldn't breathe. Connor rescued Max from a sleeping Bryson, and it was time for everyone to head their separate ways.

As soon as I padded across the kitchen, Jared came back inside and lingered quietly by the front door. His broad frame looked even bigger under his winter layers.

"Forget something?" I asked, cleaning up the glasses and cans scattered on the coffee table. Not having cabinets or counters made hosting in the kitchen difficult. I wasn't complaining, but my living room always looked like a rager was thrown after our crew came over.

"Yeah." Jared gestured toward the couch. "I drove him here."

I recognized the position Bryson was sleeping in and knew it was no use. He was down for the count, and it wasn't worth waking him up when I was heading in the direction of his place tomorrow.

"I'll drop him off on my way to work," I assured him.

Jared furrowed his brow. "You sure?"

I nodded. "Go enjoy the rest of Valentine's Day with your beautiful wife."

"I'll probably be back in a few days so I can actually hang a cabinet. We'll order your counter and countertops when—"

"Jared," I threatened playfully. "Go!"

Jared reached for the handle of the front door and smiled. "Night, Mace."

After the headlights backed out of the driveway, I tossed a quilt on Bryson and locked the front door. Since there was a chance Bryson might wander upstairs, I opted for a baggy T-shirt and athletic shorts to sleep in. He claimed that my couch hurt his back, but I saw right through his hard exterior. He wasn't a fan of sleeping alone, and I offered a friendly, very platonic option for him on the nights he stayed.

Even though I barely took up half of my bed, I couldn't get comfortable among the pillows and blankets that covered it. So many pieces of my life fit together perfectly, but there were times when I felt like I was missing a corner.

After three years of hard work, late nights, and countless efforts to get my name in front of the board, I finally got the call from Owen.

I had Chase, who checked in when he could and constantly invited me to stay with him and Trey. I had parents who kept their distance while they figured out their new life paths.

I had amazing friends to share the news with. I had Katie and Spencer, who both embraced our girls' nights and made me feel sane through my countless attempts to put myself back together. I had Jared, who was the first person to watch me fall apart and was helping me make a house into a home. I had Bryson, who, by some crazy turn of fate, became a friend I couldn't imagine my life without.

All of my pieces, but I was still missing the full picture. All of my happy moments were muddled by the image I thought would be there.

My king-size bed felt incredibly small on the nights when I stumbled over my thoughts. Tonight, as I fell comfortably into a dreamless sleep, it felt as big as the state of California.

Chapter Eight

JAXON

August 2021

After all of those times I spent complaining about having to travel, it felt good to get off an airplane again. The pandemic frenzy began to ease, and in-person meetings became acceptable again. It was nice living the remote life for a little while, but there was nothing like doing business on pen and paper in front of a client.

Plus, it added tasks to my schedule. I could only do so much from home, and I was running out of books to read and shows to watch. While I was doing my part to social distance from broads, I discovered I was a reader with a weakness for thrillers and plot twists I couldn't see coming from a mile away.

The plane pulled up to John F. Kennedy International Airport, and I noted the time change on my phone. The first time I flew into this airport, I was getting an Uber to an apartment in Chelsea and picking up flowers at a corner market.

It was also the *last* time I ever flew into this airport, until now. Irony was always fun when it happened in stories, but I hated it when it showed up in real life.

My next potential client lived just outside Manhattan, and after the year he had at Penn State, he was a guaranteed first-round NBA draft pick. He had multiple agencies trying to book meetings with him, but I was the only one who hadn't offered a Zoom link. When I mentioned flying out to meet him in person, I could tell he was excited to have someone sitting in front of him.

My phone rang as soon as I passed the first sign for Rental Cars and Ground Pickup. Over the years, Helen proved how impeccable an assistant could be with timing. She was my dad's best hire, and I was dreading the day when she told me she was retiring.

"Good morning, Hel—"

"Jaxon? It's Connor."

I stepped off the escalator. "Connor?"

"From BG," he added.

"I know who this is, man." I chuckled at his unnecessary detail. "It's been a long time, but it hasn't been that long—"

"I don't know how to tell you this, J, so I'm just going to say it. There was an accident—" His voice cracked, slowly falling off as he grew quiet on the line.

Everything around me moved in slow motion. People arrived for their flights. Travelers buzzed around in a frenzy, trying to get to their gates on time, while security yelled for people to step forward.

The silence between me and Connor was louder than the typical airport chaos I was used to while traveling. This wasn't a call to catch up and see how I was doing. This didn't end with us laughing about good news. Time might have passed, but I knew Connor's voice.

There was an accident. Connor wouldn't call me about her. Would he?

He wouldn't call me unless she weren't here to argue about it. My heart pounded in my chest as I prepared a question I didn't know how to ask.

"Jared's gone, J," Connor said through a staggering breath. "Jared's gone and Bryson's in the hospital."

My knees buckled, and I gripped the handle of my luggage so I wouldn't fall to the floor.

"Spencer called us this morning. I'm sorry to tell you like this." Connor cleared his throat, sounding more like himself. "J, did you hear me?"

"I heard you," I said, the floor blurring in front of me.

Jared was twenty-six years old. I was twenty-seven. People didn't die at twenty-six. People didn't lose friends at twenty-seven.

Friends.

I thought about the desk in my office—the Jared Foster Original that received so many compliments. He couldn't be gone. The person who called me every other month just to see how I was doing couldn't be *gone.*

"I heard you," I repeated softly, trying to silence the arguments in my head.

"Katie is with Spencer now," Connor explained. "His service will probably be this weekend."

"And Bryson?"

"No news yet," Connor answered quickly. "But they are hopeful that they will have some updates for us by tonight."

I nodded, dragging my hand down my face. Across the waiting area was a screen with all of the flight information for that day. I scanned the list, my eyes falling on the twelfth line from the top. Without any hesitation, I typed out a text to Helen and hit send.

"I'm at the airport now," I said, guiding my bag toward security. "I'll be on the next flight to Chicago."

Chapter Nine

JAXON

"I love you, Mace."

"I love you, too."

"But I—" I swallowed the lump in my throat. "Baby, I just don't know if it's enough anymore."

My heart sank as I watched the tears trickle down her cheeks. "You don't mean that. You can't call me baby and expect me to think you mean it."

Those words tormented me on repeat since the day I spoke them into existence. They wrapped themselves around every person, place, and memory in my life at Bowling Green State University. After I ended things with Maci, I expected to lose Katie. She eventually dropped off, and our meme and text exchanges became nonexistent.

It was the unexpected that made me feel like I had to make a choice.

Every phone call I had with Bryson reminded me of the day I fell for Maci. Every text message with Connor made me think of Thursday dinners at her apartment. Every life update from Jared reminded me of the promises I made and didn't keep. The unexpected reminders drove me to skip board meetings and ignore client emails. They were contradicting every reason I made for losing the love of my life.

I started resenting my parents for making me choose, and when I recognized that I was the only one to blame for my decisions, I knew I had to cut off the unexpected.

One of the last conversations I had with Jared was when he told me he was serious about starting a contracting business. He had the vision and the space picked out for his first brick-and-mortar shop; he just needed a backboard for the legal jargon and the steps to get started. Fortunately for him, my dad loved to invest in people with great potential and even better hearts. It was an opportunity for Jared to get the help he never asked for and the distraction I knew my dad desperately needed.

I pictured the desk in my office, the one Jared custom made as a thank-you for setting him up with my dad's lawyer. Before boarding my flight, I called my parents. I couldn't even begin to imagine what Spencer was going through, but if I could save her a few steps when she was ready, I wanted to.

As soon as I broke the news about Jared, my mom burst into hysterics, apologizing over and over again in complete disbelief that what I was telling her was true. She handed the phone to my dad, who barely got a word in before I told him I needed him to do something for me.

"Spencer was the most important thing to him, Dad," I explained. "I don't want her having to deal with—"

"I'll take care of everything, J," he assured me. "You focus on being present and take all the time you need."

Hearing his voice gave me just enough strength to hold it together for my flight. I closed my eyes as I descended into Chicago, feeling totally and utterly unprepared for the next unexpected.

Connor and Katie lived on a quiet street lined with colorful houses that mirrored the charm of their neighbors. Even under the glow of the streetlights, colorful garden flags and attention to detail made their lawns look like they belonged on the cover of a magazine. There wasn't a car parked out of place, making my Uber stand out on a street consumed by the patterns of day-to-day life.

Just as I was about to call Helen and ask her to book me a room at a nearby hotel, Connor insisted on coming to his house instead. After receiving multiple invitations with their address in curly-twirly font, it felt surreal to stand in front of it. It was uncomfortably quiet when I shut the car door, alerting everyone on the block that I had arrived. There was no going back. With my luggage in hand, I quickly closed the space between me and their bright yellow front door.

I knocked once before Connor answered, his giant frame taking up most of the entrance. His hair was short, highlighting the bags under his eyes and his pale cheeks. It was as if someone muted all of the color in his features. His light was completely gone.

"Hey, J," he murmured, extending his arm and pulling me in for a hug. His shoulders relaxed in a motion we did so many times in college, and when he squeezed harder, I knew better than to pull away.

I lost track of how long we stood in the doorway before he invited me in. He gave me a brief tour of the rooms we passed as he led me into the kitchen. It was near the back of the house, with a giant window that faced an impressive backyard. A small swingset sat in the middle of the grass, the rest of the green littered with toy cars, animals, and a few soccer balls. For the first time since Connor's call, I smiled.

"It's a mess, isn't it? Getting a one-year-old to clean up is a nightmare." Connor placed his hands on his hips, looking like a total dad. "Shit. You want a drink?"

"A drink would be good," I said, taking a seat at the table. My stomach would hate me for the whiskey, but it would have to do. Nothing seemed like a good antidote for the nausea.

He quickly averted his gaze outside. For a moment, he forgot why I was here. He didn't invite me over to show me the house or to meet his son. He took the seat across from me and slid me my drink.

"What happened?" I prompted softly.

Connor cleared his throat. "There was a shooting."

A shooting? There couldn't have been a shooting—

"They don't cover them like they used to," Connor murmured as if he read my mind. "Who can keep track? Just another day in America's news."

My mind raced faster than I could formulate my next question. "Where were they?"

I took short, shallow breaths. "Bryson. Bryson, is he—"

"J." Connor extended his hand on the table. "Breathe, man."

I took a sip of my drink and gestured for him to continue.

"Bryson had a lot of internal bleeding, but he made it through the night. The doctor is optimistic about his recovery."

"What happened?" My question sounded more like a desperate plea.

Connor set the scene of a gruesome narrative at a local middle school, where Jared and Bryson were dropping off a desk to celebrate a vice principal's twentieth year in the district. A twelve-year-old kid brought his father's gun to school and did as much damage as he possibly could before taking his own life.

"It happened fast. The security footage isn't even five minutes long. The kid couldn't get past the front office, so that's when he—"

His sentence hung unfinished, but the image he painted was more than enough to make me sick to my stomach. I pushed my glass away and crossed my arms in front of my chest.

We sat in a comfortable silence, neither of us knowing what to say. It wasn't until Connor tipped his empty glass in my direction and stood up that I realized what time it was.

"Want another?" he offered.

I shook my head.

"Probably best not to," he admitted. "I was going to head out early to see Bryson tomorrow morning. You should come with me."

I wanted to see Bryson. I wanted to apologize. I hoped that he would let me explain why I went dark for three years and that we are reuniting under these circumstances.

I succeeded in taking over my dad's company. I took care of my family. But as Connor waited patiently for my answer, I was reminded that as a friend, I faltered. In all other parts of my life, I failed.

"I haven't spoken to Bryson since I told him I couldn't come to your wedding," I admitted lamely. "I'm sorry, man. I was still in my first year at my dad's company. I would've had to fly out on Saturday, and by the time I landed, I wouldn't have made it."

Connor rested his elbows on the counter. "I was never sure if that was the *exact* reason why, but I understood. Katie doesn't. She probably never will."

He was no longer referring to the wedding.

"She's on her way home from Spencer's," he added. "She should be—"

A loud buzzing sound came from the front of the house, and a few seconds later, Katie emerged from a door on the other side of the kitchen. Her dark curls framed her face, almost making me believe there wasn't a force to be reckoned with underneath her delicate features. She stared at me, her brown eyes softening the moment I smiled in her direction. I couldn't help it. She looked as if no time had passed at all.

She drew in a shaky breath. "It's you."

"It's you," I echoed playfully.

Her hand flew to her mouth, and she closed the space between us. She wrapped her arms around me, and the harder I squeezed, the more she fell apart. I took advantage of the gesture, trying to make up for every single moment I missed over the last three years.

The explanation I should've given her after I ended things with Maci.

The hug I should've had ready for her after she got married.

The tears of joy I should've shown her after her son was born.

"Damn you," she murmured.

I rested my chin on the top of her head. "I'm sorry."

She sighed against my chest. "I know."

Chapter Ten

JAXON

AUGUST 2021

I HATED THE SMELL of hospitals. It brought back memories of my mom in a bed with more tubes winding around her than I could count. It made me relive the betrayal I felt when the doctors told us that the cancer was back—after my mom rang a bell two years ago to let everyone know it was gone.

Her oncologist stared at us from behind his desk, guarded by his impressive awards and framed certifications. While Dad and Alex responded with stunned silence, I couldn't contain the fury as it flew in all directions.

"What do you mean it came *back*?" I demanded as I paced along the back of the room. "She rang the bell. You said it was gone—"

Alex cleared his throat. "J—"

"Fuck off," I warned. "You're supposed to be the best. All the money and energy you cost our family—and you're telling me it's just *back*?"

I'll never forget the stoic shine in Dr. Ottoman's eyes when he said, "Money doesn't buy miracles, Mr. Hayes."

Everything was a blur after that.

As Connor and I stepped into Bryson's room, I reminded myself that this time was different. There would be no follow-up appointments. I assumed there would be physical therapy, but Bryson was on track to be released tomorrow morning. He was going to be okay.

"He should be waking up soon," the nurse explained, adjusting the clipboard in his hand. "His vitals sound good, and he's recovering well. As long as the doctor gives us the okay, we can have him discharged tomorrow morning."

"How can we support him?" Connor asked. "We've tried to call his family, but we haven't had any luck. My wife and I were going to help him get set up with us—"

"He's headed down a long road of recovery," the nurse explained calmly, relieving Connor of his nervous rambling. "He won't be able to do any heavy lifting or strenuous activity for several weeks. No working out or running. Walking is okay as long as he doesn't overdo it—"

Their words faded into the background as I stared at Bryson. His shoulders were almost too big for the hospital gown, which pulled at the patterned fabric and rested over the sides of the bed. A new emotion climbed into my chest and declared residency.

Anger. And the longer I looked at Bryson with Connor's description of what happened, the bigger it grew.

I took the chair next to his bed and placed my hand on his forearm. My anger had no clear direction. There was the twelve-year-old kid who shot up the school. The parent who probably shouldn't have had the gun in the first place. This fucking country that didn't give a shit about gun laws.

Connor rested his hand on my shoulder, taking the seat beside me. I hadn't even noticed that the nurse had left the room.

"What else did they say?" I murmured, watching the monitors keep a steady beat.

Connor dragged his free hand down his face. It was etched with the lines of another sleepless night, thanks to his son, who was way too young to understand what was going on. I couldn't imagine having a little one like Max, knowing one day he would grow up and have to be sent to the same place of safety that resulted in so many tragedies.

"He's going to be limited for a while. I don't see how he can stay at our place," Connor admitted softly. "With the stairs and all of our bedrooms being on the second floor . . . I can't put him out in the living room. Max would eventually drive him crazy—"

"Stop," I said through a breathy laugh. It felt weird to laugh. Why was I laughing? And once I started to question why I was laughing, I couldn't stop.

Connor eyed me carefully, searching for some loophole in the crazy vortex I was spiraling in.

"I just imagined Max waking Bryson up the same way I got woken up this morning."

Connor smirked. "Captain America or Black Panther?"

"Black Panther!" I laughed. "Right to the fucking forehead. The kid's got an arm, man."

Bryson inhaled sharply, and my hand flew from his forearm. He stirred slightly, taking in his surroundings and adjusting to the lights above him.

I pushed the call button on the side of his bed. One thing I learned from being in the hospital with my mom was never to do anything without a nurse's permission. I hesitated to offer Bryson water at this point. The last thing I wanted to do was fuck up any chance he had of leaving here tomorrow.

"Welcome back, man," Connor said, patting Bryson on the hand.

Bryson's face twisted in pain as his other hand flew to his chest. "Fuck."

"Everything okay?" a nurse asked as she entered the room. "Oh, you're awake!" Her voice flew up two octaves as she adjusted Bryson's bed, sitting him up straight. "How are you feeling?"

"Like I was shot," he admitted harshly. "Shit, I'm sorry."

She smiled sweetly at him. "No apologies necessary. I'm gonna get you another dose of pain medication, and that should help some."

All of us watched as she fed some fluids into his IV.

"I'll let the doctor know you're up and eager to leave," she added, shooting Bryson a look that informed me this wasn't their first meeting. "Just let me know if you need anything else."

Bryson tried to mimic her sweet expression through an exhausted grin as she set a giant mug of water on his tray. He thanked her as she left, leaving the three of us alone for the first time since college.

There was so much I wanted to say, but as the silence grew louder, I decided to go with the first coherent sentence that formed in my head. "It's good to see you, Kennedy."

Bryson eyed me cautiously, his mouth forming a hard line. I could handle a pissed off Bryson, but a quiet one? The begging happening inside my head was so loud, I swore he could hear it. I needed him to say *something. Anything.*

Bryson's silence was practically a death sentence for everything we built. If he didn't say something before I left this hospital room, I might as well board a plane back to Los Angeles tonight.

Chapter Eleven

MACI

Augustus 2021

In between my third and fourth pour of vodka, I officially lost track of time.

I said I wouldn't do this. I promised Spencer that I *wouldn't* do this. But after I encouraged her to triple her dose of melatonin, she had fallen asleep exactly two hours ago, leaving me alone in my living room surrounded by Jared's unfinished projects.

Signs that he was here only a few days ago.

Reminders that he would never come back to finish them.

While I found it challenging to be here, Spencer didn't seem to mind. Since the news of Jared's passing, Spencer spent most of her time at my house, seeking refuge from the space that she and Jared built together. She didn't want to sleep in the bed they shared or take coffee in the kitchen where they used to relax in the morning. She wanted space while Elle sorted through family memorabilia and dealt with his parents.

Jared's mother was pleasant, but his father? He barely deserved the title.

I sat quietly on the couch in my living room, waiting for cars to drive by the giant window that faced the front yard. Jared had just reframed the trim after convincing me that he couldn't mess with the original structure. He assured me that I would eventually appreciate the home's character, and he was absolutely right. I appreciated everything about this home.

With every car that passed came a new guess as to where the driver was going. It was a little after one, and my curiosity was starting to get the best of me.

Where was someone heading this late at night? Why were they up? To be fair, I was up. I was trying to come to terms with the idea of going to Jared's Celebration of Life tomorrow, a small gathering thrown together by Spencer and his family.

My phone buzzed on the coffee table, and I caught myself slipping. I *hated* that after all this time, I thought it might be Jaxon's name on the screen.

Why would he call? He had no reason to call. Katie reached out to say that Connor had called him, but that didn't mean he would reach out to me.

I silenced my pathetic monologing before I whispered, "Hi, Derek."

He sighed heavily through the phone. "Damn. I was hoping for voicemail."

I stretched, placing my glass on the table. "Sorry to disappoint you."

"I was hoping you were asleep."

I threw my head back against the couch and closed my eyes. Derek always felt the need to explain himself. It shouldn't have annoyed me. He was incredibly transparent. He could've told me he just won a million dollars, and my chuckle still would've been void of any humor.

"I'm about to try," I admitted softly. "Why are you up?"

"I'm just worried about you, that's all. Just because you dumped me doesn't mean I don't care about you. Do you want me to come over? We could *not* sleep together if you want. *Just* friends."

"*Just* friends?" I challenged him playfully. His offer tugged at what was left of my heartstrings. "I want Spencer to have her space when she wakes up in the morning. Tomorrow is going to be—" I drew in a shaky breath, unable to blink away the tears as they started to form.

Goddammit.

"It's going to be hard," Derek added.

Hard didn't even begin to describe the feeling. Part of me wanted to hide away in my bed, completely ignore the event and the milestone it represented. Jared wouldn't mind. He'd probably recommend some movies for me to pass the time.

A Marvel movie, naturally.

"Did you want a ride tomorrow?" Derek offered. His tone was laced with genuine innocence, which made this entire situationship even harder. He'd always put our friendship first, regardless of how many times I led him on. Anyone who witnessed us together probably assumed I was crazy.

On paper, he was incredible. But he wasn't for me.

I swallowed around the lump in my throat. "That would be great."

"Try to get some sleep, Maci. I'll be there at nine with some smoothies. I'm sure you need to get something in your stomach, too."

Fortunately for me, the aftermath of my empty glass was starting to impact my empty stomach. Exhaustion felt heavy on my eyelids as I sank further into the couch, dreaming of raccoons with machine guns and baskets of cherry Fun Dip.

Chapter Twelve

JAXON

August 2021

One thing I never took for granted about Bryson was his ability to ignore conflict. He hated it with a passion, always blaming it on his parents' inability to coparent when he was younger. While it shook his family dynamic, it did wonders for his friendships.

He didn't hold grudges, and he didn't want to hear my apologies for the way I dropped off a few years ago. Hearing the words "I'm sorry" come out of my mouth caused more of a visceral reaction than seeing his gunshot wound for the first time.

"We never did bullshit apologies before," he explained once the nurses changed his dressings. "Let's not start now."

It was a classic case of two very different things existing side by side. I was grateful for the easy reunion, but I was worried about how easygoing Bryson had been since I brought him back to his place. He made only one comment about his condition, and it was to draw attention to my choice of rental cars.

"If you're gonna be driving me around while you're here, you're gonna need a lower car," he noted as he shifted himself into his wheelchair.

I patted the side of the bright red Jeep affectionately. "Easy fix."

As soon as Bryson accepted my offer to stay with him, I booked an exchange for the next day. I traded in my Jeep for a medium-sized sedan, and I swore I heard Jared's cocky-ass laugh when they pulled around with the newest Hyundai Elantra.

We couldn't pick a song on our way to the service. Everything we chose seemed too happy or too irrelevant. Throwbacks from when we were scouring the college bars flooded my playlists, making it impossible to escape reality as we pulled into a crowded parking lot.

"A small service, huh?" Bryson noted softly.

I cut the engine, and both of us sat in silence, watching groups of people make their way to the service hall. "Do you need another minute?"

Bryson shook his head. "It's been ten minutes. If we sit here any longer, I don't know if I'm going to get out of the car."

I stepped out into the humidity, my dress shirt clinging to my chest and making it even harder to take a full breath. Mother Nature thought it would be hilarious to give us a gorgeous day to celebrate life. While the sentiment was clear, the name was misleading. We were celebrating the life of a twenty-six-year-old whose time was cut short.

Bryson and I made our way up the winding path toward the back entrance of the building. The room was outlined with barn-style hanging lights that extended out onto the patio, where there was a beautiful view of the lake. Green fields rolled behind the water, where it met the indigo skyline as the sun began to set behind the hills. It was a piece of country living in the big city. It was one last piece of Jared.

Elle, Jared's sister, stood outside the entrance. People walked around her, choosing to give her space rather than interrupt her solitude. She looked so small, standing alone with her arms crossed as she looked across the water. Bryson and I shared the same intuition, making a direct line to her instead of the doors.

I didn't say anything. I just pulled gently at Elle's shoulder until she fell into my chest. Her hands gripped my shirt, making their way across my back as she realized Bryson was next to me. The two of them shared a silent exchange, and I backed away to give them some space. Bryson murmured something into her ear that I couldn't understand, and she pulled away slowly, wiping her eyes and tucking her hair behind her ears.

"I needed some air," she explained. "It only started thirty minutes ago, and I already need a break. I can't hear another 'I'm sorry for your loss.' Like, I get it, but you get to go back to your life after this. I don't." She took a deep breath, turning to me with fresh tears in her eyes. "He was my brother."

I nodded, pulling her in again for another hug.

"I don't know how to do this," she sobbed.

It hit me. Hard. I hadn't realized I was crying until I tried to speak. "I don't know either, Foster."

She pulled back and grabbed Bryson's hand. "Will you stay out here for a few more minutes?"

Bryson softened his gaze, and I took that as my cue to leave.

To say that the room was packed was an understatement. A giant line of people moved slowly through the standing crowd, leading the way toward Jared's family. Soft piano music played overhead, and as much as I tried to block it out, I couldn't help but recognize "Let It Be" by The Beatles. Muffles and more tears surrounded me as the room began to shrink.

I spotted Jared's picture next to a beautiful blue-and-gold urn. His smile sent another stab of pain to my chest, threatening to make me fall apart. I needed to keep it together until I could get back outside.

Spencer stood out in a dark red dress instead of the expected black attire. Jared would have wanted her to shine—to stand out among the masses. Her face shifted quickly between soft smiles of appreciation and moments of sadness. It was typical Spencer, managing the show to make Jared proud. She was grateful for the love and support, and for the massive crowd that demonstrated what an amazing person her husband was. But she was also hurting. I couldn't imagine the thoughts running through her head.

Her hand flew to her mouth when she saw me, her facade breaking for only a millisecond while I pulled her into a hug.

"I'm so sorry, Spence," I managed through a raspy voice. I kissed the top of her head and gave her one last squeeze.

"I spoke to your dad this morning." She paused to regain her composure. "I am so grateful. I don't even know what to say—"

"Jared had everything in place," I said. "When you're ready to go over details, we're here for you. *I* am here for you."

"How long are you here for?"

I stuck my hands in my pockets and shrugged. "I'm not sure. I'm staying with Bryson and keeping him in check."

Spencer rolled her eyes, and I caught a glimpse of her from three years ago. "Someone has to." She ran her hand down my arm and hugged me again. "It's good to see you, Jaxon."

To keep the line going, I made my way to Jared's parents. Elle joined them just as I gave my condolences to Jared's dad, who could barely create a complete sentence. If the whiskey that laced his breath didn't give him away, his bloodshot eyes would. I couldn't judge him. I only knew him as the man Jared described him to be, and right now, he looked like a father who wished he had put more effort into loving his son.

Elle patted my shoulder as I passed, giving me space to exit into the crowd as more people entered the hall. I scanned the room for Bryson, needing another familiar face as the anxiety started to rise in my chest. I searched for Connor and then Katie until my eyes found someone I only dreamed of seeing again.

Blue eyes, dark hair pulled back, and her hands relying on someone who wasn't me. He guided her toward the back of the room, where he took her face into his hands and spoke in a way that made her focus on him.

Him. Not me.

I was spiraling. My mind was heading to a dangerous place while I was at my best friend's *funeral.*

I blamed the grief. It has to be the grief. What the fuck was wrong with me?

"Connor and Katie are walking up now," Bryson said, noticing the expression on my face. "Need some air?"

"How about a drink?" I prompted desperately.

I forced a laugh, and Bryson gestured toward the doors behind me. "I'll be out there in a second."

Without another word, I pushed open the doors and flew outside. My hands gripped the railing, and I leaned over the side so the blood could rush to my head. The lake below illuminated the last moments of sunlight, and a gorgeous orange hue spread toward the sky.

"One last time, Jared," I said, pulling a joint from the pocket of my dress pants. Through the closed doors behind me, I recognized the piano rendition of one of his favorite songs.

"I miss you, man." I blinked away another round of tears and swallowed around the lump in my throat. "And I hear you."

Chapter Thirteen

MACI

THE SMOOTHIES DEREK SHOWED up with this morning were real.

Driving in his truck to the service was real.

The sunset in the background of the hall was real.

But as my hand hovered over the handle, my third panic attack of the day threatened to unleash itself.

Today wasn't real. It couldn't be real. I wasn't walking into my friend's funeral.

"Maci," Derek's husky voice came with a reassuring squeeze to my forearms. "We don't have to go in. We can meet Spencer back at her place—"

"No," I stated firmly. "No, I can do this." I had to do this. I wasn't the one who lost everything.

Derek led us through the crowd, guiding me by the hand toward the back of the room so we could adjust to the space. A line of people led up to where Spencer, Elle, and Jared's parents were standing. Jared smiled at us from the other end of the hall, almost as if he were proud of the blue-and-gold urn we picked out for him.

Derek gently took my face in his hands. "Still with me?"

I nodded.

Derek kept my hand as we joined the line. I tried to block out the scene and calm my senses. Goosebumps lined my arms, making me regret my sleeveless dress instead of my long-sleeve romper. Traces of deli meat teased my empty stomach, restarting the whirlwind of nausea I thought I had tamed back in the truck. Visions of black surrounded me, the only saving grace being Spencer's choice of bright red in the front of the room. Derek's thumb stroked against the back of my hand while I tried to guess whatever piano cover was playing over the loudspeaker. My attempt to ground myself brought us to the middle of the room.

One more song and I'd be hugging Spencer. One more song, unless that song request came directly from heaven and Jared was fucking with me from the other side.

"Come and Get You Love" by Redbone played triumphantly in the background. Spencer's eyes scanned the crowd for someone who would understand the reference, and when she found mine, we both exchanged a chuckle. She brushed past the few people that separated us, bringing me in for a hug so both of us could escape.

"Damn him," she choked.

"And this song," I added, barely making it through my comment. The next few moments were a blur. I remembered the chorus picking up, Derek calling my name, and Spencer encouraging him to let me go.

I burst through the side door, using the railing as a lifeline when my body tried to collapse. The weight of it all was too heavy. It was like levitating when all I wanted to do was land.

I pushed the restart button on my grounding. The railing was warm on my hands after being in the sun all day. The last seconds of sunlight glimmered against the small waves creeping up onto the shoreline. A blend of white grape and sour earth floated in with the cool summer breeze—a smell I knew too well from college nights spent with Bryson.

Bryson. I needed to find Bryson.

I exploded outside so quickly that I hadn't even noticed the person on the other end of the balcony. The bright orange glow told me that he was the one responsible for the college nostalgia. He tossed the blunt on the ground and pressed into it with his foot. He took a few steps toward the door, halting when he caught me out of the corner of his eye.

His dark green eyes—eyes that drew me in so many times before, only to drag me down to my lowest point.

My mouth stayed put, and my knees didn't crumble. I didn't search his face for some sort of explanation, and I didn't beg him to give me one. Instead, I stood tall next to the railing, keeping one hand on the bar in case my body decided to betray me at the last minute.

He swallowed, his lips—*God, those lips*—parting slightly at the sight of me standing in front of him.

Jaxon Hayes—the man who broke my heart.

The deafening silence between us would eventually draw the attention of someone inside. It had to. There was no way the world just continued spinning after this interaction.

"Hey, Mace," Jaxon said, his raspy voice effortlessly etching the words under my skin.

Mace. The fucking nerve of him—acting like he knew me well enough to call me that.

I brushed past him, ignoring the smell of his cologne and the heat that radiated off his body.

Jaxon Hayes had been real. *We* were real, and when Bryson intercepted me on my way to Katie, his soft grip told me everything I needed to know.

Jared was gone. Jaxon was here. Spencer was grieving. Bryson was healing.

And nothing would ever be the same.

Chapter Fourteen

JAXON

AUGUST 2021

BEAUTIFUL. GORGEOUS. MACI LAWSON.

She was right there in front of me, and I couldn't go to her. She wasn't mine to hold.

"Baby, I just don't know if it's enough anymore."

When I ended things, there was no doubt in my mind that some lucky bastard would find her. I wasn't naive enough to think that she wouldn't fall for someone else. It was a thought that crept into my mind at the worst times, imagining her life with someone who wasn't me. It was an entirely different feeling to see it—to watch it happening in real time.

Three years dissolved into three seconds when her eyes met mine—a captivating blue gaze that ignited something inside me. A flame waiting to be fed, a fire that never went out.

Chapter Fifteen

MACI

September 2021

Time had a funny way of dragging its ass when you least expected it—my days at work had me feeling like I never had enough time to get anything done. But when I took a step back, the crushing weight of reality pulled me even further from where I wanted to be. While work kept me busy and my friends kept me sane, it had only been thirty days.

Thirty days since Jared's Celebration of Life.

Thirty days since Bryson called me drunk at two in the morning to tell me he shouldn't have lived.

Thirty days since Spencer came home with Jared's ashes.

Thirty days since I walked outside to find Jaxon Hayes on a balcony.

Yet, life went on as if we hadn't shattered, and we were all just struggling to keep it together.

I took advantage of the red light right before Katie's street and took a long sip of my smoothie. The frothy, fruity beverage had been one of the only items I could keep down in the morning, but today it was hard to stomach. It tasted like it had selfishly overstayed its welcome. It tasted like guilt.

Derek had proved to be an amazing friend—never pushing the boundary or drawing attention to the fact that we were strictly platonic. He'd show up in the mornings to make sure I was eating, and when he stayed the night, he slept on the couch.

I knew he wanted more. He told me multiple times since we started talking that he wanted more. Yet, I kept pushing, taking advantage of a guy who made it clear what his intentions were when I couldn't be more sure about what I wanted.

Before I made any rash decisions this morning, I tabled my Derek saga as a discussion topic for this afternoon. I was meeting Spencer at Katie's house today for a much-needed girls' lunch. It was our first attempt at a typical Saturday, and it wouldn't be one without me having some relationship drama to add to the pot.

I was relieved to see that Spencer's car replaced Connor's in the driveway. Part of me worried that she might not show up, that Katie and I would receive another text saying she wasn't feeling well or just needed some time to herself today. I kept track of how many times she left the house and how many text threads and phone calls she responded to. Since I met Spencer, she has tried to do everything on her own. Katie and I did our best to make sure that grieving her husband wasn't one of those things.

"Hello?" I sang as I stepped into the foyer.

"In here!" Katie shouted over the music.

I followed the delicious smells of coffee and cinnamon to the kitchen, where Katie was whisking something in a bowl behind the counter. Spencer sat with Max at the table, keeping his attention with a small dog dressed up like a firefighter.

I hugged Spencer and planted a kiss on top of Max's head. "What happened to the pink one?"

"Skye was last week," Katie explained.

"It's kind of bullshit that she's the only girl on the team," Spencer said.

Katie and I nodded in agreement, sharing a small laugh when I pulled her in for a side hug only to sneak a taste of her batter.

"Oh my *god*." I groaned, trying to take another sample before she swatted my hand. "What is this?"

Katie prepped her first tray with liners. "They *will* be maple-cinnamon muffins."

"She's helping me create thank you baskets," Spencer added, averting her glossy gaze to Max. "It's about time I clean out all of the cards, vases, and leftovers."

"We cleared out your fridge last time I was over," I said, vaguely remembering Derek stuffing his trunk with foil tins.

Spencer winced. "A delivery came yesterday that took up our entire deep freezer."

"Damn," Katie murmured.

"Food is the universal language of love," I said through a pathetic laugh. The mountains of gift baskets and DoorDash gift cards were enough to make anyone a believer. "Wait, your *entire* deep freezer?"

"Do you have that list for me?" Katie prompted, placing her first batch in the oven.

"Yeah." Spencer pulled a piece of paper from her sweatshirt pocket. "Can you hand this to Katie?"

I snatched the list from her hand and did a quick scan. My eyes fell on the very reason Spencer made it sound illegal to talk about a deep freezer.

Twelve-Month supply of Soups for the Soul – *Hayes Sports & Entertainment (Reed and Evelyn Hayes)*

I passed the paper to Katie, hiding the annoying stab of sadness behind a reassuring grin. When it sent Max into a fit of giggles in Spencer's arms, I knew I was safe. There was no sadness here, just a painful pinch of a reminder that two names I used to know everything about were now recipients of a piece of paper in a thank-you basket.

"Can we just burst this bubble wide open, please?" Spencer practically begged. "I need all your inner thoughts right now."

Katie's high-pitched chuckle shocked me from behind the counter. Clearly, there was a debriefing session I missed before my arrival. It didn't bother me. If anything, I was glad the topic offered a minor distraction from the recent conversations we'd been having.

I couldn't ignore the spark in Spencer's eyes. "Where do you want me to start? How I was completely unprepared to run into him"—I took the seat across from Spencer and shot Katie an eye roll—"or that *some of us* knew exactly when he got into Chicago and didn't tell me."

"Do you think you'd *ever* be prepared to run into him, though?" Katie countered, keeping her focus on her whisk. Her snarky tone made it clear that she already knew the answer.

Someone could have given me the exact time and day when I'd run into Jaxon Hayes again, and I still wouldn't be prepared.

"I'm just giving you shit," I added. "Obviously, it wasn't a priority then, but I'm happy we can laugh about it now."

"Good." Spencer chuckled. "Because I can assure you that Jared would want you to—"

Her voice wavered, and I reached my hand across the table to grab hers. Jared would've loved the entire interaction. He was probably smiling ear to ear now that Jaxon and I were in the same zip code.

"How is Bryson doing?" Spencer pressed gently, tugging a stray curl from Max's hand and tucking it behind her ear. "Have you talked to him? I call and text him every day, but I keep getting the same responses back. And he never *calls* back, it's always a text."

"I think he's doing the best he can," I admitted sadly. "Just like all of us are. I know he struggles with the guilt, but when I saw him a few days ago, he seemed okay."

Katie shook her head. "Guilt?"

I exhaled slowly, looking between her and Spencer. "He's struggling with the fact that he is still here—"

"And Jared isn't," Spencer interjected, looking down at the table. "My therapist calls it survivor's guilt. I can't imagine how that is affecting him. I know it hits me hard sometimes."

"You?"

She nodded. "How could it not? Why him and not me? It's a scary rabbit hole to go into."

Katie grabbed both of our hands and took a deep breath to steady herself.

"Not that I *enjoy* sharing custody of one of my best friends," I joked. "But I'm glad Bryson has Jaxon here. We can't be with him all the time, and since he can't drive or do, well, *anything* that he usually does to pass time, I think it's been good for him."

"He should be cleared to drive in a few weeks, right?" Spencer asked. "Wait—how did you see him a few days ago?"

I smiled sweetly, and Katie bit her lip to keep from laughing. She had already heard that part of the saga where I felt like the enemy had discovered my home. "Jaxon dropped him off for an evening visit."

Katie burst into a fit of giggles, dragging Spencer along with her. I didn't care if our desperate cravings for joy prompted them. I was going with the flow.

The timer dinged, pulling Katie from her seat at the table to prep another round of muffins. I waited to share more of the story until she returned from putting Max down for a nap.

"And the best part was that Derek was parked in the driveway," I continued through a breathy laugh. "He had to wait for Jaxon to leave before he could pull out."

Katie laughed even harder from the kitchen, and Spencer covered her mouth to try to downplay her reaction. I knew she felt bad for Derek; both of them did. But for just a glimmer of a second, I felt like we were in college again—us girls sharing embarrassing stories and relishing in the mouthwatering aroma that came with Katie's baking.

"I'm officially breaking it off with Derek tonight," I added, shifting my body toward Spencer.

Spencer winced. "Didn't you already do that?"

"Kind of," I murmured. "Sort of."

"And we're just going to gloss over the timing of this breakup?" Katie probed.

I rolled my eyes, keeping my focus on Spencer. "How are *you* doing? I was being serious about my offer to sleep over anytime you want some company."

"And I appreciate that." Spencer placed her folded hands on the table. "But you guys, I . . . I need to find out how to do this. I need to find out how to keep going, knowing that no matter how badly I want it, Jared isn't coming home."

I lost count of how many times I stared at my front door, wishing Jared would walk through it with his arms full of tools and supplies. He'd wear his goofy grin and tease me about how cluttered the living room looked, even though he was the reason for the clutter. Eventually, I'd have to do something about my unfinished kitchen. I just didn't have the heart to make space for anything else. Every time Derek offered to put something together, I told him not to touch it, as if his interfering would somehow taint the memories.

Before I could swipe them away, a few tears escaped down my cheeks.

"I'm going to figure it out because *I have to*." Spencer shrugged. "He'd want me to."

"Cheers!" Katie exclaimed proudly from behind the counter. She held up her coffee cup, and Spencer and I did the same.

"And it's only been a month," I reminded her gently. "Spence, you can take all the time you need."

"I'm going back to work next week, which should help," she said, her voice laced with caution. "The only problem is that my office is directly above Jared's workshop, and I'm almost positive I'm going to have a mental breakdown as soon as I step inside."

"Do you want us to go with you?"

"I can do it. I think it will be nice to have that moment alone with him." Spencer took a deep breath, and I prepared myself for another round of tears. Instead, she hit me with, "So you did or *didn't* break up with Derek?"

I chuckled. "Oh my god."

"As one man left her zip code," Katie muttered fondly, "another man returned."

"Stop it," I warned her.

"What?" she exclaimed through an innocent grin. "Technically, Derek has a different zip code than you and Bryson. And since Jaxon is staying with Bryson . . ."

My stomach twisted at the way Jaxon's name left Katie's mouth. It was like the word didn't even belong in her vocabulary.

Later that night, I sent my official break-off message to Derek. As soon as it said DELIVERED, I placed my phone on the counter and walked away. It felt worse than a phone call, and an hour later, there was still no response.

Time had a funny way of dragging its ass when you least expected it. Especially when you were waiting to hear back from a text you hesitated to send in the first place.

Chapter Sixteen

JAXON

September 2021

Every morning after my jog, I stopped by Jared's workshop. I expected to see it left in an organized chaos that only Jared could understand. His college bedroom was always in shambles, but I was impressed to see that his workspace was the complete opposite.

It took a few weeks, but I finally tied up the last loose ends on the unfinished projects in his shop. His inbox was empty, and a portion of his life insurance check had paid off the last of his rent. Spencer officially owned Jared's space, and I swore the sun shone a little brighter through the front windows.

I wasn't sure if Jared could hear me. I wasn't sure how I felt at all about the afterlife. Regardless of whether he could or not, I always told him that I'd make sure Spencer was taken care of. I'd make sure everything Jared left her found its way to whatever future she decided for herself.

Since the business was still open and Bryson couldn't drive, I took it upon myself to handle projects as they came in. I used the free time between my meetings and client calls to organize the resources Jared left behind. He had a few crews he contracted through, and they were more than happy to help me fill in the blanks. Jared Foster was a lover of people, and his ability to put relationships above everything else showed even beyond the grave.

"Where the fuck are your business cards, J?" Alex demanded. "You're the only person I know who doesn't have a holder on their desk."

I smirked at the decorated wooden holder that housed Jared's business cards. "First drawer on the left. Why would I have them on display in my home office? That's weird."

Alex mumbled something I couldn't make out. He'd shown an incredible amount of patience during my unexpected trip to Chicago. When I expressed my need to stick around for a while, he offered to stay at my place with Bella and the girls to run my in-person meetings. Granted, I didn't have random broads showing up for a good time.

Fortunately, I was able to handle most of my responsibilities virtually. With Helen working on things in the background, Alex basically rode out an extended invitation to revisit the West Coast. I was grateful as fuck for everything they were doing.

I leaned back in Jared's desk chair, glancing around at the photos that lined his walls. Pictures of him and Spencer on trips and vacations. Collages of Connor, Katie, and Bryson. Group photos that included the one person who hadn't left my mind since I saw her.

What the fuck are you still doing here?

The unhelpful answer to that question? I had no idea. But I had a nagging feeling that I owed it to Jared to help out where Spencer and Bryson needed me.

It's not for her.

"J?"

I sat up straight. "What?"

Alex chuckled. "I asked about Bryson's next appointment."

"Wednesday," I said, dragging a hand down my face. "His next therapy appointment is Wednesday, and I'm hoping for some good news. He needs it."

"How's Spencer? Mom mentioned sending her more food yesterday, and I told her to simmer down."

I laughed, picturing what Mom's face would look like if that ever left Alex's mouth. "You did not tell our mother to simmer down."

"Nah," he said through a chuckle. "But I convinced her that a year's supply of soup was plenty for one person."

The tiny bell above the workshop door rang, alerting me that a customer was here.

"Let me call you back later," I said quickly. "Someone just walked in."

"Wait! Bella wanted me to ask if you've seen—"

I hung up before he could mutter her name into his question. Spencer rounded the corner of the office, looking just as surprised to see me as I was to see her.

"Jaxon?" she breathed, putting a hand to her chest. "Shit, you scared me."

"I'm sorry," I said, rising slowly from the chair.

She tried waving me back into the seat. "You're fine! It's nice to see someone sitting there." Redness flooded her cheeks, and her eyes grew glossy. She crossed her arms over her chest and glanced nervously around the workshop.

I kept my distance as I moved silently through the space behind her. Her eyes skimmed the bulletin board where Jared kept handwritten notes and his project calendar. Her fingers traced the blue penmanship that covered his scraps of paper.

Someone might as well have taken Jared's sledgehammer to my heart. I watched the love of my friend's life take in more tiny remnants that he left behind. Evidence that her husband was here a month ago, cracking jokes and probably singing whatever song was in his head that day at the top of his lungs.

"I can feel him here," she said, her voice cracking. "It's like he still has things he's working on."

She turned into my chest, and I rested my chin on top of her head, letting her wrap her arms around me as tightly as she needed. My eyes wandered to the picture of Jared and Spencer from their college graduation, both dressed in black robes, with giant smiles on their faces, blissfully unaware that this was in their future.

"I've got you, Foster," I murmured.

Spencer steadied her breathing, leaning back to wipe her face of any rogue tears. "I'm glad you're here. I've been putting off coming by. I wasn't sure what would happen once I got inside."

"I can take care of the place for as long as you need me to," I assured her.

"You've done so much already. A letter came from the bank yesterday saying that they received our payoff amount."

"Good." My mouth curved into an involuntary grin. "Now I don't have to bug them next week." That earned me a small chuckle, and I hugged her again. "Jared didn't want you dealing with any of this, Spence. I know I haven't been around—" I swallowed around the lump in my throat. "I'm here to make sure you don't have to."

"I think I'm going to see if Bryson wants to take over. I think Jared would want that."

I cocked my head at the thought of Bryson doing any sort of manual labor. Spencer chuckled again, making it clear that I was doing a shitty job at hiding my reaction.

"More like a *project manager*," she explained through a toothy grin. My god, it felt good to see this girl smile again.

"Bryson was here way more than a part-time employee should've been. He knows exactly how Jared ran the business."

"Let me handle things until Bryson gets back on his feet. We should know more at his appointment this week."

Spencer eyed me cautiously, her warning glance full of reasons for her to say no.

"Please," I begged through a pathetic plea. "Let me do this for him."

She shook her head. "Your job. California. Jaxon, I have to ask why—"

My silence hung between us as she weighed the pros and cons.

She took a deep breath as her lips curved into a slight smile. "Please don't make me regret this."

Spencer and I took a few hours to sort her studio into totes and boxes. We moved her books and trinkets safely into the storage unit in the back and packed her car with the essentials. She'd be working from home for a little while, hoping it would help with her transition back. With Jared no longer downstairs, I wasn't sure if she'd ever come back here to work.

Either way, I was happy to hear she was excited to start writing again.

Chapter Seventeen

Jaxon

September 2021

Bryson and I spent the evening sorting through Jared's calendar and outlining projects we needed to finish. I had no idea how Jared managed this. He had a lengthy list of clients, and even with three crews to help, it still felt like we were running on fumes. In one conversation, I went from running my family business to running two. It was only the second week, and my head was already heavy with the pressure.

"I'm working on a few emails to send out before the end of the day," I explained as I put the finishing touches on the pancake batter. "With us extending the timelines on these projects, some of his customers might decide to go with someone else."

Bryson chuckled. "I don't think we're getting off that easy. People will wait."

From a business perspective, that was amazing to hear. From where I was standing behind this hot-ass griddle? The heat was starting to make me dizzy. The only thing keeping me upright was the good news Bryson received at his last appointment. By the end of October, he'd be out of his wheelchair, and he could get back to light exercise again.

His entire energy shifted after that appointment, and for the first time since I got here, I started to see glimpses of my best friend.

Bryson and I fell into a comfortable routine of living together, as if we rolled right out of Bowling Green and into his Chicago penthouse. It was an impressive upgrade from Falcon's Pointe, but the ambiance was the same. It was the two of us trying to figure out what the hell we were doing.

I kept waiting for him to ask why I was here or when I was leaving. While I didn't blame him for the questions, I feared the moment he would voice them. The fact that I had no answers put me a little on edge. It also wasn't helpful that packages from my apartment in LA kept showing up in bulk at his front door. Every day, it was either clothes, client files, or something I needed from my office.

"When's your Jeep arriving?" Bryson teased after I tore open another box last night. For a moment, I considered his suggestion. But the message it would send to my family and everyone here was what stopped me.

I slid a plate of pancakes in front of Bryson, just as his phone buzzed on the counter.

He answered the call with a smug grin. "I was beginning to think you were ignoring me," he said, sending the person on the other line into a fit of laughter. Their reaction made him pause his next bite of pancakes. "Don't be like that! What's up?"

I drizzled some syrup onto my plate before opening up my email. I had a few items from Helen that needed my signature, and I had to confirm next month's calendar. Dad always gave customers at least one month's notice if he had to move a meeting, and I tried to provide them with the same courtesy. It was unusual for me to cancel, since my entire life revolved around my role in the business. But when I saw the stacks of colored blocks that flooded my schedule, my caffeine withdrawal went into overdrive.

"Gimme one second," Bryson said, shifting his phone from his ear to the counter. His attempt to balance the speaker near his mouth was suffering due to his inability to wait for breakfast. "I'm putting you on speaker so I can check."

"Bryson, don't put me on speaker!" the voice said through a high-pitched laugh. "You did it already, didn't you? Why are you so annoying?"

It wasn't just a voice. It was *her* voice, and it sounded just like I remembered it.

"I'm looking at Jared's notes!" Bryson exclaimed, offering me a half-assed shoulder shrug.

I shook my head to make it seem like hearing Maci's voice didn't make me forget everything I just read in my email. I started back at the top, only to have to repeat the process when she spoke again.

"If it's too much, just tell me," she pressed.

"It's not too much," Bryson reassured her, his eyes softening as he sifted through paperwork.

I felt like a third wheel in their conversation. These weren't two people who picked up the phone when they needed something from the other. These were two friends who spoke often.

When I failed to read another email, I shifted my focus to the espresso machine behind me.

"It gives me another reason to order from that sushi place we like," Maci offered.

"So I can listen to you complain about how much money you're spending?" Bryson teased. "Mace, you need a working kitchen. Plus, the plumbing in your laundry room is shit."

There was silence on her end of the line, and I smiled at the slow drip of espresso. I pictured her face as I had done so many times before. She furrowed her brow and pulled up the right side of her mouth. Her nose would crinkle slightly, and she'd act like she had no idea what you were talking about.

It was the look I got five years ago when I asked about the miles on her car—right before I helped fix it on College Drive.

"I'll work on getting a team over there by the end of this week," Bryson said.

"You know I have new classes starting—"

"And I have your spare key," Bryson stated as if she already should've known that.

Maybe she does. What the fuck do you know?

I poured my shot of espresso over ice and layered it with milk and creamer.

Maci sighed as a car door slammed in the background. "Thank you, Bryson. Just text me when you know more. I'm about to head into my seminar."

They said their goodbyes, and the questions flooded my head.

So I didn't sound like a complete lunatic, I went with one that was completely unrelated to the person who just left speakerphone. "Can we pull from another project this week?"

Bryson shook his head. "Nope."

"Is there another team Jared uses other than the three we have?"

Bryson echoed his answer from before. "Nope."

I rested my elbows on the counter. Could Bryson ask the guy she was with at Jared's service for some help? At least I'd no longer have to guess what his name was.

"If we post the work, someone will pick it up," Bryson insisted. "Her house is pretty much in pieces. The outside structure is fine, but Jared just finished ripping out her kitchen right before—point is, it needs to get done."

I took a sip of my latte to buy time for my next question. "How much?"

Bryson prepared his next bite of pancakes. "A lot. Most companies charge for their materials, which is usually double what we pay anyway. It'll be a dent, but Jared wouldn't want it sitting there like that."

"Why can't we move another project?"

"Because those clients signed a contract with Jared. Jared worked on Maci's place when he had the time," he explained.

I stared at the colorful calendar on my laptop screen. The next tab over was Jared's projections for next month and last month's budget.

"Does Jared have an outline for what needs to be done?" The words flew from my mouth before I ran them through my head first. I barely recognized my voice as my offer continued, "I can do what I can."

Bryson's eyebrows shot to the top of his forehead. "You do what you can, as in . . . what, exactly?" He let out a cocky laugh. "I can't just send you over there, man. She wouldn't even let you in."

I shrugged my shoulders, digging myself deeper into the hole of craziness. "Tell her you hired someone. I'll go over when she's at work. She won't even know."

"What is this, J?" he demanded. "I'm happy you're here—fuck—but why—how long are you even staying? Why this?"

Welp. He voiced them.

I stared at my drink, unable to look at Bryson while he waited patiently for an answer. I left so easily before. Why was I inserting myself everywhere now?

"Two weeks before Connor called me to tell me what happened, I got a desk from Jared. I told everyone who came in that it was a Jared Foster Original. No matter how many texts I ignored—" I shook my head as an uneasy feeling brewed in my stomach. "He never stopped calling me, man. No matter how many times I ignored his texts or how many excuses I had for not showing up, he never stopped calling me."

"That's just who Jared was," Bryson answered calmly.

"I fucked up, Kennedy."

"Yeah, you did," he stated.

There were so many layers to that sentence, I wasn't even sure where to begin. I could've told Bryson the truth. I could've said why I never went back to North Carolina. I could've given him all of the reasons I ran through my head until I convinced myself that they were the right ones.

But I didn't want to hear that they were enough. So instead I said, "And I'm sorry."

"Stoooooop." He groaned, making us both laugh. "Look, do what you have to do. But don't keep doing this shit because you feel bad."

"Come on, you know I'm not. If I didn't want to do it, I wouldn't offer."

He raised his hands defensively. "I'm just saying! When your real life starts to get too loud because you're here instead of there, I'm not gonna blame you for having to get back to it."

I sorted my meetings into groups that I could afford to reschedule and ones that couldn't wait. I wasn't sure what was right or what was wrong. But my choice to stay, my choice to help—everything about it felt right.

Chapter Eighteen

MACI

September 2021

Something had to give eventually, and it wasn't going to be my bank account. My phone call with Bryson last week made it clear that I couldn't keep accepting food through a drive-thru window or tracking it with the DoorDash app. I bought this fixer-upper with a vision in mind, and those visions included me hosting a holiday and actually using my stove.

But still, the guilt was consuming me. I knew that Bryson was doing everything he could to run Jared's business with the help of what's-his-face. A crew would be at my house this morning whether I liked it or not.

"Are you *ever* going to say his name again?" Katie asked through an annoying cackle. She was keeping me company on my commute to work. She was also the perfect person to distract me from the fact that this would be the third time I was late this week.

Apparently, alarms didn't wake the guilty. We were too busy drowning in our own emotions to come up for air.

I bit into my chocolate croissant. "I do say his name."

"You don't. You pass right over it."

I rolled my eyes. "And? Do you need me to bring anything else on Saturday?"

"Just your positive attitude since Jaxon might come," Katie answered as if she were asking me to bring an extra bag of chips.

Suddenly, I no longer wanted the rest of my croissant. I set the pastry aside and pulled into the parking garage. "That's no secret, Katie. Bryson told me he was riding with Jaxon."

There was only one phrase I imagined saying to Jaxon, and I was positive that "Fuck off" would be frowned upon at Jared and Spencer's anniversary party. The day was about being there for Spencer. No one should have to spend their first anniversary alone because their spouse didn't make it to the date.

Damn you, Jared.

He appreciated the random jabs I sent his way. I considered them tiny letters of my love since he was no longer here to send me memes. What I wouldn't give to see any of the Avengers flash across my screen from his number.

"You said his name and that's good enough for me," Katie murmured.

"I just don't know why he's still here," I blurted. I put my car in park and dragged my hands down my face, ashamed of my admission. Since it was loud and out, I decided to roll with it. "I get it, he's helping Bryson. But *I* could've done that. Spencer has what she needs for Jared's policies. Other than handling some of the business, what is he doing?"

"Finally, you've cracked," Katie exclaimed. "Give it to me, girl. I've been waiting for you to say something for *weeks*."

I chuckled, wishing we were having this conversation in person with a bottle of wine. "You know I had a thought last night, and I hate myself for it."

"Go on," she prompted.

"It was so easy for him to rearrange his life—to drop every-thing and be here at the last minute. It's been over a month—"

"—and it was never an option for him while you guys were together?" Katie added. "I can say it so you don't have to. You're not a bad person for thinking it."

I sighed. "No. Just pathetic."

"You aren't that either. Jaxon hurt you, and he came back into your life unannounced. Regardless of the reason, you're allowed to feel what you feel."

I noted the time on my dashboard. 8:20.

Fuck.

"You know it's just me and you in this conversation, Mace. You don't have to hold it all together for Spencer right now. Two things can exist at the same time."

"Force of habit," I said, throwing my tote over my shoul-der. "Thanks for letting me vent."

"Anytime, bitch," Katie noted. "I'll text you."

I tucked my phone into my purse and pushed open the door to our office. I couldn't avoid Owen's lingering gaze even if I tried.

"Good morning, Maci," Owen said. He plucked a pen from the holder on his desk and smiled. "I wanted to talk to you about something."

Here we go.

"Owen, I'm so sorry I'm late. It won't happen again—"

"Take a seat, kid." He gestured to his empty desk chair. "You're here, and that's honestly all I care about. I'm worried about you."

I let my bags drop to the floor, unapologetically slouching into the seat across from him. "Why?"

"I'm just gonna give it to you straight because that's always how we've operated." Owen took a deep breath and clasped his hands. "When my wife died, I didn't come back to work for three months. You lost a good friend, and you're other is still recovering, and you came back two weeks later."

I pursed my lips at what he was suggesting. It was hard to ignore the red flags when Owen's soft brown eyes waved them in my face.

"Let me know if I'm overstepping," he added gently. "I just wanted to make it clear that I don't expect you to bounce back this soon."

"And I appreciate that, I do," I said, noting the hesitation in my voice. Every time anyone showed a drop of sympathy, I completely shut it down. I wasn't the one who lost everything. Spencer was. "Coming back to work has given me something to focus on. I can't just sit around."

"Fair enough. If for whatever reason that changes, you let me know, okay?"

I popped out of my seat and grabbed my tote. "Are we good?"

Owen motioned for me to sit back down. "Not yet."

I tried not to roll my eyes. This chair was beginning to feel more like a witness stand.

"I'm planning my schedule for the winter semester, and I want to run something by you."

I quirked a brow. "What kind of something?"

"If it isn't too much—" Owen paused, choosing his following words carefully. I wasn't sure if the sigh that escaped him stemmed from regret or exhaustion. Either way, the anticipation was driving me crazy. "I have another Learning Theories course that needs coverage in the winter semester. Do you want it?"

"Like on my own?" I exclaimed. "Absolutely!"

"You can decide the day and time as long as it meets the requirement. You've earned it."

I was already planning out the first week of class in my head. This called for a new binder. I'd need to adjust the syllabus, and then there was getting the course set up online—

Breath, bitch! Your boss is still waiting for you to say something back.

"Thank you, Owen," I said, standing up for what I hoped would be the last time.

When I made it to my desk, I got to work on a course outline. Excitement seeped into the energy around me, making me feel lighter than I had in weeks. It was the first time I recognized myself in over a month.

Two things could exist at the same time. I could still enjoy parts of my life while I struggled with others. We could still hold celebrations for anniversaries and birthdays without forgetting the people who took up empty chairs at the table.

Jaxon could be here to help Spencer and Bryson during their darkest time and still be a stranger. I could be grateful for everything he'd done for my friends and still hate him as best as I could from afar.

Chapter Nineteen

JAXON

September 2021

Part of me hoped that the key Bryson gave me wouldn't work. When the knob turned effortlessly in my hand, I froze. There was no car in the driveway. I knew she wasn't home. Still, I craved for her to appear when I stepped inside.

A few sweatshirts hung on the hooks behind the door. I recognized the Converse sitting next to the entry rug. Picture frames and photos covered the living room walls, adding a homey touch to the disheveled space. A black shaggy carpet covered the floor between the TV and the set of couches she had pushed together in an L-shape fashion.

This was the place she disappeared to—free from the baggage of the past. I was a stranger who stood in the middle of it all.

I took a deep breath, searching for more reminders—evidence that we were *something*. Fuck, Maci was more than something. She was everything I gave up to try to give her better.

Familiar traces of her perfume lingered in the kitchen, where she probably rushed to get out of the house. The light on her coffee maker was still on, and when I opened the fridge, I knew I'd find coffee creamer and Dr. Pepper.

I pulled up the list Bryson sent me on my phone to regain focus. He was taking a huge risk, and I couldn't afford to waste any time. I was his last resort, and he was trusting me not to fuck it up.

Walking into the kitchen, it wasn't hard to guess what needed finishing. Jared installed a few counters and cabinets, but some didn't have the fixtures. Unopened boxes surrounded the dining table, which I assumed housed most of the missing pieces. I took a few pictures for reference before looking under the sink. Blue painters' tape marked which pipes were for what, and I knew they weren't for Jared's reference. His labeling system continued in the bathroom, the laundry room, and near the water heater.

In the garage, I opened the fuse box to find his scribbled handwriting next to each switch. He'd thought of everything.

"Well played, Foster," I said through a breathy laugh.

I helped myself to a seat at the dining table and took a page from the Koll Construction playbook. I needed an outline that didn't consist of Bryson's word vomit and pieces of Jared's notes.

After opening a few boxes in the kitchen, I decided to sort them by room and project. Instead of an endless ring of packages, I had four clearly marked piles. While the kitchen and living room housed most of the materials, items were still missing. Jared would never leave anything outside, so I checked the garage. It was empty except for a lawn mower and some gardening supplies.

Maci gardens? She couldn't even keep a vase of flowers alive.

I texted Bryson to see if there were any pending deliveries. It might explain the lack of countertops and cabinets. I had a few weeks' worth of work sitting in front of me, and I was starting to understand why Jared had Maci on a five-year plan.

A picture on her fridge caught my attention. It was of Maci and Bryson, both wearing winter hats and smiling into the camera. Her face was clean of any makeup, and I knew the redness in her cheeks was from the cold. The memory was important enough for her to want to see it every day. I searched for the guy I saw her with last month, but there was no evidence that she even knew him. He was still a mystery, just like everything else she had going on in her life.

More pictures of my college friend group continued on the side of the fridge, where a calendar took up most of the space. Her handwriting noted the classes she had for the month and the events she needed to attend. September seemed bare compared to her summer agenda.

August was when her world shifted. It was the reason I stood in her kitchen in the first place.

Maci wrote Spencer and Jared's Anniversary party in purple for tomorrow. A little heart she drew sat underneath it, the same personalization she included on every note she gave me and every card she signed.

I dragged a hand through my hair and did a final look around the kitchen. In another life, I had a jacket by the door. My shoes sat next to hers on the floor, and she wanted to keep pictures of me. It was my handwriting on the fuse box, and I told her where the main was in case she had to turn off the water.

In another life, I wasn't looking at a text from Bryson that told me a delivery was expected on Monday. In another life, I didn't have to choose and lose her.

Chapter Twenty

MACI

September 2021

Jared was lucky I appreciated his love for Marvel. It was the only logical explanation for the dozens of balloons knocking together in my backseat. They provided some comedic relief as I rounded the corner of Katie's street. I wasn't sure what the vibe was going to be once I passed through the front door, and it gave me a moment to pretend like Jared wasn't missing his first anniversary.

Spencer sounded okay when I called this morning, but I didn't expect her to hold it together all day. She'd grow tired of being social and eventually retire to her living room, where pictures of her and Jared would become wallflowers to how much she was truly hurting.

I teared up at the thought and quickly regained my composure. It wasn't in my role description to be emotional today. I was the positive backboard for all of the distractions Spencer would bounce off me today. It was our job to show her that we could still celebrate a milestone and that she wasn't alone.

Katie's reminder played in my head, *"You know it's just me and you in this conversation, Mace. You don't have to hold it all together for Spencer right now. Two things can exist at the same time."*

Katie and I should've programmed while Connor set up the backyard. Maybe my stomach wouldn't be in knots from the thought of having to see Jaxon again. Per Katie's instructions,

I threw on my positive attitude and made sure I was smiling when I walked through her front door. Connor met me with an appreciative grin, motioning that he would take the balloons off my hands.

"Thank you," I panted, as if I had lugged coolers of drinks into the backyard like he was in the middle of doing. We managed a hug through the mess of strings before he placed the decorations on the counter. "Is Spencer here yet?"

Connor shook his head. "Katie is in the back with Max."

"Hey." I caught his gaze. "How are you holding up?"

He shrugged, his smile tapering slightly. "It's hard, Mace."

"I know." I patted him on the shoulder as I passed. "We'll get through it together."

When he looked back at the microwave, I made my exit to the backyard. Like me, Connor needed permission to have a moment where he didn't have to have it all together. It was the part he played for his best friend—carry on with a smile and get the most out of the day. We tried to take turns wearing the mask.

When Spencer arrived, she gushed over the decorations and the shots we had ready on the dining room table. Her hair was down in soft curls, resting on the straps of her white sundress. She looked beautiful.

"You take a shot"—Connor threw back the green liquid and smacked the glass on the table—"send it up, and have a good time."

Spencer laughed through a few tears as Connor demonstrated Jared's party instructions. We all clapped and hollered when she slammed her shot glass down.

Elle came in next with her mom. A few of Jared's crew members and their families made themselves at home as kids flooded into the backyard, taking advantage of the water toys.

Eventually, everyone found space on the patio, only getting up to refresh their drinks or grab a plateful of food.

"I really wish you had let me use a caterer," Spencer said, her words slightly slurred after taking a few more shots.

Katie scoffed, switching out her empty White Claw for a fresh one. "Don't insult me like that." She turned to me with wide eyes. "I forgot about the brownies."

My offer to help with the missing dessert bought me a much-needed moment of solitude. The sliding door to the kitchen muffled the sounds from outside, loosening the tension in the screws that were holding up my smile.

A round of cheering exploded outside, probably announcing Bryson's arrival. He was the only one missing from our crew, and in typical Bryson fashion, he was over half an hour late.

I reached behind me for a potholder, putting the straps on my sandals to the test. The heat from the oven was making me sweat. Once I hit twenty-five, everything counted as a workout. Spencer and Katie had mentioned joining a cycling class once or twice last summer. It might be time for me to take their offer seriously and start picking out shoes.

Just as I was deciding on what color bike shorts to invest in for my imaginary cycling class, I heard the patio door shut behind me.

The one time I offered myself up as a second-string Betty Crocker, I became stuck in what could only be considered an advertisement for the same cologne that embedded itself in every hoodie I borrowed. Even with freshly baked brownies cooling on the stovetop, it found me.

I knew Jaxon would be here, but what were the fucking odds? I felt him before I saw him.

Maybe the universe had some sick agenda it had to follow. Maybe Jared really did have a pull in what happened from the other side. It was easier to blame him and then laugh later. It kept part of him alive.

"You wouldn't happen to know where cookies would go, would you?"

Is he really *asking me about cookies?*

Maybe he didn't recognize me from behind.

You should turn around and find out.

My body betrayed me, slowly turning until I had no choice but to face him. Everything around me halted—drawing my focus to the steady breaths I pulled into my chest. At least I *was* breathing. The way his eyes searched my face made me worried.

Time had erased every boyish feature I knew in college. Jaxon's hair was shorter, eliminating any evidence of the dark curls I loved to hang onto. His full lips were surrounded by a delicious five o'clock shadow, accentuating his sharp jawline. My favorite shade of green popped against his sun-kissed skin, looking completely unbothered behind long lashes that should've been illegal.

It was unfair, really. My mascara could never.

His gaze lingered on my mouth before he pushed a hand through his short hair. His nervous tick, his reaction when he was unsure what to say next.

Stop noting things. You don't know him. He isn't yours anymore.

His gray T-shirt pulled at his shoulders, emphasizing the defined muscles in his arms.

Fuck me.

Jaxon cleared his throat, setting his container of store-bought cookies on the kitchen table. "Did you need any help? Katie mentioned there were a few things that still need—"

"Nope," I snapped. "I'm fine."

Only I wasn't fine. In my attempt to get out of here as quickly as possible with Katie's decadent dessert, my elbow knocked into the corner of her glass baking dish, sending the tray to the floor along with the last scrap of my dignity.

Chapter Twenty-One

JAXON

September 2021

It was in the way that she looked at me. Her blue eyes were unable to convince the voice in her head that I was actually in front of her. They skimmed down my throat, crossing over my chest and rising again when she noticed I was still staring. I couldn't help but stare. I drank her in, sipping on the slightest chance to be close to her again. Like the first time I kissed her at Nate and Wally's—tongue red with cherry and eager to taste more.

She looked good that night—a black lace crop top and white jeans that hung on her hips. Her bare stomach drove me crazy, begging my hands to be on her skin and tracing the freckles that disappeared below her waistline. But nothing pushed me over the edge like her ass in a sundress—especially one that barely fell to her knees and emphasized her curves.

I rested my weight on my heels since she wasn't answering my question. I asked her if she was okay, but I could wait. I was in no hurry to rush the first and only moment I had alone with her since I saw her at Jared's service. Our interaction in Connor and Katie's kitchen would have a lengthy run time, and I'd lose track of how many times I replayed it.

I cleared my throat, prompting her to regain focus. "Are you good?"

She nodded fervently, as if my asking was some dramatized attempt to get close to her. She stood up, and I followed her lead, taking a step back to offer her the space she needed to adjust to my presence. I knew she'd—

Stop. You don't *know her.*

I had memories and snippets and everything in between from three years ago. I knew nothing about the woman standing in front of me. She had no clue that she could make my heart want to pound out of my chest just to prove that it was hers.

For the love of—

Get it together, Jaxon.

"My brownies!" Katie screeched. If it weren't for Max resting on her hip, she'd probably drop to her knees and try to piece them together. She pressed her free hand to her forehead, her eyes bouncing between Maci and me from underneath. "What happened?"

Maci shrugged. "I slipped?"

"Mhm." Katie pouted, adjusting her grip on Max.

I tried not to smile, pretending to have a sudden interest in the photos that covered the fridge. The scowl on Katie's face was one we received dozens of times.

"He wants a banana," Katie added, making her way across the kitchen. She shoved Max into my arms, and he smiled. "Do you mind getting him one? Random, I know."

Maci crossed her arms in front of her chest, looking me up and down once more before speaking directly to me. "Maybe I should do that."

I couldn't help but grin at what she was insinuating. "I've got two nieces back home. I promise I've got this."

Her face fell, and I pretended not to notice.

"Who brought these?" Katie demanded, picking up Bryson's cookie contribution.

"Who do you think?" Maci murmured.

Max let out a screech comparable to something I imagined a small dinosaur would make. It was the same sound Evie made whenever I took too long with cereal, blueberries, or really anything her little hands wanted.

"How's it going?" Katie prompted playfully from the floor. She held the dustpan steady as Maci swept the brownies into it.

"My man has no patience," I said, getting a chuckle from both of them. I placed a few banana slices on his tray to satisfy him.

"Did you take the initiation shot for the party?" Katie asked, smoothing out her red dress.

"Not yet."

"We need to bring one for Bryson, too," Katie added, handing Maci a shot to take outside.

"Just make sure he—" I hesitated to keep going, swallowing around the lump in my throat before I continued. "Give Bryson a water, please. He's been drinking since ten this morning."

An uncomfortable silence fell over the kitchen. Maci stared out into the yard while Katie rested her back against the counter, her eyes focused on the clean floor near her feet. The only sounds came from Max demanding more bananas from his high chair.

Maci took a deep breath before stepping outside, where more cheering and an enthusiastic Bryson met her. Katie rounded the kitchen island and stood beside me. I wasn't sure if it was the loud noise or the fact that I was in her space again. Whatever the reason, she leaned her head into my bicep and closed her eyes.

It wouldn't matter how much time passed. There was no denying the pull we all felt to what Jared's death left behind.

Chapter Twenty-Two

MACI

It could've been worse. Sure, I dropped some baked goods and couldn't formulate sentences, but at least I didn't shove my fist into Jaxon's face. It was a tiny baby step toward progress.

A baby step—like the ones his *nieces* took one day. The idea of Alex and Bella having two little girls left an embarrassing ache in my chest. It was foolish to feel hurt by the idea that they could've been mine, too.

On the wall behind me, my master's degree was framed and centered. Rows of literature I had poured over and high-lighted were proudly displayed as the background for all my Zoom meetings. I just finalized my course calendar for next semester.

I was smart. I was determined. I was proud of everything I had become. But on the days when my intrusive thoughts won and memories from the past poured in, I felt incapable of doing anything.

One comment. One fact about Jaxon's life I didn't know. That's all it took for me to place myself under the microscope again. And *oh*, how I hated him for it.

It was foolish to keep my ringer on loud, hoping he would call. It was ridiculous to delete some of my favorite songs from my playlist because they reminded me of him. It was wild to feel sentimental about the frost on my windows before I warmed up my car. But I was not foolish for believing in the life we talked about. I was *not* foolish for believing *him.*

There was a brief moment between Jaxon and me after I helped Bryson get into his car. A silent exchange so familiar that I almost believed the history that separated us was no longer there.

He wanted to ask me how I was doing. He'd phrase it in a way that would allow him to probe just a little bit. Maybe ask about a boyfriend or if I had someone at home who could get me if I decided to stay and drink more.

Part of me wanted him to ask. I wanted him to be curious. But as I patted my hand lightly against his car door to say goodbye, I reminded myself that I didn't need the question.

I was fine. *You're fine.* I was always fine.

When my parents split and rooted themselves in their new lives, I was fine.

When Chase followed Trey to Europe, I was fine.

When it took all three of my family members two weeks to call after Jared's death, I was fine.

As weeks turned into months, "fine" started to feel like holding my breath. It was only a matter of time before it dragged me under.

Chapter Twenty-Three

JAXON

October 2021

Summer trickled away slowly as September drifted into October. The breeze was no longer warm and inviting, and the greenery turned to a comforting fall palette overnight. It was a Tuesday morning when I showed up at Maci's house, and the tree in her front yard was no longer full of flowers. Another reminder that I couldn't be further from where I thought I would be.

After Jared and Spencer's anniversary party, it was no secret that Bryson wasn't doing well. On the days I knew I'd be at Maci's, Elle or Connor would swing by to make sure he wasn't disintegrating into the couch. Even with the playlist of low-impact workouts I made for him and the to-do list we shared on the computer, his free time still worried me. It was killing him not to be able to run or take a drive somewhere on his own.

While I was handling onsite projects and working from Jared's office when I could, Bryson was struggling to find a sense of purpose. Watching someone you loved struggle was beyond anything I had ever experienced. No matter how much you spoke, the words were never helpful, and no matter how much you did to try to help, you couldn't erase what happened or what they were going through.

I couldn't find the balance between what I was supposed to do and what I *should* do. In one week, I was supposed to be back in California, leading a board meeting that required my presence rather than a Zoom meeting. It was hard to convince investors that their money was backing a person when the person was never around. While people in business weren't complete robots, they lacked empathy when your personal choices moved past the deadline on their calendar.

Regardless of how my company felt about me being gone, I knew that finishing what I started was the right decision. Working on my ex-girlfriend's remodel might not have been what I was *supposed* to do, but finishing what Jared started? It was the first "should" that I was sure of in a hell of a long time.

Since Jared's labeling system saved me the headache of guessing which pipe went to where, it wasn't hard to get the washing machine hooked up and running. Bryson wasn't kidding when he mentioned that the system was shit. No one would've ever known that behind the water heater was a mismatched entanglement of gray and white snakes.

I threw in a small load of junk towels I'd set aside for cleanup and kept an eye on the standpipe. Before I finished the rest of the flooring, I wanted to make sure that any errors I might have made on my end didn't cost me my time or Maci's materials. She'd ordered one extra box of the planks, but it wouldn't be enough if the plumbing decided to work against me.

I pulled out my phone and dialed Bryson. His laughter tapered off as he answered, "What's up?"

I rested my lower back against the cabinet. "Am I on speaker?" A small giggle in the background told me I wasn't. "Take me off speaker."

"What's up?" Bryson repeated, sounding clearer than before. "You good?"

"Elle?" I prompted playfully.

"Yes," Bryson mocked my tone.

"Can you tell Maci that the team needs another hour or so?"

"How's the team doing?" He sighed. "Fuck. What happened? I knew I should've found you some help."

"I'm good!" I assured him. "Nothing happened, I just wanna check the laundry room off the list if I can."

As soon as I hung up with Bryson, I went to work. I laid out the flooring pieces, cutting them where they met the trim and layering them so the grain wouldn't repeat. It wasn't a ton of space to cover, but there was a lot to cut around. Some pieces required a little more attention than the table saw, and I realized I would need more than an hour.

I was just about to open another box of flooring when I heard the front door shut. I froze, as if my lack of movement would suddenly turn me invisible. Maci could head right upstairs, and I could sneak out the back. Maybe she was just dropping by to change, then heading back out.

When I finally looked over my shoulder, I saw Katie standing in the kitchen doorway.

"Maci's not here," I said.

"No shit," she snapped, her smirk curving into a smile. "Just wanted to drop in and see how the *crew* was doing. She'd lose her mind if she saw you here."

I unplugged the saw and helped myself to a bottle of water in the fridge. Katie's eyes followed my every step, watching me as I navigated a space I'd clearly been to before.

"How'd you know I was here?" I asked before sneaking a sip.

She leaned her back against the cabinet next to me. "Connor sucks at lying, and Bryson talks a lot when he drinks."

"Fair enough," I murmured.

"What are you doing?" Katie straightened up, unable to stand still. "Here. Like, what are you doing *here*?"

"Katie—"

"You made her look like an idiot for loving you, Jaxon. You completely broke my best friend. And the fact—" She pressed her fingertips to her temple. "The fact that I saw you as the good guy kills me. I don't know what your reason was—if there even was one. I couldn't do anything back then to help her, but I can help her now. You can't be here."

Her words hit harder than she realized. "Katie—"

"Stop," she warned, her eyes meeting mine. "When you walked away, it wasn't just Maci you left. She wasn't the only one who was disappointed. I don't know why you're still here, but I sure as hell hope that you don't prove me wrong again."

"I'm not here for her, Katie," I admitted quickly, unable to avert my focus from the floor. I couldn't look at her or pretend that what I had just said made any sense.

Because it didn't, and because she was Katie, she didn't wait to call me out on my bullshit.

She scoffed. "Really? You would've fooled me since you're standing in her kitchen." Her eyes softened as they followed the layout of the cabinets. "It looks good, though."

"I asked Bryson to let me help where I could while I was staying with him. I *wanted* to. I'm finishing up the floor in there, and then I'm out. I'm going back to Cali next week."

That news seemed to startle her more than me being here. "For how long?"

Since it was clear she wasn't leaving, I went back to the saw and picked up where I left off. "What do you mean, how long?" I chuckled. "That's where I live."

"Yeah, but—"

"But nothing," I added gently. "I'm not here for her, Katie."

I'm not here for her.

It wasn't worth admitting a third time, at least not out loud. Because I still wasn't sure if I believed it.

Chapter Twenty-Four

MACI

October 2021

"Spencer! Your windows are down, and I'm pretty sure it's going to—" I stepped over a pile of clothes and fell into a stack of boxes. I assessed the wine bottle in my hand for any damage. "Rain."

Spencer came running around the corner, blonde hair flying in all directions. "I'm sorry for the mess!" she exclaimed, making a dive for her car keys. Apparently, getting her windows rolled up took priority over saving me from her cardboard prison. "I got sidetracked."

"I'll say." I heaved myself up and kicked off my moccasins. "Do you have any sweatpants I can borrow?"

"Another late day at work?"

"Another day of the contractors needing more time at the house," I said, doing my best not to sound ungrateful. "Just one step closer, right?"

Spencer took the bottle from my hand and smiled. "Right. Let's pop this open, shall we? Katie should be here in a few minutes."

I took a seat at the breakfast counter, noting more boxes behind me.

"Sweatpants! Gimme one second." Spencer took off down the hall, leaving me alone and confused on a barstool.

"Hello!" Katie sang from the living room. She rounded the corner into the kitchen, scanning the space when she noticed I was by myself. "Where's Spence?"

Since our hostess was a little preoccupied, I took it upon myself to pour the wine. "Getting me pants."

Katie's smile grew just a tad. "Again?"

I exhaled slowly. "Again. But, hey! One step closer to having Christmas." I handed her a glass so we could cheers.

Katie peered over my shoulder to look down the hall. "Geez, how many pairs of pants does she have to choose from?"

I chuckled into my drink, setting it down just in time for Spencer to throw me a pair of black sweatpants. Because of the size, I assumed they were Jared's. I felt the soft material in between my fingers, hesitant to take them into the bathroom to change.

Spencer noticed me staring. "You're good. I have like ten other pairs."

Katie and I exchanged a glance before she gently asked, "Spencer, what's with all the boxes?"

Spencer raised a brow, taken aback by the question. She finished her sip of wine and gestured toward the bathroom. "Why don't you go ahead and change?"

I looked at Katie again, and she silently scolded me to follow Spencer's request.

"I'll get the dips in the oven," Katie offered. "I also have another bottle of red in my bag that I think will go well with these."

As Katie continued to pull from her Mary Poppins bag of goodies, I locked myself into the guest bathroom to change. I slipped on the sweatpants, laughing at how massive they were around the waist.

Why do this? Why give me these?

I was losing my grip, and no matter how hard I tried to hold on, I was falling. A few tears slipped down my cheeks, and I swiped them away.

Absolutely not. Not today.

Not ever, really. Every time there was a moment of weakness, I stood taller. However, no matter how tall I stood in these pants, they'd never leave the floor.

That's right. Find some sort of humor. That will make it pass.

There was laughter on the other side of the door. The sound of two friends preparing appetizers for our girls' gathering. A sign that things could still be good despite everything that had happened.

I splashed some water on my face and patted it dry with an Iron Man towel.

Endgame. God, he was everywhere.

"So the boxes," Spencer started once I took my seat. "I'm—I'm starting to go through things. I'm redecorating the space."

Katie threw her hands out in front of her. "That's great!"

"Jared would want you to make it your own," I added, my throat tightening as I said his name.

Spencer's eyes bounced around the room. "So things like clothes, trinkets, things we—*I* won't use . . . I'm just trying to cut down, you know?"

Considering I just had a moment over a hand towel, I knew exactly what she was saying. I imagined it was hard trying to find your own way when it was sprinkled with reminders of who was missing.

"Have you thought about storage?" Katie suggested taking a bubbling cheese dip out of the oven. It smelled heavenly.

Spencer tore open a box of crackers, ready to dig in. "Uhm, no, not exactly," she said, her voice skipping a few octaves. "I don't think I want more to move or keep track of."

Katie and I exchanged another glance. Our ability to have an unspoken conversation was immaculate at this point, and it was my turn to poke the fire.

"That's a lot of boxes," I commented. "They almost swallowed me whole."

Spencer stared at the steam coming from the dip on her cracker. "I spoke to Jaxon's dad a few days ago, and he mentioned an option that I hadn't thought of. I'm going to sell the house."

Katie and I watched the weight slip from Spencer's shoulders.

"I'm a writer," she added desperately. "I want to *find* myself again, and I don't think I can do it here. I'm only twenty-six. How can I already lose myself at twenty-six?"

"Sweetie, look at everything you've been through," I emphasized. "Your entire world shifted overnight."

"But even before Jar—" She paused, gathering herself before she continued. "Even before Jared passed, I had no idea what I was doing."

"Oh, honey," Katie spat, shoving a cracker full of dip into her mouth. "I *still* don't know what I'm doing."

"Neither do I," I said through a breathy laugh, sending all of us into an easy chuckle that we couldn't stop. Soon, we were laughing, and when we couldn't think of a good reason as to why we should be, we laughed even harder.

"But seriously—" Spencer wiped away a lingering tear. "*You* don't know what you're doing?"

Since I knew she wasn't talking to me, I took this opportunity to catch up on the wine I missed out on while I was changing. Katie had a fantastic husband, an adorable son, and was kicking ass at her job at the hospital. It wasn't a contest.

"Welp, if we really want to run down the list." Katie drummed her fingers on the countertop and smirked. "My uterus tapped out a few months ago, earning me the title of *infertile*. And then, there's the aching sense of dread that I don't want to do my job anymore. Which one do we want to target first?"

I cocked my head, as if I were the one weighing the options.

"Well, first of all, fuck your doctor," Spencer stated.

"You can't fuck science." Katie chuckled half-heartedly. "But I appreciate what you're trying to say."

"I didn't realize you guys were trying to have another baby," I said slowly, tiptoeing around the idea of my not knowing about something in Katie's life. It was the bittersweet passage that a best friend went through when they got a significant other. I was no longer in the top tier of support.

"We stopped trying after that appointment," Katie admitted. "But, it's okay! I've been focusing all of my energy on work."

"You mean the job you're not sure that you want," Spencer deadpanned.

Katie rolled her eyes. "Yeah."

"So what's the new dream?" I asked, eager to keep the silence stayed away.

"New dream?" Katie poured herself more wine. "I'm only a few years into my old one."

"Uhm, so am I, and you're not making me feel any better about it," Spencer said.

"I can't just quit my job and go to culinary school."

I smiled. "I knew it."

Katie shot me a menacing side-eye.

"Why can't you?" Spencer demanded through a gasp prompted by wine and a dip-filled stomach. She had to be feeling good. I was creeping up behind her, and I at least had a few tacos for lunch.

"I went to college," Katie argued. "I got the degree and I did the work. Fuck, I have a kid!"

We could see the heaviness of it all. Everything Katie had been carrying lately was placed on the counter for us to decipher. This entire time, I thought I was the only one with the mask. It turned out that I wasn't the only one good at hiding it.

"So you're not allowed to dream?" Spencer softly asked, her voice growing louder with each question. "Like, that's it? Do we get one shot to get what we want? You went to college and got a piece of paper." Her mouth split into a half-hearted grin. "Don't spend another minute of your life doing something that you no longer love."

Katie planned her following words carefully. She didn't want to rock this boat, not when we were already struggling in a canoe without oars. "Well, I don't know how much yours was, but I paid a lot of money for that piece of paper."

"Would you return it?" I challenged, lifting a brow as I shoveled in another mouthful of dip.

Katie winced. "Probably."

I mimicked her expression. "I think you have your answer, sweetie."

After another ten minutes of dip and wine, we spent the rest of the evening helping Spencer pack her life into boxes. It didn't take long to get the ball rolling. Once Katie and I provided the bumpers, Spencer rolled with confidence, striking down every single pin that might have stood in the way of her decision.

When I walked into my living room a few hours later, the lack of boxes and piles of clothing made the space look incredibly clean. I flicked on the kitchen lights, noting that every time the crew left after a late afternoon shift, they left the living room lamp on. Whatever company Bryson contracted through, they were moving quickly. The only evidence of their arrival was the finished projects, and I was eager to see what was behind my laundry room doors.

The smell of fresh wood and detergent greeted me when I stepped inside. The light flooring looked beautiful, complementing the black fixtures on the sink and the dark cabinetry above the appliances. There was a quirky line of trim that was original to the home, and it made me smile to see that the team left it, cutting the floor so it ran along the winding wall instead of straightening it out.

It was a finished laundry room, and it was *mine*.

I giggled as I ran upstairs, eager to throw in a load of laundry that didn't come from Katie or Spencer's house. I reached a new level of adulting.

I tossed in a capful of scent beads, turned the dial, and watched with joy as the water poured in. While the washer warmed up for its first official cycle, I decided to pre-treat a pair of dress pants that were victimized by salsa verde. Only when I stepped forward did I notice it wasn't just me who dipped downward; the floor did too.

Putting pressure on my foot, I listened again to the agonizing sound coming from beneath the floor.

Water—and a shit ton of it.

I gasped as a small trickle of water emerged from beneath the washing machine, meeting another line that came from beneath the sink. Which one was the culprit? I turned off the water, but the steady trickle still rolled across the floor.

"What the fuck!" I exclaimed to the empty room of witnesses.

I began to spiral. I couldn't call a plumber. This late at night? The rates would be ridiculous and probably drain the rest of the budget I had for the bathroom upstairs.

The alarm bells went off, and I darted back into the living room to grab my phone, so I could dial the one person I knew who might be able to provide a lifeline.

Chapter Twenty-Five

JAXON

October 2021

After my third touchdown in a row, Bryson began to pace in front of the TV. Usually, I'd yell at him to get out of the way, but I kept the rage inside. A few days ago, his doctor cleared him to stop using his wheelchair. Bryson was up and walking around again, and I was happy to see him back on his feet.

"Best two out of three?" he offered, helping himself to another slice of pizza.

I couldn't tell him no. I wanted to continue his alcohol-free celebration and feed into his excitement. "Yeah, one more game."

He slumped back into the recliner, and I gave it five minutes before he was up and walking around again.

Working over at Maci's house was draining me of any extra energy I had to give out. I even skipped the gym this morning, exhausted at the idea of having to wake up early tomorrow to catch my flight back to California. I needed a reset, and watching Bryson fly out of his seat reassured me that it was okay for me to head back to my obligations.

Only this time, it wouldn't be such a long goodbye. I wouldn't disappear, and I'd make the effort. Somehow, I'd find the balance between what I should do and what I wanted to do.

"Timeout," Bryson muttered, reaching for his phone. He furrowed his brow before taking the call. "Everything good?"

The high-pitched response he received to a simple question alerted me that this was no ordinary late-night call. Suddenly, we were back in our college apartment, waiting to continue our game while Bryson took care of some broad he had happened to piss off the night before.

I took a sip of my water to hide my amused grin.

"Maci, you know I don't know the answer to that," Bryson said through a humorless chuckle. He pressed his palm to his forehead, eyeing me from under his arm. "How bad is it?"

I slowly lowered my drink while Bryson nodded at something she said.

"Fuck," he muttered, muting her so she couldn't hear what he was saying. "She's got some sort of leak coming from the washer and the sink downstairs."

"Did she turn off the main?" I couldn't hide the urgency in my voice. "I just did those floors."

Bryson repeated my question to her.

I was already slipping my hoodie over my head. "Tell her you'll have someone over there soon."

"Someone?"

"Well, you can't say it's me!" I exclaimed, mimicking his cocky grin. "She might choose to let the kitchen flood, too!"

Maci's muffled voice continued as I shut the door behind me. Fuck, it was cold out. I didn't miss the winter in the Midwest. I also didn't miss having to warm up my car to leave.

Frost covered the windshield, preventing me from peeling out of the driveway. I rubbed my hands together as the heat made its way through the cabin, slowly creeping up the glass and clearing my view. It reminded me of a night in

November—four years ago, when I wasn't alone and waiting didn't seem so bad.

Maci couldn't have gotten any closer to me in the backseat if she had tried. We were parked near a lake outside of the city, away from the noise of her New York apartment and surrounded by dark skies and a breeze that shook the car.

"Jaxon, you said this wouldn't take long!" she exclaimed through a whiny laugh. Her chattering teeth made me hug her even harder, and I chose not to remind her that only a few moments ago, she was hot and heavy underneath me with no clothes on at all.

I glanced over the driver's seat to sneak a peek at the dashboard. "The warm air is coming. I told you we should've kept the car on."

"And risk getting caught by some eager park ranger? No, thank you."

I rolled my eyes. "No one is out here in this cold."

She scoffed. "Please. You spend a few winter months out in the sunshine of California, and suddenly you forget that people can survive outside in the cold."

"At two o'clock in the morning!" My hand shot out in front of me to survey the space in front of us, sending her into a fit of giggles. "The only audience we'd have is probably deer or some shit."

"Can you just let me whine?" She turned to face me. The color in her cheeks made me smile, igniting a much-needed rush of warmth to my chest. "I hate how you have to go back tomorrow."

When she averted her gaze to the windshield, I pulled her close again. She was trying not to cry, and I didn't want her to carry anything by herself during our last few hours together.

"It's just hard," she added, her voice shaky. "I miss you."

"I know, pretty girl," I whispered, planting a kiss on her temple. "I miss you, too."

As her mouth traveled up my neck and found its way to mine, I remembered willing the heat to cloak her instead, and when I leaned us back so she was on top of me, I snaked my hands up her hoodie, urging it to move faster. I wanted to give her everything. I wanted to *be* everything that she needed. Always.

We made love as the windows cleared around us, and it was the last time we were together in her car. That was the last time I ever flew out to see her in New York.

⁓

Traffic moved slowly on my way to Maci's, and as my fear for her flooring grew, it allowed me to clear my head.

Time had changed so much between us. How did a person who was your everything become a stranger you were nervous to face again?

Maybe nervous wasn't the right word. Was it excited? Nah. If I was excited, *that* made me nervous. I couldn't be excited. I wasn't here for Maci. But as I pulled into her driveway, I realized it didn't matter what I wanted or how I felt.

Maci Lawson accepted my heart five years ago. I'd say she stole it, but that would make it sound like I was unwilling. The truth was, I gave it to her, and she took it gladly. As I stood in front of her, I realized why everything still hurt.

The ache in my chest surfaced right after I ended things. I remained empty.

It wasn't that my heart couldn't belong to anyone else. The pain never left because I didn't want it to.

Chapter Twenty-Six

MACI

October 2021

I couldn't make this shit up even if I tried. I called one man from my past, and he sent the other. In what twisted universe was my first flood happening in?

"Can I come in?" Jaxon asked. He was being polite, but he couldn't hide the urgency in his voice.

I stepped aside and he flew past me, leading us to the scene of the crime.

It all happened so fast. His cologne sent my body into panic mode, seeking refuge from a scent that wasn't allowed here. We banned that trigger years ago when it had the power to perk me up and pull me under.

Jaxon pulled the washer from the wall and examined the pipes behind it. He dipped around the basin of the sink, following the trickle of water as it flowed from underneath the trim of the wall.

Water sprayed up his sleeve as he turned a knob on one of the pipes. "Reach above the water heater and turn off the main!"

I peered into the closet around the corner. "How do I know it's the main?"

"Because Jared labeled all of them for you."

I examined the labels on the blue painter's tape hanging from the pipes. In my moment of panic, I forgot to look up.

With one twist, the spray of water meeting Jaxon's forehead subsided.

He stood slowly, allowing droplets of water to roll down his face as he examined the damage. I wanted to look away. I *tried* to look away. When the water trailed down his jawline, I focused on the sink to avoid biting my lip.

He ran a hand through his short hair, sending a small spray of water in all directions. "You said you turned off the main."

I crossed my arms in front of my chest, barely holding it together so I could muster up a response without laughing. "I thought I did."

Jaxon slowly shifted his gaze from my hands until his eyes met mine. Deep and green—waiting for me to say something else that would give him direction on what to do next.

I had no guidance to offer. Jaxon found the source of the problem quickly and seemed to know his way around. He knew about Jared's tape labels and—

"How did you know Jared labeled the pipes?" I asked.

He gestured to the closet. "Lucky guess."

"Fucking Bryson," I said through a laugh. My smile tapered as the pieces fell into place. "It's been you coming over, hasn't it?"

He seemed encaptured by our silent exchange, as if any sudden movement might spook me back to pretending he didn't exist. Most of me wished he would. But a small part of me still lingered in the noise.

"I knew he found someone too quickly," I added. "Bryson couldn't hang a shelf if I asked him to, let alone interview a contractor."

Jaxon stripped off his wet hoodie and placed it on top of the dryer. "Mind if I get a towel?"

My eyes drifted unwillingly down his shirt. "You know where they are."

He brushed past me, his body taking up most of the doorway. I couldn't believe I thought an actual crew had been here for the past few weeks. All of the work that had gone into my home suddenly felt tainted, blurred by a vision that I tried like hell to keep clear.

"Don't you leave tomorrow?" I blurted.

He smothered his cocky grin with a towel. "Been counting down the days, have you?"

"And if I was?"

Jaxon tossed the towel over his shoulder and grabbed a few more out of the box. "I'd expect nothing less." He passed me again, only this time he made more of an effort to ensure there was no space between us.

My mouth dried up so fast that I had to clear my throat to speak. "The water is off. I can call a plumber tomorrow morning."

He assessed the damage in front of him. "I wanna get this flooring up so it can start to dry for whoever is coming over tomorrow."

I furrowed my brow. "So, there really is a crew?"

Jaxon hit me with a look that could've knocked me out right there in the doorway. The right side of his mouth deepened into his dimple, and his eyes crinkled slightly in the corners.

"Listen—" He ran another hand through his hair. It felt good to see him nervous for a change. So far, I thought I was alone in this unexpected reunion. "I told Bryson I would cover the work until his doctor cleared him. I'll be back in—"

"Bryson?" An exasperated laugh escaped me. "He might have helped Jared in the background, but he didn't actually do any of the handiwork."

"A crew will take over once I'm gone," he assured me. "I was trying to help him save money where he could."

I saw right through his innocent grin. "You did this for Jared."

His mouth twisted slightly before he answered. "Yeah."

The pressure behind my eyes started to build. I stared down at Jared's sweatpants, unable to believe that my girls' night with Katie and Spencer had only happened a few hours ago.

Jaxon looked up and down the wall behind the sink. "Do you have any plumbing upstairs?"

The impending cloud of betrayal returned overhead.

You've been coming over for weeks. Wouldn't you know?

"I haven't been upstairs," he said, reading my mind. The hands that used to coax my body over and over again slid along the walls, reminding me of what it felt like to have his fingers trail the sensitive line of my lower back.

I tucked my hair behind my ears and nodded.

"I'll let the team that's coming on Monday know. As for your bathroom and kitchen, I'm happy to come and—"

"Wait, my kitchen?" I whined, spinning around to try to locate the damage. "What's wrong with the kitchen?"

His words were hot against my neck. "There's water underneath this floor right here." He pointed down, where I could see a slight line in the wood. "See? That will need to be cut out and replaced."

My stomach dipped, and I stepped away to create some space between us. For one weak moment while Jaxon paced around the kitchen, I let myself picture it. He cared this much because it was his space to look after, too. It was our place—*together*—and it wasn't just about finishing what Jared started or helping Bryson because he needed the additional support.

It was because this was the version of our lives where it worked out. This was the part where we stayed up all night, frustrated with each other because a DIY project went south. It was a night when he drove me crazy, and I tested his patience. It was supposed to be us.

"I can come by when I'm in town and help finish what I started," he offered, unable to look at me. "It could at least get you a finished space by Christmas. I know that was important to you."

It felt like the room was shrinking around us, pushing me closer to him, and I had no way of escaping. When Katie told me he was leaving, I felt relieved. His time here in Chicago had an end date. He'd go his way, and I would go mine. Our friends would move forward, and everything would snap back to the way it was before Jared passed.

Only that wasn't what was happening. Jaxon would be back, and there was nothing I could do about it. I worked too hard over the years to build my walls and draw my boundaries. I knew what letting him back in would do. Even if it was on a professional level, I couldn't do it.

And I didn't have to.

"I'm sure whatever team Jared has on deck will be great," I said, my voice a little raspy. "But thank you for everything you've done. It looks really good."

With a slight nod of his head, he understood what I was saying. There was nothing left to respond with. He cleaned up what he could, and I offered him a bottle of water for the road.

"Take care of yourself, Maci," he said, offering me a small, half-hearted smile before he closed my door behind him.

I watched him leave from behind my curtain, and when the taillights turned at the corner, I did nothing to stop the tears from slipping down my cheeks.

Chapter Twenty-Seven

JAXON

October 2021

Even though I'd be smiling in the Halloween-inspired selfies my mom snapped of us tonight, when I saw them hanging in her office, I'd know that I wasn't happy.

Happy to see her? Always.

Happy that she traveled across the country by herself to see me? Furious.

Her immune system wasn't what it used to be. If one wrong bug weaseled its way into her system, she could be back in the hospital. Dad was no help. When I called, he assured me that she insisted on coming by herself. Something about "A boy needing his mama," or whatever persuasive nonsense she swayed him into believing before she hopped on a plane.

I hadn't even had time to unpack my interaction with Maci. Being in the same room with her like that—having a conversation as if we didn't have a past. Seeing her in baggy sweatpants that I guessed belonged to some guy, while she looked completely pissed to be in my presence. I was a stranger to her, and every time I found myself feeling upset about it, I shut it down. I wasn't allowed to feel a certain way about it. I created it. I chose this, and this was the aftermath of that choice.

Evelyn Hayes sat next to me on the love seat, wearing a glittery purple witch hat and counting down the seconds until another eager trick-or-treater knocked on my door.

"Ma, if you wanted to go trick-or-treating so badly, why didn't you just stay home so you could take Evie and Peyton?" I took a sip of beer, flipping from *Scream* to *Hocus Pocus*. I was in the mood for something nostalgic, and a masked person running around with a knife wasn't cutting it. Plus, I loved me some Sanderson Sisters.

There was a knock on the door, and before I could even get a slight grip on the bowl, Mom swatted my hand.

"Honestly, Jaxon—Jaxon Reed!" She laughed when I tried to push her back onto the couch. "Stop trying to beat me to it!"

If I could bubble wrap this woman while she was here, I would. I watched her tiny frame cross my living room, eager to greet the costumes behind the door. Her mouth lifted into a giant grin, carefully scanning each kid's character choice and making sure everyone got a compliment.

Instead of enjoying Halloween with her grandkids, she was forcing me to wear cat ears and fuzzy gloves that made my hands look like paws. Yeah, it was cute, but nothing beat Evie in her Little Red Riding Hood getup, and Peyton as a wolf pup. Mom was on a mission; she just hadn't filled me in on what it was yet. I knew she'd break eventually. I had a way with my mom that my dad never understood.

She was the first person I ever truly saw standing in my corner, and I was terrified to lose her.

"Where's the wine I brought?" Mom surveyed the kitchen. "We also have those fun skeleton wine glasses we got from that local gift shop."

I used my free paw to direct her to the cabinet next to the microwave. "Can you just pour me some whiskey?"

Mom raised a brow in question. "Anything with it?"

I shook my head, getting up to throw my empty beer bottle in the trash. "But please don't rob me of a skeleton wine glass."

"I swear you're more and more like your father each time I see you."

"Lucky you." My smile tapered when she struggled to keep the bottle steady. "Ma—"

She whipped around to face me. "Stop."

I held up my hands in defeat. "I just worry, that's all."

"I know you do. Everyone is *always* worrying. You spend more time worrying than just being present with me." Her shoulders slumped, and she closed her eyes. "I only mean . . . this thing has taken so much from us already. I refuse to give it any more time."

I swallowed around the lump in my throat, refusing to crack under the pressure. Mom didn't need me to tear up or sound upset. She didn't need me to coddle her with excuses or try to protect her. It was up to me to carry it, the idea that I couldn't save her. I couldn't do anything but the exact opposite of what I had been doing since she showed up on my doorstep.

"We've got those cookies too," I offered. There was another knock on the door. "I'll get the next one while you put them in the oven?"

Her mouth curved into a soft smile, and she went back to pouring the drinks.

After we baked the cookies, we spent the rest of *Hocus Pocus* sipping from our skeleton wine glasses and reminiscing on Halloween from when Alex and I were kids. We'd been fortunate enough to spend them all in the same house, knowing which streets were best to hit up for the king-size candy bars and which places had the best decorations. It seemed so long ago—back when my mind was taken up by sports, friends, and girls.

"What was the girl's name who wanted to dress up with you in high school?" Mom asked, flushed and with glossy eyes. She could barely hold in her laughter to finish her question. "Was it Peter Pan?"

I put my drink down on the coffee table so I wouldn't spill it. "It was Jess. She had fucking tights and everything."

"Jess from Bella's wedding?"

"Yes!" I exclaimed, making her laugh even harder. "That girl drove me nuts in high school."

"Well, you were kind of a jackass to her."

I inhaled sharply. "Not my proudest era."

Mom placed her drink next to mine and turned to face me. I hadn't realized I was bouncing my knee until she calmed it with her hand. "You were gone for a while. Can I ask about it now that you're back?"

An exasperated laugh slipped from my chest. "There's not much to say. I just wanted to help where I could. I've—" I thought of the pictures that covered Maci's fridge. "I just missed so much. I owed it to Jared to finish some of what he started, and Bryson . . . I should've been there for him a long time ago."

Mom leaned back on the couch. "I wasn't surprised when you mentioned you were staying. I think it was a great idea." She sat up again, unable to sit still with her questions. "How is she?"

"Spencer might sell the house. I don't blame her. I'm not sure if I could keep it."

Mom nodded slowly, her lips pressed into a tight line. Wine was an excellent weakness in Evelyn Hayes' poker face.

I ran a hand through my hair. "That's not the she you were asking about, was it?"

Her silence was so fucking loud, I was positive she woke up the neighbors across the street. There was no follow-up question or guesses. Instead, she mocked me with her sweet little skeleton glass.

I unwillingly smiled as a montage of tiny memories played in my head. It started back on day one, when I met her in a small-town Dairy Queen with a Cotton Candy Blizzard in her hand. It blended into the first night I kissed her, with the taste of cherry and sangria on my tongue, eager for more but unable to continue what I started. The first night we slept together on Spring Break, and when I chased her down the street on St. Patrick's Day.

One Tree Hill. College graduation. New York City and everything in between.

My first and only "I love you." Hundreds of memories wrapped around one girl.

"She's better than anything I could have imagined about her," I said, my voice barely above a whisper.

Damn. You couldn't even try to play off what you just spent five minutes thinking about.

"Good." Mom patted my wrist. "Because you're going back."

My bittersweet walk down memory lane came to a screeching halt. "What?"

She stood up, gathering the glasses and making a beeline toward the sink. The energy around her quickly shifted from bubbly and carefree to eager and rigid.

Was this the big news she had to say in person? My dad was so disappointed that he sent my mom to do it. That had to be it. There was no other reason they'd strip me from my office and suggest I go back.

My heart pounded in my chest as I followed her into the kitchen. "Look, I took some time, but I'm back now. I'm sorry."

She furrowed her brow. "Why are you apologizing?"

"Because I failed. I wasn't here. I didn't do what I told you I would do."

It might have been the whiskey, but I swore the room was spinning. I gripped the counter to steady myself, drawing in deep breaths to try and convince my body that we weren't running for our lives.

Or maybe we were, and I wasn't overreacting.

"Baby, you have—"

"I haven't," I countered quickly. "That's why you're here."

You failed, and they aren't surprised.

You'll always fail. You had one purpose. It's easier just to let you go than to keep you.

"I'm here because you're my son," she said, unable to hide the urgency in her voice. I felt her hand on my forearm. "And it's *my* job to come when you need me, even when you don't ask me to."

"You shouldn't be here. You should be resting or taking the girls trick-or-treating."

She chuckled softly, and my grip on the counter relaxed. "I've done a ton of resting, baby. I want to be here . . . *with* your dad. He wants to do this for you while you—"

"No," I snapped, pushing off from the counter. "I owe Dad this. *You* this. When I stepped into this role, I knew what it meant. I chose this."

"You don't *owe* him anything."

"I owe you and Reed *everything*," I practically shouted. Her eyes widened, and I took a step back. This space wasn't big enough, and I feared I might snap. "You've given me *everything*, and running Hayes Sports & Entertainment is the best way to pay you back—"

"Stop." Mom threw up her hands. "Stop with the owing and the paying and the next way you were thinking of phrasing it." She placed her hands on my chest. "I need you to hear me when I say this."

I shifted my focus to her, staring into eyes that were the same green as mine. The gloss grew more apparent in her patient gaze.

"I am so sorry that the two people who were supposed to love you more than anything made you feel like that was something you had to *earn* from us, and made you feel like you weren't worthy enough to give it to someone else."

Her words hit me like a fucking freight train.

"When you love someone—" She wiped a few tears from her cheeks. "You really do try to give them everything, regardless of what sacrifices you have to make. To say we gave you *everything*, boy, that's a bold-faced lie."

"You gave me a pretty damn good life, Ma."

"And what gives you the right to speak like it's over?" she spat. "There are some things that we will never be able to give you, but we don't want you compromising parts of your life because you feel like you have some sort of debt to pay."

"I'm going back to Chicago for Thanksgiving," I argued. "I can do what I need to do here and still visit." She started shaking her head, and an unconvincing laugh worked its way into my plea. "I didn't stay there for her, Ma."

"Not saying you did. But I won't watch this job eat you alive. What you need now . . . your *everything* . . . you aren't going to find it here. Maybe one day it'll bring you back. But that day isn't today."

My everything. The idea of going back without an end date forced a calm sweep throughout my nervous system. I wasn't sure what the endgame was, or where it would lead me, but I was relieved. And it felt pretty damn good.

Chapter Twenty-Eight

MACI

ANOTHER HOLIDAY, ANOTHER EVENING with Bryson Kennedy. It felt nice to have some normalcy back in my routine. While Katie and Connor indulged with Max at a local Trunk Or Treat, Bryson was keeping me company for my first official Halloween as a homeowner. My neighborhood was full of eager trick-or-treaters, and I was loving the distractions.

Today marked a week since Jaxon left for California. He'd gone just as quickly as he arrived, slowly and unexpectedly, with a long trail of unidentified emotions behind him.

I might have been complex with my inner thoughts, but I wasn't an idiot. There were things Jaxon wanted to say to me. He was never one to stay quiet when he had a point to make. Or I was just in my head about it all, longing for an explanation that I would never receive. It could be as simple for him to leave it all behind, the same way it was the first time.

Jesus, Maci. Have another White Claw, please. You're pathetic as fuck.

My head whipped around to Bryson, as if he had muttered the dig instead of me. They say the first step to recovery is admitting that you have a problem. Katie mentioned getting therapy after Jared passed. Perhaps this was the final step in acknowledging that I needed help.

"Want another beer?" Bryson asked from halfway inside my fridge.

Or I needed another drink. Beer was cheaper than therapy anyway.

There was a knock on the door, and I almost twisted my ankle sprinting to see what costumes were on the other side.

"Are you going to do that every time someone knocks?" Bryson chuckled, switching on the TV.

I waved goodbye to Woody and Buzz Lightyear and closed the door. "Just because you're the Halloween grump in your complex—"

"I'm not a grump." He handed me my drink as I fell onto the couch. "I'm usually out on Halloween."

"Did you not have plans tonight?"

He shrugged his shoulders, side-eyeing me as my mouth curved into a heartfelt grin.

I lovingly patted his hand. "You *wanted* to hang out with me, didn't you?"

He recoiled at my touch, laughing as I hit him with an obnoxious, "Aww."

"You won't come to my place!" he argued. "It seemed like a good night to just chill."

"You had an infestation there for a while, my man. Were your usuals taken already for the evening?"

"Yes, they were." He clicked on *Jeepers Creepers* and placed the remote on the coffee table. "And don't be bitter."

"I'm not being bitter," I muttered.

"Whatever you say," he countered playfully. "In all seriousness, is that how it's going to be when he's back in town? Like, should I just not plan to see you?"

"You did it for over two months. A long weekend here and there won't put you out."

He hit me with a cocky grin. "Bitter ass. Exactly why did you end things with Derek? When's the last time you got some?"

I laughed into my beer bottle. It didn't matter what Bryson called me next. I missed him. I missed *this*. And I was grateful to see some of his light shine through again.

"It was time to let Derek go. As for Jaxon, I have no reason to be around him," I explained. "He's your friend, not mine."

"And the timing is just, what, a coincidence?" he prompted. It was only a matter of time before he dove into that timeline. "What about holidays?"

I bounced my head back and forth to weigh my answer. "Birthdays?"

"I think you're giving him a ton of credit for someone who so easily cut you off for three years," I admitted, sounding harsher than I wanted to. "Okay, *now* you can call me bitter."

"Touché, though."

We both winced at the same part in *Jeepers Creepers*, and I sensed a subject change. I'd happily greet whatever topic he decided on with open arms. There was no reason to delve into something that might not even happen yet. Either way, the time spent with Jaxon helped bring Bryson out of the shadows, and for that, I was grateful.

The doorbell rang again, and I snatched my bowl of candy from the coffee table. When I opened the door, I let out an obnoxious squeal.

Bryson leaped off the couch, confusing my excitement with a cry for help. His shoulders relaxed when Max came waddling in dressed up as a cow.

"Well, that's fucking cute," Bryson swooned, crouching to get eye-level with Max.

Katie held up two bottles of wine and invited herself in. "We brought rations."

"The trunk thing ended early, so we invited ourselves to crash," Connor added. "Hope that's okay."

They looked relieved to have shortened plans, so relieved that Katie was already unscrewing her first bottle of wine.

"Yeah, you can have one of these!" Bryson said, holding Max in one arm and his pumpkin pail in the other. "Only if you let me have a Reese's Cup." He disappeared into the kitchen, and with one look from Katie, Connor followed closely behind them.

"The last thing I need is a trip to the emergency room because Bryson gave my toddler a gumball," Katie said. "Your decorations look great, by the way. The house is super cute."

"Thank you," I beamed, surveying the spider webs on the mantel.

"You're sure you can't do Friendsgiving?" Katie scrunched her nose. "We could totally fit a few tables in here."

"I'll be lucky if I can have Christmas." I sighed into my palm. "Jaxon said the water from the laundry room got underneath the flooring in the kitchen, too."

She tapped her freshly manicured nails against her wine glass. The innocent little ghosts on her ring finger almost convinced me that she didn't have a comment brewing. "I mean, you *could* host Christmas. You have an offer."

This bitch. I knew I shouldn't have mentioned Jaxon's offer. When I shared the recap of my discovery about the so-called crew that had been coming to my house, I may have provided too many details about our conversation before he left.

Katie held up a defensive hand. "Look, I'm not saying to forget or forgive. Buuuut you guys were twenty-four when you broke up."

"Okay, *and?*"

She shrugged, slipping in a quick sip of wine before continuing. "*And* you might as well have been babies."

I cackled at the fact that we were even having this conversation. "It wasn't that long ago!"

Katie lowered her voice. "Look how much has changed in three years. You're not the same person you were when he—"

"Shattered my heart," I mumbled pathetically.

She gave me a sympathetic grin. "I'm just saying, you might be able to host Christmas. If it speeds up the process, then why not?"

I hated how the more she spoke, the more it made sense. The thought of waiting until next year for construction to be over made my stomach churn. Every day I woke up, reminded by power tools and random wood planks that the man who poured so much love, time, and effort into my home wasn't coming back. I'd never watch Jared walk through the front door, tapping the frame and making some sort of comment like, "It's coming along!" or "It's looking good, Lawson!"

The day after I found out it was Jaxon coming over to work on the house, "Unwritten" by Natasha Bedingfield came on when I was in the shower. I had a borderline panic attack. It was the same song that Jared and I sang right after Jaxon ended us. Jared held my hand and stayed with me the entire night, giving me the perfect balance of space and support.

My mind raced as the lyrics surfaced conversations about endgames and happy endings. I was so tired of the reminders. I was ready for the pain surrounding Jared to transform into moments of peace where I could feel him here—embedded in the work he did to build me back up after Jaxon buried me.

So how the fuck was I supposed to depend on the man who held the shovel?

When Connor and Katie left a few hours later with a sleepy and sugar-filled Max, Bryson and I turned off the lights and put on one last movie.

Heart hammering, I leaned into his side and crossed my ankles, willing the words to come out so I could stop sitting with them. "Can I ask you something without you being an ass?"

He stared down at me, a slight look of concern settling in his gorgeous, golden-brown eyes. "Hit me."

"Does the offer still stand so I can have Christmas?"

His eyebrows shot to the top of his forehead, but to my pleasant surprise, there was no witty comeback or unwanted comment. Instead, he just rested his arm around my shoulders and sank deeper into the couch. "I was just about to send him the dates for Friendsgiving."

With a quick nod, I ended the conversation. We fell asleep on the couch under a few fluffy blankets, only to wake up to a crisp November morning, where winter announced its arrival with cold air and an unforgiving breeze.

Last night, I chose to prioritize my peace. I just hoped, with everything I had, that it was worth it.

Chapter Twenty-Nine

MACI

November 2021

Indefinitely. I hadn't realized that word was in Bryson's vocabulary until it was leaving his perfectly full lips.

Jaxon Hayes was coming back to Chicago indefinitely, booking a one-way ticket with no idea when he'd return to California. The plot line made no sense. The entire time we were together, Jaxon stressed the importance of being there. Suddenly, he had unlimited miles to use and a knack for catching me off guard.

When I woke up this morning, I expected a message from Bryson saying Jaxon would be over while I was at work. My dear friend failed to mention that it would be an evening visit since Jaxon's flight wouldn't arrive until late in the afternoon.

I glanced at the time on my screen—5:04 PM. Bryson said five o'clock, so it was only a matter of time before—

There was a knock at the door, and I regretted choosing chai tea over wine for tonight's lesson planning beverage.

Jaxon looked surprised when the door opened between us, almost as if he wasn't expecting me to answer it. He wore a solid black hoodie, blue jeans, and tennis shoes.

It was simple. It was Jaxon.

The Carolina Panthers beanie that I borrowed more times than I could count covered his head. The black cat was taunting me, denting the relaxed expression I had practiced a few times in the mirror with an unnecessary smirk.

"Hi." I gestured to the room behind me. "Come on in."

He brushed past me with a smile that one gives to a stranger in the grocery store aisle. The silence between us was so loud that the furnace kicking on made me jump. Jaxon sensed it too, and when he took his hat off to run a hand through his short hair, I knew it was driving him crazy.

"Bryson told me that the team couldn't come?" He placed his hat on the dining table. With the hot air pushing through the vents, it was only a matter of time before his hoodie came off next.

"I guess a few of their contractors got sick." I shrugged my shoulders. "I haven't touched anything since you were last here."

The slight curve of his mouth betrayed his efforts to remain professional. "No more water?"

I failed at suppressing my smile. "No."

Fuck me.

"If you're cool with it, I can rip this out right now."

"Like . . . right now, right now?" I looked back at my computer in the living room.

"Yeah," he said, unbothered by my hesitation. "I'll have to go upstairs to take a look at that bathroom. Do you care?"

The only place in the house that he hadn't touched. "Yeah, that's fine."

He licked the center of his top lip, sending a rush of butterflies to my stomach. The shock of it almost knocked me to the ground. I was beginning to think those fuckers retired.

"I'll be quick," he promised. "And I'll try to be quiet."

The universe was really testing me this evening. I knew from a lengthy list of experience that Jaxon Hayes was neither quick nor quiet.

My fingers raced across my keyboard, eager to draw me back into my focused flow of work. I was just about to publish the final exam for my fall semester, and I couldn't be prouder of what I accomplished.

Since I was still a new instructor, I sent a draft over to Owen for his opinion. While I used the bones of his exam to create my own questions, I still wanted to make it clear that I wasn't drifting too far from the university's typical model. Everyone loved to claim how good change was until what they wanted was attacked. Then, suddenly, change became "woke," and your opinions on improvement were deemed dangerous.

A loud squeaking sound came from upstairs, followed by some pounding. Was that a drill?

I pulled up my calendar for next semester in another attempt to distract myself. After a long chat with Connor, Katie agreed to give culinary classes a try after the holidays. To show my support, I offered to watch Max on Tuesdays after my last session so Connor wouldn't have to take time off work. It was a small contribution, but I knew it gave them one less thing to worry about.

"It isn't as bad as I thought."

I whipped my head around to the stairs. "Huh?"

Jaxon tried to ease the tension with a chuckle while he held up a pipe. "It isn't as bad as I thought. This pipe needs to be replaced, but it seems to be the only one that was leaking."

I furrowed my brow. "And where did you *get* that pipe?"

"Well, your wall," he stated plainly, "but again, it's an easy fix."

I closed my eyes. "Is there a hole in my bathroom wall, Jaxon?"

There was a moment of silence, and I opened my eyes to find Jaxon staring at me. He watched me intently, as if every thought in his pretty dark-haired head suddenly disappeared. "Yeah, Mace."

Message received. Loud and fucking clear. I said his name, and I remembered how I longed to hear him say mine.

Had he yearned for it the way I had? Tried to play the sound of it from memory when he needed to reassure himself that what we had was real?

"I can swing by tomorrow to fix the floor," Jaxon said, stepping into the foyer but still keeping his distance. "I should have enough leftovers from the extra that Jared ordered."

I nodded.

"His notes mentioned you want to paint the kitchen, too?"

"Oh my god. I almost forgot about that! I was supposed to order it from the hardware store up the street once I had a color. Something about a discount if it gets shipped to a business address?"

Jaxon rocked slightly on his heels. "Do you have a color?"

"Nope," I said, proudly popping the "P."

He chuckled softly, and I couldn't fight my smitten smile. Apparently, it wasn't just the sound of my name that was a weakness. His laugh also threatened to break my guarded exterior.

"It can take a few days for it to come in. Think you might have one soon?"

"Yeah, I can go tomorrow after work."

"At the university?" he prompted as he slipped on his shoes. I hadn't realized he took them off.

"Yeah," I stated, making it clear that this wasn't an invitation for him to ask more questions. "Thank you for coming over. If I'm not here tomorrow when you swing by, just use Bryson's key."

Jaxon pulled his hoodie over his head. "No problem." He tapped the doorframe on his way out and spoke over his shoulder. "A Ring doorbell should be here tomorrow. I'll install that for you, too."

"I didn't ask for a new doorbell. Was that in Jared's notes?"

"Nah, that's from mine." Jaxon grabbed the handle and started pulling the door shut behind him. "Have a good night."

When he turned over the engine in the driveway, my phone buzzed next to my laptop. My heart skipped a beat at the sight of the name on my screen. The twisted dagger came from the fact that, after all this time, I still hadn't changed the profile picture.

Jaxon

Lock your door.

My first text from Jaxon Hayes in over three years—it read as if no time had passed at all.

Chapter Thirty

JAXON

November 2021

Even with the brand new memory foam mattress Bryson purchased for his guest room, I slept like shit. Last night, regret tried to wrap itself around every anxious thought I had, tightening its grip with every second I spent considering it. The only relief came from replaying the sound of my mom's voice.

"What you need now . . . your everything . . . you aren't going to find it here. Maybe one day it'll bring you back. But that day isn't today."

Like all good overthinkers, I started my day as if nothing had happened. It was about a twenty-minute drive to Maci's from Bryson's place, giving me just enough time to suck down the coffee Bryson made me. I'd need all of the caffeine I could get since I planned to fix her bathroom wall and finish her floor today. The flooring alone would take a few hours.

There were two packages at Maci's front door, and when I read the return address, I brought them inside. One was her Ring doorbell, and the other was the handles for her kitchen cabinets.

"Just add it to the list," I muttered happily.

I started to lose steam around three. No matter how hard I tried to ignore the taunting from Maci's Keurig, it tempted me. Even thinking of going inside her fridge and snagging some creamer felt illegal. I didn't want to leave evidence of a used mug in her dishwasher since she clearly didn't like to keep dish soap handy.

I sat against the fridge door, resting my head against the cool stainless steel. My eyes closed just a little, and if my phone hadn't rang, I might've fallen asleep on Maci's kitchen floor.

For a moment, I thought I did, because there was no way her name was on my screen. I wasn't sure what I was thinking when I texted her last night. It was only an innocent reminder, but it was no longer my place to send it.

I cleared my throat before answering, "Hello?"

"Hey," she breathed, her voice laced with hesitation. Or was it regret? "I had a quick question for you about paint."

I was grateful that we were chatting on the phone instead of in person. I couldn't smile as much as I wanted to in person—I'd look like an idiot.

"I texted Bryson, but he isn't responding. They are asking about the sheen?"

"You can do satin or semi-gloss," I explained.

She let out a humorless chuckle. "Okay, let me rephrase my question. Which one do I choose?"

"I would go with semi-gloss."

She repeated my recommendation to the worker. "And I'm having them ship it to the workshop?"

"Yes." I searched every folder in my brain for something else to say, something else to keep her talking to me. But each one was empty.

"Okay," she said, sounding peppier than before. "Thank you for your help."

"Your doorbell came today," I practically blurted, "and so did the handles for your cabinets. I was going to try and get those done before I head out."

"Okay," she repeated. "I'll see you in a bit."

It was best that she hung up before I served her any more word vomit. Hearing her voice recharged me better than any cup of coffee would, and my heart pounded in my chest at the thought of her walking through the front door.

Agreeing to do this might have been the second-worst decision I've ever made.

A few minutes after Maci came home, I finished up the last of her flooring. A giant smile spread across her face at the sight of it, making my entire morning worth it.

"It's one color," she swooned. "Thank you."

"You know you don't have to thank me after every little thing," I teased, catching her eye before she placed her brief-case on the dining table. "When you have a second, I can give you the directions to set up your Ring account."

"Yes, I saw the doorbell." She pressed her lips into a hard line. "I'd thank you, but you just told me not to."

I unwillingly traced the outline of her mouth, thinking of all of the creative ways she used to thank me in the past. Before she could catch me staring, I picked up the drill and lined up one of the cabinet handles. She put a few things away in the kitchen—a Tupperware that held her lunch this morning, a thermos for her coffee, and a giant cup with a handle for her water. Without me even realizing it, she ran upstairs and came back down wearing leggings and a T-shirt.

It just had to be leggings, and Maci just had to have the ass for them.

I drilled into another cabinet and kept my eyes in front of me.

"I can do that," she protested.

I looked down at the drill, then back up at her. "You sure?"

She held out her hand, and I passed her the tool. It took her a little longer, but after her third handle, she got the hang of it. I watched her line up the metal, sneaking glances at me when she thought I wasn't looking.

Is she sneaking glances, or is she wondering why you're still here?

Fuck. It was already almost four.

"Just say the word when you want me to leave," I suggested, keeping my tone casual. "I don't want to make you uncomfortable, and we don't have to make this weird."

Maci kept drilling, reaching into the cardboard box and pulling out another handle.

"If you have work to do," I added cautiously, "or have someone coming over, or just want your space—"

"Oh my god," she murmured, whipping her head around to face me. She gestured to the drill with a cocky grin. "If I give this back to you, will you stop talking?"

I dragged a hand over my mouth. I could take her little digs and attitude—actually, I encouraged it. *Loved* it even. It was the silence and the tiptoeing around me that drove me insane.

She passed me the drill on her way to the living room. "I have a few things to finish up for work, but I was going to order pizza. If I get a large, will you eat some? The place I order from isn't good reheated."

Her offer left me so speechless that I almost didn't answer her question. I noted the length of her leggings and how even under the bagginess of her shirt, they accentuated her hips. Her skin was probably warm under the fabric, and I ached to explore it, reunite with territory I used to cherish instead of admire from afar.

My mouth curved into the sly smile that caused me more trouble than I could keep track of. "I could eat."

Chapter Thirty-One

MACI

November 2021

What the actual *FUCK* was she doing?

This bitch really said, "You know what, you broke my heart three years ago. Shattered it, actually. But did you wanna stay for pizza? I'll pay!"

She didn't have to ask what he liked. She already knew. She'd gotten pizza with him dozens of times before this moment. There was no reason to waste dialogue on unnecessary questions.

So now, she has to eat dinner with him. She couldn't just hang out in a different room of the house once the food arrived.

Seriously, who did that shit?

I sank into the couch, pulled my laptop onto my lap, and clicked Submit on my order. It was me, Maci Lawson. I was the bitch, and I had no idea what I was doing.

Could he *eat*? Of course, he could eat. Memories spun around in my head on a carousel, reminding me of every meal we'd shared and times when it didn't even involve food.

Do not *let your head go there.*

Too late. I slammed my laptop shut, burying my face in my hands and hoping I could smother the next flashback in the queue. It didn't help that I wanted to see it. I suddenly *needed* to see it—evidence that the man in the kitchen had once been someone I couldn't imagine my life without.

I swallowed, remembering the intensity in his gaze as he looked up at me from the floor. He knelt in between my legs, his green eyes never leaving mine as he pushed my knees further apart so he could hoist them over his shoulders.

"We should go into your room," I warned, struggling to keep my voice steady while his mouth kissed the inside of my thighs. I gripped his hair with my fingers while his slid inside me. "Won't they be here soon?"

Jaxon smirked before lowering his mouth. "Alex is never on time."

"But Bella is," I managed weakly when his tongue met my clit. I arched my back, my free hand holding onto the couch so I wouldn't slide off.

Jaxon wrapped his forearms around my thighs, pressing his mouth into my center so I couldn't move. I groaned, unable to break free from the intense amount of pressure building in my core. I stared down at him, watching him tenderly stroke and suck, only stopping to shoot me a devilish grin.

If this were hell, pull me all the way under. So far down that I would find the pleasure in burning.

⁓ele⁓

When the pizza arrived twenty minutes later, I was still burning from a memory that left a familiar throbbing between my legs. It was unexpected, yet I welcomed it like an old friend I hadn't seen in a long time.

I had gotten off with other partners. I had my moments of intense foreplay and spent plenty of time taking care of myself. But with Jaxon, it was different. It had always been different. The fact that I was eating with my legs still crossed proved that his touch left a mark.

Easing the throbbing wasn't hard when I knew there would eventually be a release. My body from the waist down didn't understand why we weren't jumping over the table. While my heart struggled to remain on the right side of history, my brain was molding into a nauseating version of Switzerland.

Katie's words rang in the back of my head.

"Look how much has changed in three years. You're not the same person you were when he—"

"Shattered my heart," I mumbled pathetically.

I could've gone upstairs to work. I could've had Jaxon let me know when he was heading out for the night. Instead, I invited myself to the table with him—*literally* pulled out the chair—and decided to get closer. Even after everything he'd put me through, I still ached to be near him.

"Ranch?" Jaxon held up the bottle, resting his elbow on top of my fridge door.

I pulled a few napkins from the holder and placed them in the center of the table. "Yeah. Thanks."

"Did you ever choose a paint color?"

I pretended to wipe my mouth so he wouldn't see me smile. His eyes softened from across the table, watching my every move as I helped myself to another slice of pizza.

"Green," I said, my heart hammering in my chest. "I need a beer. Would you like a beer?"

I wasn't even sure if he heard me, but I saw him nod. The words thread together so quickly that I barely stitched them together. Every part of me was one bad cut away from unraveling.

With a quirk of his lip, he asked, "What kind of green?"

I placed his drink in front of him. "Dark green."

"Interesting," he said, screwing off the top of his beer.

While I was anxious and stressed, Jaxon was trying not to laugh. Suddenly, we were back in my apartment in Bowling Green, where we had exchanged this interaction more times than I could count.

I followed his lead. "What?"

He no longer stifled his smile. "Just a little surprised to hear green, that's all."

"What color were you expecting to hear?"

"Blue, maybe? Some shade of grey?"

"Jared said I wasn't allowed to choose grey." I chuckled as I opened my beer. "He said he couldn't possibly paint another kitchen the color of concrete."

Jaxon laughed, allowing me the space to take a much-needed sip. It also let him get a few bites of pizza in before I asked a question. If he didn't clear a few slices soon, this dinner would never end.

"So, was there ever a crew?" I prompted. "You can tell me."

"Ask Bryson," he suggested. "I arranged everything before I left."

"And now you're back again. Eating pizza at my dinner table."

"You invited me," Jaxon stated it so matter-of-factly that I couldn't help but laugh. He blinked a few times, probably gauging my sanity, before he joined me in my response to something that shouldn't have been funny. "I told you this didn't have to be weird."

"So don't make it weird," I challenged, the alcohol making its way into my bloodstream. "Another one?"

His green eyes lingered on the neckline of my shirt that slipped slightly off my shoulder.

He nodded, handing me his empty bottle.

We still shared—it, the wavelength between us that indicated we were thinking about the other. I couldn't ignore it. No matter how hard I tried, there were still parts of Jaxon Hayes that I could pick up on. They settled deep inside me years ago, threading themselves into pieces that I couldn't let go of.

"Jared used to tell me all the time that you'd come back eventually." I hesitated to hand him another drink. "Can I ask you a question?"

He eyed me cautiously.

"Why didn't you?"

Jaxon rested his elbows on the table, dragging his teeth over his bottom lip—a tell-tale sign that I wouldn't get the complete answer. "I was juggling a lot with Hayes Sports and Entertainment."

I decided not to push for more. "Who is taking care of things while you're here?"

"Mom and Dad," he said with a soft chuckle. "My mom came to my place and practically drove me to the airport. I think they understood more than I thought they did. Fuck, they usually do. They knew that I was helping Spencer with a few things and that I was living with Bryson."

"And that you'd never ask to come back on your own," I offered simply.

"Yeah, that too. Are you ever going to visit Bryson at his place?"

I rolled my eyes.

Jaxon threw his arms to the side. "Just going off of what he's said."

"And what exactly has Bryson said?"

"Or maybe what he *hasn't* said," Jaxon corrected with a grin. "You guys are close. Took me a second to wrap my head around that, but you used to come to his place all the time."

There was no nice way to tell Jaxon that once he left my life, Bryson immediately stepped into it.

"I'm glad he has you right now," I said, tasting the caution in my admission. "While no one can replace me as his best friend, I can't be there as often as I'd like to. I check in on him when I can, and he's been over a few times. But it isn't the same."

"You have a lot going on," he noted.

I wasn't sure if he meant to sound proud, but I stifled a grin anyway. "Yeah."

We spent the next few drinks asking each other questions you'd ask any new friend. All surface level. All marked safe from oversharing.

Jaxon told me about his office in Los Angeles. I told him about my classes at the university. He asked about Chase, and I shared that he and Trey couldn't be happier in Europe. Questions about my parents followed shortly after that, and I kept it brief. There wasn't much to say about my family tree, and for reasons I didn't want to admit out loud, I couldn't bring myself to ask about his.

There were certain things I wasn't sure I could handle yet. I wasn't ready to hear about Jaxon's family. Not after I loved them like my own.

When we said goodbye, there was no hug or awkward exchange.

I held the front door open, and before he stepped outside, he asked, "I'll see you Saturday?"

"Saturday?"

What was Saturday? Fuck, what was today?

"Friendsgiving," he reminded me. "You still going?"

"Fuck." I gasped. "I have to get a pie."

He chuckled, making it impossible not to smile. We'd done so much of it tonight, my cheeks would mock me when I came down from the high. "Good night, Maci. Lock the door behind me."

I followed his direction, leaning my back against the door that separated us.

Maybe I was unraveling. Maybe I didn't know what to call it. Perhaps, regardless of how bad I didn't want to admit it, it was no better than burning.

Chapter Thirty-Two

JAXON

November 2021

Growing up with a mom who loved to cook, I knew my way around a kitchen. I learned to taste the batch for salt before assuming it needed more at the end of the cook and to let the meat rest before serving.

I also knew that surrounding yourself with as little stress as possible made directions much easier to follow.

"Elle," I said over the buzzing of the range hood. When she didn't turn around, I added a little bass to my already irritated tone, "Elle?"

She and Spencer threw their heads back on the couch cushions. Elle rolled her eyes, silently daring me to continue.

I pressed my lips together, limiting any smart-ass comments that might slip through. Elle was in town for Friendsgiving, and while she was staying with Spencer, she texted Bryson to see if they could come hang out this afternoon. Only Bryson was still at the office, and I was left to share my living space with two hangry females.

"This is now the *third* time you've asked us to pause *Pride and Prejudice*," Elle growled. "What do you want?"

"Bangs can wait," I spat. "I need you to tell me if these almonds are almost burnt."

Spencer cackled from the couch as Elle joined me behind the counter.

"You *did not* refer to Elizabeth Bennet as Bangs," Spencer shouted.

"Always leave it to Jaxon Hayes for the comic relief," Elle murmured, poking a few of the almonds in the pan with a spatula.

I wiped the sweat from my brow. "I'm here to please, Foster."

Elle scrunched her nose. "What does it even mean, *almost* burnt?"

"I don't know!" I exclaimed. "Katie's recipe is called Green Bean Casserole with Almost-Burnt Almonds."

"That's oddly specific," Spencer noted.

"Are you sure you're supposed to have these in this pan?" Elle turned around and pointed to the stove. "And not *that* pan?"

I looked between the two pans. "The recipe says—"

"And you read the recipe?"

I closed my eyes, exhaling slowly so I wouldn't scrap the entire process and reach for the Campbell's Cream of Mushroom soup in the pantry. "Yes."

"Liar," Elle said with a sly smile. She snatched the recipe from my hand and scanned the page. "It literally says to roast the almonds in the oven before the green beans go in. Why are they on the stovetop?"

"He seems a little distracted," Spencer chimed in.

I whipped my head around to respond, my gaze softening at the sight of her on the couch. She looked happy to be a wallflower to the banter happening in the kitchen.

When Dad told me that Spencer had decided on the house, I wasn't sure what would follow. But the truth was, I couldn't ignore the way she no longer crossed her arms in front of her chest when she was speaking or how her shoulders relaxed when she began to wear the loose sweaters that she favored.

Spencer stepped back into a version of herself that I recognized. She was excited to post the house after Thanksgiving, and I was grateful for the parts of her that were returning.

Elle, on the other hand, was harder to read. She loved to act like nothing was ever bothering her.

"I'm not distracted," I countered. Before Elle could poke any more at the popping almonds in the pan, I pulled them from the stove. "Enough with the almonds!"

"You called me over here for this," Elle snapped. "Did you mess up the recipe because you were busy thinking about something else?"

I knew what they were implying. Maci Lawson and I were on speaking terms. Yeah, I was fucking distracted. But I wasn't about to admit that to the two gossip gurus in front of me.

As if he had heard my silent call for help, Bryson burst through the front door. He placed a cardboard box on the dining table and tossed his keys on the counter.

"Rough day at the office?" Elle prompted playfully.

Bryson looked over his shoulder, his irritated scowl quickly replaced with a sly smirk. Now that he was Elle's center of attention, I knew I was halfway off the hook from any more questioning. The other half still smiled at me from the couch, fashioning her long blonde hair into a bun. It was the same style Bella utilized to probe me.

Bryson hovered over the stovetop. "What's up with the peanuts?"

"They're almonds," I snapped.

"Scrap these." Elle walked the pan across the kitchen to dump the evidence into the trash can. "I'll roast some almonds tomorrow morning, and we can sprinkle them onto the beans before Katie reheats them tomorrow."

"You think that will work?" Spencer asked.

Elle shrugged. "Maybe not. But Katie will have like ten other dishes she's managing. It'll be fine."

We agreed with a round of nods and quickly dispersed from the kitchen. No one wanted to be the last one in the room with the green beans. I had no idea what I was thinking when I offered to make an important side dish. I figured Katie would pull the option away from me and hand me something I couldn't possibly mess up—like chocolate chip cookies or brownies.

Well, the last time you were involved with brownies . . .

My chuckle must've sounded quieter in my head since Spencer said, "Oh, Jaxon."

My phone vibrated on the table between us. "You'll have to wait a few more minutes to drill me, Foster. My nieces are calling me." I answered Bella's FaceTime, mimicking the scrunching motion Evie was doing with her tiny nose. "What's up, girl?"

"What's up, Uncle Jax?" Evie laughed, her high-pitched voice deepening the dimples in Spencer's cheeks. "What are you doing?"

"I'm hanging out with my friend, Spencer." I turned the phone so Evie could see.

"Hi!" Spencer squealed. "I loved your Halloween costume. Is Red Riding Hood your favorite story?"

"And Peyton was a wolf!" Evie exclaimed. The rustling and bustling alerted us that she was on the move. I shifted next to Spencer just in time for her to show Peyton's angry scowl on the screen. "She has angry eyebrows. See?"

Spencer and I laughed at Peyton's furrowed blonde brow.

"Yes, she does look pretty angry," Spencer added.

"Jax, are you coming in for Thanksgiving?" Bella shouted in the background. A few seconds later, she grabbed her phone from Evie's hands. Her flustered expression quickly shifted when she realized Spencer was sitting next to me. "Oh, sorry! Spencer, right?"

"Nice to meet you," Spencer said. "Your girls are adorable."

"Yeah, yeah, she knows," I interjected. Bella rolled her eyes while Spencer swatted my shoulder. "Since I'm coming in for Christmas, probably not."

"Okay, I figured," Bella said. "We'll probably just go to your parents, then."

We shared a silent exchange over the screen, understanding that it was better for them to travel to my mom than for my mom to return to North Carolina. I was grateful for Bella's decision, and I was relieved when Alex confirmed with me later that night that they would land two days before the holiday.

Chapter Thirty-Three

MACI

November 2021

Since the first time she hosted it at our apartment in Bowling Green, Friendsgiving had quickly become Katie's Super Bowl. She couldn't care less about what was playing on the TV or how guests entertained themselves in between courses. The preparation and presentation were the first half of the game, and carving the turkey was the halftime show.

The second half consisted of more drinking and pulling out the desserts, and I personally couldn't wait for her to bust out her specialty sangria. It was a play on the Blood Orange drink she attempted in college, only this time she perfected it through various recipes on the internet and her own trial and error.

"Putting those culinary skills to work, huh?" I teased, swiping a candied pecan from the top of the sweet potatoes.

Katie shot her dark brown daggers at me from across the counter. She held her tongue since I was the only one keeping her company in the kitchen. While everyone else sat in the living room with eyes on either Max or the football game, I was helping myself to test bites.

"Still keeping your distance from Jaxon, huh?" Katie whispered, raising a suggestive brow.

Well, there was that, too. "That's not funny."

"Isn't it, though?" Katie swatted my hand as I made a move for another pecan. "You fed the man pizza. You didn't ask him to spend the night."

I rolled my eyes. Katie received a rundown the next morning when I was driving to work. I might have left out the flashback of Jaxon kneeling between my legs, but Katie was no dummy.

"You know—" Katie halted her sentence and decided to put the sweet potatoes in the oven instead. When she straightened up, I gestured for her to continue, practically lying myself over the countertop. She met me halfway so she could keep her voice low. "You know, just because you aren't trying to set the man on fire doesn't mean you've forgotten. You can be cordial and friendly with someone and still choose not to forgive them. It doesn't have to be black and white."

I scrunched my nose at her proposition. "And if I'm trying to avoid the grey area?"

Katie placed her hands over mine. "It's you and Jaxon. You guys *invented* the grey area."

I sucked my teeth. "Bitch."

Katie snuck a quick sip of her white wine. "Dinner is in ten!" she shouted, brushing past me so she could make last-minute adjustments to the table settings.

"Is the sangria out yet?" A hushed voice hovered over my shoulder. Bryson strained himself, reaching over me for the bottle of sauvignon blanc. "This wine isn't cutting it."

I batted my lashes. "I will sneak you a glass from the fridge right now if you can pronounce what you're about to pour."

Bryson stared at the label, his gorgeous face shifting into ten different combinations as he contemplated his response. He was naturally pretty, and he didn't even have to try. He'd been spending his free time back in the gym, and he was still attending his physical therapy. His body was slowly changing back into a version he felt most comfortable in, and his cocky confidence was starting to show.

I gave his forearm a light squeeze. "We're about a half-hour away from the third quarter. Hang in there."

Everyone filed in from the living room to find their place. Connor strapped Max into his high chair, and Katie stood at the head of the table. Elle snagged the seat on the other side of Bryson, and Spencer sat across from her. As everyone claimed their spot, I waited for the inevitable to happen. Even though it wasn't her fault, I'd blame Katie later.

Jaxon lowered himself into the seat across from me, unable to hide the humor he found in this situation from his disgustingly handsome face. Over the rim of my glass, I admired his exposed forearms. I traced the tight fabric of his black Henley to where it hugged his shoulders, crossed his chest, and noticed two buttons undone at the collar.

Conversation happened effortlessly around us, friends and family gathered around a gorgeous table as if there wasn't a flock of obnoxious turkeys in the room.

Spencer stared longingly at the empty chair where Jared should have been telling a cheesy joke.

The bottle of prenatal gummies sat next to the Keurig.

Connor's inability to take a break from searching his wife's face for some sort of hint.

Bryson and Elle's hands were underneath the table.

Jaxon's infectious grin—a result of holding Max's attention even through the layers of distractions.

It was all happening so fast. Another holiday, another milestone that we had to step over because time gave us no other options. As I glanced around at the masks of smiling faces, an unpleasant yet familiar weight settled onto my chest. It was minutes away from sinking into my stomach, threatening to spoil my appetite for a meal I knew Katie would comment on if I presented an untouched plate.

What was the endgame here? What was the point of it all?

On a day I was supposed to be thankful, I couldn't ignore the anchor that sat across from me. I spent the last three years of my life trying to stay afloat—navigating unforgiving waters I never thought I'd be thrown into.

Jared handed me a life preserver, and I was terrified that Jaxon brought another chain.

Katie tapped the side of her glass with her fork.

Thank god. It was getting dark in here.

Katie cleared her throat, drawing everyone's attention to the head of the table. "I know I usually have some sort of sappy speech to deliver, but not this year. I just want you all to know how incredibly grateful we are for everyone who is sitting at this table." Katie grabbed Connor's hand. "Thank you for being here. We love you guys."

Various versions of "We love you too!" echoed back at her.

No sooner than our glasses clinked, Bryson leaned across his plate and asked, "Can we have the sangria now?"

"Sangria?" Jaxon asked.

It was hard to ignore his eyes on me. At least three other people knew about the iconic sangria. Someone else could fill in the blanks.

"Blood orange," Connor teased, scooping a giant spoonful of mashed potatoes onto Max's plate. "It tastes ten times better than what you had back in college."

"I don't know about that." Jaxon smothered his smirk with his glass, draining his drink to prepare for the next course.

This time, I couldn't look away. Warmth rushed to my cheeks.

"Can I have some green beans?" Spencer held out her plate. "I've been dying to try them."

A silence fell over the table, making Katie's pour of sangria sound like a whimsical babbling brook.

"Damn," Spencer said, surveying the quiet crowd. "Jared would have laughed at that."

Elle giggled nervously, granting the rest of us permission to loosen up our masks.

"Don't try to use Jared as a cover for why you're asking," Jaxon argued playfully. "These are about to be the best beans you've ever had."

Bryson and Elle added their plates to the queue.

Katie groaned. "What did you—you know what, never mind. I don't want to know."

I steadied my pour of sangria and handed the pitcher to Bryson.

"How did you mess up a recipe I *gave* you?" Katie exclaimed, causing the rest of us to burst into hysterics.

Jaxon furrowed his brow since he was trying not to respond with a smart-ass comment. He loved to ruffle Katie's feathers, but he knew better than to cause a mess over a holiday spread.

Watching Katie and Jaxon go back and forth across the table brought back a comforting warmth of nostalgia. A Thursday dinner, a study session, a movie marathon—all opportunities for them to butt heads. Jaxon's natural way with Katie was one of my favorite parts about him. I missed having a front row seat to their heated discussions.

"Wait a second," I said through a breathless laugh. "You told me to bring a pie, but *he* got to bring an actual side dish?"

Jaxon whipped his head around to face me. "What's that supposed to mean?"

"You don't have a kitchen!" Katie protested.

"She does have a kitchen," Jaxon noted.

"If I may," Spencer interjected with a mouthful of beans, "these are incredible."

"Really?" Katie swooned. "Pass them down."

I smirked at Spencer. "Lemme taste."

Before Spencer could add more beans to her fork, Bryson offered me a bite from his.

"Here," he said, practically shoving it past my lips.

I covered my mouth with my hand. The last thing I wanted was to spit a wad of beans onto someone's plate because I couldn't stop laughing. I also couldn't deny the flavor. They were delicious.

"Wow," I exclaimed, giving Jaxon my full attention. "They're—"

While everyone else had already moved on to other side dishes, Jaxon's gaze remained fixated on my mouth. I licked my lips, erasing whatever pattern he'd been tracing. It was the first time I'd felt it—in a room full of our closest friends, even though we'd spent multiple minutes alone in my house.

The moment Bryson offered me his fork, Jaxon joined me in the neutral zone. Instead of watching his roommate do something that seemed so incredibly natural, he pictured himself giving me a taste. He pictured it—a glimpse of what we could've been before he secured the chain.

It was in the little things where I missed Jaxon the most. After all this time—the good, the bad, and everything in between—regardless of how much I wanted to hate him, I still saw everything with the man who dragged me under.

Chapter Thirty-Four

JAXON

November

AFTER I DROVE AROUND the block so Maci and Elle could
finish out their duet of "Untouched" by The Veronicas, we
waited in the driveway to make sure Maci made it inside.
She had the doorbell and the floodlight above her garage,
but it was still dark enough that I wanted to watch her walk
through the front door.

"You're sure you don't wanna just stay over?" Elle yelled
out the window.

Maci looked over her shoulder as she stepped onto the
porch. "I'm okay!"

"Night, Mace!" Bryson shouted. Between him and Elle, the
entire street was about to be invited to this conversation. It
was already a little after eleven.

Maci pushed open her door, giving Bryson one last smile
before she waved goodbye. Our eyes met briefly, lingering
long enough for me to see a slight quiver near the right side
of her mouth.

I shifted slowly into reverse, waiting until the door closed
behind her before I started to move.

The ride back to Bryson's place was quiet, giving me just
enough time to get into my own head. While Elle dozed
off in the back seat and Bryson typed away on his phone, I
tried to remember the last time I had dropped Maci off at her

apartment in Bowling Green. It had been a long time since I left her at a place where I didn't stay.

"Fuck," Elle murmured, pressing a hand to her forehead. She rose slowly, glancing around the back seat as if she had already forgotten where she was. "Is this yours?"

She held a phone between the front seats. It couldn't have been Bryson's since he barely put his down on the ride over here. Which meant the dark blue phone case could only belong to one person.

Bryson gestured for my keys, slurring, "I'll take it over to her."

"You aren't taking shit," I said through a breathy laugh. "You guys go inside. I'll run it over really quick."

If they both hadn't lost to Katie's sangria, they might have been able to talk me into waiting until tomorrow morning. A left-behind phone didn't require immediate attention. It could have waited until Bryson or me went to the gym in a few hours.

Well, at least when *I* went to the gym. The way Bryson struggled to open the front door just solidified that he probably wasn't doing anything tomorrow. At least not until he had some of the leftovers Katie sent us home with and a few naps to recharge.

It sucked getting older. We couldn't bounce back after a night out with just a Gatorade and a greasy sandwich. It took one to two business days to start to feel human again.

When I pulled into Maci's driveway, the porch light was still on. As I rounded the front of the car, I saw that the front door was slightly ajar, with no light from the living room to indicate that anyone was inside.

My heart hammered in my chest. I crossed the yard in a few steps and pushed gently on the door, letting myself in unannounced as I searched the room for any signs of an intruder. It took a total of forty-two minutes to return after we dropped her off—long enough for some shit to happen that no one was here for.

Without thinking, I let the scenarios I was making up in my head get the best of me. "Maci?" I said, my voice loud enough to echo throughout the first floor.

Welp. If there wasn't an uninvited person in her house before, there was now. What the fuck was I doing? I couldn't stop myself. When more silence met me, I repeated her name louder, peering into the kitchen and checking back in the laundry room.

"Mace?" I shouted, taking the stairs two at a time. There was only one light on, and I followed it to her bedroom. Music played softly from the speaker on her nightstand. When "Unwritten" by Natasha Bedingfield ended, it started up again, the upbeat melody picking up right where it left off.

Maci sat on the floor, leaning against the bottom of her bedframe. There was an empty bottle of vodka next to her and one in her left hand that was missing a few sips.

"Mace?" I prompted softly, squatting down so I was at her eye level. "Your door was open. I'm just dropping off your phone."

My heart sank when her glossy blue eyes registered who was in front of her. Her mouth lifted into a tiny bittersweet smile. "That's why I couldn't find it."

I shifted so I could join her on the floor. "You tried to look outside?"

"I was not successful," she muttered.

I turned my head to see a fresh stream of tears rolling down her cheeks. What I thought was sinking before had nothing on this. The sight of her alone with a bottle made me feel like I was fucking drowning.

She closed her eyes, and when she opened them, she was staring at the ceiling. "I miss him."

I followed her gaze, afraid that if I looked at her any longer, I'd lose what was left of my composure. "Me too."

"Like what the fuck am I doing?" She paused so she could catch her breath. "I just had a great night with everyone, and still, I come back here, put on a pair of his sweatpants, and drink like I'm the one who lost a husband."

The sweatpants I questioned that night in her laundry room—they were Jared's.

Of course, they were Jared's. I was just giving him more material to make fun of. Wherever he was, I knew he got a kick out of my internal dialogue surrounding his clothing.

Meanwhile, Maci was comparing grief when grief wasn't a contest, and she wasn't in her right mind for me to try to explain that to her now.

"You loved him," I said softly. "You loved him and you miss him and it's okay to be sad that he's not here."

Her eyes were softer now but didn't lack the pain from before. We exchanged a heavy silence, neither of us able to look away from the other. I knew she was drunk, so far gone that she probably wouldn't remember any of this tomorrow morning. But I'd never felt so sober, so attuned to what I was feeling and missing and wanting all at the same time.

The urge to reach out and touch her, stroke her cheek with my thumb so she would know she wasn't alone. Her gaze fell to my mouth, and I knew that look. I fucking *craved* that look. She no longer wanted words. She wanted me to fix what I could.

"It's not supposed to be like this, Jaxon," she whispered.

"No," I said, my voice growing raspy. "No, it's not."

Maci let her forehead fall to my shoulder, and I wrapped my arm around her, pulling her into me. Her body shook as tears soaked into my shirt, her sobs chipping away at the few sets of heartstrings I had left that were keeping me together.

I held her as tight as I could, and she let me. No one else existed. It was just us, along with every ounce of pain, regret, and grief we carried on our own over the last few years.

In this moment, I forfeited. I took advantage of her silence and acted out loud, not with words or a song, or some grand gesture that would ever erase what I had done. I loved her—so much that I knew better than to say anything at all.

"I'm so sorry, pretty girl," I muttered against her temple.

Maci rose from me slowly, searching my face for any indication that she might have misheard me. "Can we just pretend for a moment?"

"Pretend what?"

"That it never happened. That nothing ever changed," she said, her voice catching near the end. "That you never stopped."

I tucked her hair behind her ears. "That I never stopped?" I repeated, realizing that maybe she needed a few words after all. "You act as if I had a choice."

Her brow furrowed slightly as I cupped her chin. "Choice?"

I stared into her eyes, leaving no hints of hesitation when I said, "Not to love you."

Chapter Thirty-Five

JAXON

November 2021

Before I sat up, I felt the muscles in my upper back tighten, stretching up the side of my neck and making me wish I had opted for the couch.

In my attempt to make sure Maci fell asleep okay, I made a pit stop in the chair she had in the living room. It was poofy and soft and had the makings of a nice place to rest my eyes for a few moments. The inviting dark grey fabric betrayed me. It was a little after one when I came downstairs, and I had no idea how long I lasted before exhaustion got the better of me.

A slight creak in the wood flooring drew my attention behind me. I looked over my shoulder to see Maci leaning against the doorframe of the kitchen. She crossed her arms over her chest, her tiny frame covered by an oversized BGSU hoodie and sweatpants from the night before. Her eyes were much more alert this morning, so alert that she seemed genuinely confused to see me.

"Everything okay?" I asked, my voice still raspy with sleep.

"Oh, I don't know." She cocked her head and sighed. "I'm hungover as fuck and you're on my couch, so imma go with no."

I wasn't sure what kind of wake-up call I expected, but this wasn't it. Maci was pissed, and I had no idea why.

"I brought over your phone," I offered simply. It was clear that I'd better leave. "You left it in the backseat."

"I see that. Thank you."

I ran a hand through my hair and patted the pocket of my jeans to make sure I had my car keys. I shouldn't have stayed. It wasn't my place to think I should stay.

"I'll stop by in a few days," I said, reaching for the front door.

"Jaxon."

I froze, hoping that one day, the sound of my name coming out of her mouth wouldn't hold such a strong power.

A delicate concentration filled her soft features. "Why did you stay over?"

She was already irritated, so if there was a time for me to be honest, it was now. "It seems I can't help this pattern I have for looking out for you."

As the words from our past filled her gorgeous head, her scowl eliminated any satisfaction I felt from the throwback. "Are you serious?" She scoffed. "Fuck you."

"Fuck you?" I repeated sternly. "Wait, fuck *me*?"

"Yes," she chirped. "Fuck you. Don't pull that shit."

In a strange turn of events, she was getting an attitude with me. I was annoyed and turned on at the same time. There was a reason arguments escalated into blowouts when we were together. Being honest with one another gave us more ammo to fight with, and boy, did we love telling the truth.

Maci's hand flew to her mouth. "I'm sorry."

I stifled a grin.

"I'd be lying if I said that didn't feel amazing, though. Throwing a 'fuck you' in there in person."

"I imagine it did."

"This hasn't—" Maci tucked her loose curls behind her ears. "I don't want to *hate* you."

"I prefer if you didn't," I admitted, unable to look away. Her statement was hard to believe with the surge of electricity passing between us. It was an undeniable pull, prompting me to take a step toward her rather than maintaining the safe distance between us. "But I understand if you do."

"Evie and Peyton, huh?" she asked, forcing a smile. The switch in conversation caught me off guard, and it must've shown on my face. "Spencer mentioned seeing them."

"Yeah." I chuckled nervously, the pull from before falling flat at my feet. "She was next to me when they called."

Maci averted her gaze to the pile of shoes near the door. "It sucked hearing about them from her. Fuck, I keep saying not to make this weird, but there isn't anything *normal* about this."

"We never talked about what happened—"

She snapped her head up, shooting me a warning glance. "And I don't want to. I can't. I used to be the person you told everything to. Now, I just learn things as you choose to share them. It's like I never knew you at all."

A small huff fell from my mouth. "You knew me better than anyone."

"I thought I did," she said weakly. She gestured to the distance between us. "This has been a lot for me, that's all."

"It won't be much longer," I promised, sounding more determined than I planned to. "I told you Christmas."

We stood in silence, neither of us sure what to say next. I could turn and walk out, leaving whatever this was unfinished. Maybe that's what I should've done. Instead, I lingered a little longer, asking the obvious question that would send me in the right direction.

"You have your phone?" I asked playfully, earning me a smile. "Are you good?"

"Yeah, I'm fine."

When I pushed open the front door, a gust of chilly morning air crept into the living room. I looked over my shoulder, capturing Maci's attention one last time. "You think you're ever a little too good at being fine?"

Her smile tapered into a firm line. "Goodbye, Jaxon."

I waited until I was safely in the car to laugh at her irritated response. My words still snuck into the parts of her she tried to hide—pieces of her she thought she was taking care of just fine on her own. I'd seen enough last night to know that she wasn't okay. There was a reason I stayed downstairs. I didn't want to leave her alone.

As long as I could still get under her skin, I had a chance. Yesterday, she might have been pretending, but for me, there was nothing fake about it. It wasn't supposed to be like this, and if the smallest of chances lived in her words from last night, I'd take it. I'd hold on to it as tight as I fucking could—the way I should've done when she was mine.

Chapter Thirty-Six

MACI

December 2021

"You think you're ever a little too good at being *fine*?" Katie repeated Jaxon's annoying question for the third time since we entered the flea market. "It's just *so* spot on."

"Yes," I muttered, leading us into the next aisle of vendors. A giant hand-sewn Santa mocked me with a jolly grin. "So you've said."

Katie cackled. "I'm sorry, I just love it. I literally mentioned your lack of emotional capacity a few weeks ago. But I know the way Jaxon said it just irked the fuck out of you."

A passing mother of two scowled at Katie's language, steering her stroller away from a booth of handcrafted ornaments. Katie sucked her teeth.

"You were the same way when Max was itty," I argued.

"No, I wasn't. We value context in our household."

"Baby's first F-bomb."

Katie picked up a Jack Skellington wine glass, complete with a gorgeous backdrop from *The Nightmare Before Christmas*. "At least Max will use it correctly."

I held up Sally's glass, swooning over the matching set. It didn't take much convincing for Katie to cave and get them as a gift for Connor. *The Nightmare Before Christmas* was the first movie they ever watched together, back when I was calling Jaxon because I thought her ex-boyfriend might break into our apartment.

Good times.

We spent the next half hour moving down another aisle of local vendors, stocked with holiday decor, trinkets, and one-of-a-kind gifts. It was our yearly tradition. On the first Saturday in December, Katie and I stopped for a peppermint mocha to fuel up for the first craft fair of the season. We'd buy gifts for everyone on our lists and get some much-needed time away from the noise, trading work conversations and family needs for Christmas music and the chatter of happy shoppers.

"What about this for Spencer?" Katie held up a whimsical set of floral bookends. The details in the petals would look beautiful on Spencer's shelf of classics.

I wanted to nod—lose my mind over the perfect find. Was it enough to put into words how sorry we were that Jared wasn't here?

Katie read my reaction faster than I could answer. "Not good enough, huh?"

"I—"

"It's okay," Katie murmured. "I thought the same thing. I knew shopping for her would be hard."

"Makes gift giving seem so silly," I admitted, chucking my empty mocha cup in the trash. "Maybe we don't do a gift exchange. Is it too late to cancel?"

Katie scoffed. "Please. Connor hasn't asked for ideas, and we both know Bryson hasn't done any shopping."

I cocked my head in agreement trent. I was usually the one taking Bryson on a last-minute trip to whatever store made the most sense—just another one of our holiday traditions.

"Whatever we plan, we just have to make sure Spencer isn't alone on Christmas. *Or* Christmas Eve." Katie locked eyes with me. "I'm worried about her."

"Well, Christmas Eve, we can still do dinner at your place," I suggested.

"And . . . Christmas? Do you think you'll be able to host?"

I knew what she was getting at, carefully rerouting our conversation back to what she was really interested in. "Jaxon said Christmas."

"Okay," she stated proudly. "Once Connor's parents head out, we'll be over then."

"Just no gifts," I said, hopelessly looking down at our shopping bags.

Katie swatted the air in front of her. "We'll give them before the holiday. You only bought something for Bryson, right? What did you get again?"

I proudly revealed my find. "A Skittles phone charger. She hand-made the candies!"

Katie furrowed her brow at the colorful band.

"It's funny," I reminded her, dropping the charger back into my bag. "Bryson will laugh."

"Ah, yes." Katie smiled. "Because doesn't everyone love a reminder of how they were accused of having chlamydia?"

We burst into hysterics, reliving the memory of my Skittles purchase, back when Bryson and I could barely hold a conversation. He went from being the first one I'd call for a hookup to the first person I expected to spend Christmas with.

Katie started another lap around the topic we covered before. "So after you told him to fuck himself . . ."

I let out a hopeless chuckle. "Go on."

"Like I can feel the secondhand tension from that conversation, and I wasn't even there. You're telling me you felt *nothing*? Nada? *Zip*?" She widened her brown eyes and emphasized the "P."

There was undoubtedly a lightheaded excitement that came from being close to Jaxon. We just stared at each other, waiting for the other to give some sort of sign. I wasn't even sure if I was looking for one. Maybe I was. Clearly, I lost the definition of the word "tension" as I tried to deny it existed between us.

"No," I lied—*horribly*. "No tension."

"Are you just saying that in case he didn't feel it and you did?" Katie pressed.

"Can we please be done with this?" I begged, leading us out the back door and into the parking lot.

"You aren't even the slightest bit curious about what he's feeling? Neither of you has dated anyone seriously since you broke up—"

"Hey! I dated Derek."

"Bitch, please. We both know Derek was a placeholder."

Sheesh. Brutal shot to Derek.

"It's just—I *see* it. We *all* see it. Since you aren't friends anymore, you're dancing around what you really want to say. You replaced honesty with these god-awful filters, and it's just . . . *exhausting*."

An unforgiving gust of wind prompted us to the front seats of Katie's car instead of the trunk. Our goods sat in brightly colored bags on our laps, both of us shivering while the heat blasted through the vents.

I scrunched up my nose as I replayed Katie's last words. "What do you mean you *all* see it?"

"Look," she stated with a hefty sigh. "I won't be this invested once I start my classes next month. I think it's just weird sometimes to know Jaxon as an individual. I've only known him as yours. That's how Spencer met you guys, too. And Jared. And Bryson—in some sort of messed-up way."

"Imagine being part of the couple that isn't together," I challenged playfully. "Let's stop and get a mocha refill. I need it."

Katie chuckled. "I'm sorry. I didn't mean to stress you out. I just know you."

"Yeah." I rested my head in my hand. "I know me, too. That's why I need another mocha."

I should've kept the admission to myself. I could've shoved it further down and ignored what I couldn't stop thinking about.

His dark green eyes—daring me to take a step forward when I cussed him out at my front door. The way they looked me up and down, outlining my curves through my sweatpants, because he was so well-versed in how they moved. No matter how hard I tried to fight it, that look pulled me in. It was the same look that prompted his hands in my hair and my mouth on his neck. It was the starting point, and it was the first time in a long time since one of us didn't step in to finish it.

Katie eyed me suspiciously as we pulled into our usual coffee spot. "What's in your head?"

I succumbed to my mischievous smile. "The fucking tension."

Katie clapped her hands, squealing as we pulled up to order. We spent the drive home singing Christmas music at the top of our lungs, and when Mariah Carey's iconic hit came through the speakers, we couldn't stop laughing long enough to belt the chorus.

Chapter Thirty-Seven

Jaxon

December 2021

When Bryson asked me to come to Jared's workshop on a Sunday, I tried not to look too disappointed. In an effort to knock out as much business as we could before Christmas, I was running behind on the schedule I'd set to finish Maci's space. I hadn't seen her in two weeks, and I couldn't stop thinking about our last conversation.

Maci finally snapped at me, and a delicious satisfaction made it impossible for me to focus. Unless I wanted to hand Bryson a botched set of estimates for next week, I was going to need another dose of caffeine from the coffeehouse across the street. The owner made a mean hazelnut latte, and she became my saving grace on the long days I spent in Jared's shop.

I felt myself nodding off as Spencer came downstairs from her office. She tipped her head over, gathering her hair so she could throw it up into one of her messy buns. "You good?"

I gave her a sleepy smile. "Exhausted. But good."

"Coffee?" She raised a brow in question. "I was heading there to try their new gingerbread chai anyway."

"Hazelnut—"

"Latte." Spencer smiled, giving me a playful tap on the nose. "I know."

I looked out the window and watched her cross the street, dodging the massive piles of snow near the curb. There was a bounce in her step, one that usually appeared after she had a good writing session. The gingerbread chai was a good sign that she'd be up in her office for the rest of the day.

"Damn. You couldn't put in an order for me?" Bryson exclaimed. He walked around to my side of the desk and placed a stack of manila folders next to the computer. "There are also some buckets of paint in the back. They must've been delivered last night."

Suddenly, I had all the energy in the world to knock out this set of files. The sooner I finished with the paperwork, the sooner I could get back to the work I really wanted to be doing.

Bryson hooked his thumb over his shoulder. "Is that the paint for Maci's place? I'm about to get these numbers quick as hell, huh?"

I chuckled at his dig. It wasn't the first time he'd commented about how I acted around Maci, and it wouldn't be the last. It was in his nature to say the little things you didn't want to say out loud.

Our smiles tapered as the notorious *DING* came from the computer. Ever since Bryson took over the business, we have learned to hate the sound. The alert indicated that an email had just entered our inbox. Every time we thought we were ahead, the *DING* humbly knocked us three steps back.

At first glance, I recognized the letter heading. "It's an update about the trial," I said slowly.

Bryson leaned in to read over my shoulder. We'd been waiting for an update since last week. The parents of the school shooter—the twelve-year-old kid who shot and killed Jared—were facing criminal charges for their involvement.

I had read through enough legal jargon to know where it was going. About halfway through the third paragraph, my chest felt so tight that I feared I might snap. The anger made it impossible for my hands to hold the mouse steady.

"That's bullshit," I spat, pushing against the desk so I could stand up.

"That's America," Bryson stated. "Fuck."

I inhaled slowly through my nose to try to calm down. "Spencer can't see that. Not today."

Bryson eyed me cautiously. "J—"

"Not today," I warned.

"If she doesn't see it today, she will soon somewhere else," he said softly.

"They have proof of the father buying him the gun for his birthday," I argued. Bryson's face started to look like the visions of Jared's spreadsheets, blurred and unrecognizable through everything else my mind was trying to process. "Felony child neglect, failure to secure a weapon . . . fucking murder," I rattled off.

Bryson paced around the shop with his hands on his hips, staring at the ceiling fan as if it had all the answers. It had been four months since the shooting, and the number of lives that would remain impacted by this family was staggering—students, teachers, and loved ones of the victims.

Bryson. Spencer. The survivors. It was only a matter of time before Spencer returned and demanded some sort of explanation for the heavy silence.

"The reason we're even hearing about a trial is because of who was involved," Bryson explained calmly. "Look at Jared, look at the neighborhood, and look at the kid."

I didn't want to look any more than I already had. I didn't want Bryson to be right. But where lives were lost, there would be a next time. Nothing would change.

Spencer returned with the drinks, and we sat her down to show her the email. She wiped away a few tears, gave us both a hug, and reassured us that she was fine. At first, I didn't believe her. I spent the rest of the afternoon preparing for the crack that would break her delicate features. Instead, she sipped her gingerbread chai and offered to order pizza for a late lunch.

It was as if there were no room for anger or sadness in her day. She'd given it enough space. Regardless of what a jury decided, the outcome didn't matter. Consequences wouldn't bring Jared back. They wouldn't change what happened to Bryson or the rest of the families impacted by the shooting.

All we could do was wait for change, and it was bullshit.

Chapter Thirty-Eight

MACI

IT WAS OFFICIALLY THE end of finals week, bringing my first semester as an instructor to a close. Classes wouldn't resume until January, and I planned to spend as little time as possible thinking about them over winter break. I'd deal with the unread emails when I returned. As I drove home through the slush and the sleet, there was only one action item I could focus on, and I was getting tired of making myself feel like shit for it.

Jaxon was coming over to paint the kitchen, one of the last steps required to finish my space before Christmas. It shouldn't have been a big deal. He'd been over dozens of times. So why was I worried about background noise and what candle to light before he showed up?

Fucking Katie.

Yeah, let's blame Katie.

After I changed out of my work clothes, I ran downstairs to hunt for a casual movie.

A *casual* movie? What the fuck was a casual movie? Maybe music would be better. Or, I could play the movie on mute so we technically had people in the room with us, and music could play in the background?

Without wasting another second of my life on the things that didn't actually matter, I pressed play on *21 Jump Street* and muted the sound. I connected my phone to the speaker and hit shuffle, leaving my musical fate in the hands of my playlist.

Tonight would be no different than any other night he came over. Everything would be fine. *I* was fine.

"You think you're ever a little too good at being fine?"

I scowled.

Giving in to my need to unwind, I reached into the fridge and pulled out the white wine. I poured myself a glass, setting an empty one on the counter so Jaxon could help himself. There would be no pushing alcohol on my part, not after the last encounter we had together.

The loud alert from my new security system sounded, and I placed my drink on the counter for safekeeping. Every time someone came to my door, they scared the shit out of me. Not because they were here, but because when Jaxon installed the Ring doorbell outside, he failed to mention that the alarms went off inside, too.

"Since U Been Gone" by Kelly Clarkson came up next on the playlist. It was the perfect time. Kelly was a girl's girl. I'd channel her energy and forget all about the conversation I had with Katie about tension.

What was tension anyway? There was nothing there. There was nothing about how, when I opened the door for him, his lips curved into a grin that sent a rush of heat to my cheeks. Or how his tongue unwillingly grazed the center of his top lip when I hesitated to step aside so he could come in. His cologne lingered in the living room with me as he made his way to the kitchen, utterly oblivious to the memories that flooded my head with his scent.

On cold nights in Ohio, Jaxon would come up to my apartment and strip off his hoodie, revealing a black or white T-shirt that hugged his chest and shoulders. He'd look at me with long curls hanging just above his eyes, hooded with a heated gaze that threatened whatever movie we planned on watching. His hair was always longer in the winter months. He knew I loved it long so that I could grab it.

As he loaded buckets of paint into the kitchen, it was hard not to notice the slight curls that rested just above his ears. A few weeks ago, when I saw him, it was still short.

I snuck a sip of wine from my glass, grateful for Chicago snow. "You sure you don't need any help?" I prompted, watching him place two more gallons of paint on the dining table.

"How sweet of you to offer now that I'm almost done," he joked. "I'm good. It's getting pretty bad out there, and I only have one more box to get."

I was so fixated on his arrival that I forgot about the county weather warning. It was the reason I left campus an hour early.

Leaving his hat and jacket in the living room, he emerged in dark jeans and a black T-shirt. It was as if no time had passed at all, only this version of him somehow had broader shoulders and a deeper tan.

Jaxon eyed the bottle on the counter. "Drinking before we even get started, huh? You *do* know how to paint, right?"

I surveyed the assortment of brushes on the table. "It's just painting."

"Yeah," he emphasized, waiting for me to continue.

"I have a very steady hand," I countered.

Jaxon rolled his eyes. "Not after another glass of that, you won't."

My mouth fell slightly as he began taping off the window frames with blue painter's tape. He wasn't entirely inaccurate.

I hadn't eaten since lunch, and I was tempting a quick buzz with my empty stomach.

"I'll order some food," I offered. "Did you like that pizza?"

His mouth lifted into a sly grin. "I did like that pizza. But most places are no longer delivering because of the weather. Bryson was bitching about it when I left."

Well, fuck.

While Jaxon set up barriers around the kitchen appliances, I searched the fridge for something to throw together. Since I saved my grocery shopping for the weekends, a sad set of options stared back at me. I was no Katie, but as long as I had the essentials, I wasn't hopeless.

"Do you want a grilled cheese?" I pulled my frying pan from the cabinet. The gas clicked impatiently on the burner. "I can also offer you chips."

"Are you making it with that?"

I looked over my shoulder, and Jaxon stood behind me, barely giving me enough space to turn my head.

I swallowed. "Yeah?"

I felt him take a few steps back. "Is this for me?"

Since it was safe to turn around, I caught him holding up the empty wine glass.

"Yeah, but—" I looked between him and the frying pan. "What's wrong with the pan?"

Jaxon chuckled as he poured his wine. "What year is that pan from? You don't have to answer that, because I recognize that pan from your apartment," he muttered, sending me into a burst of hysterics.

It wasn't the wine. It was all the times that Jaxon used this pan to make us breakfast in the morning. It was another sliver from our past that came unannounced into the present, and for some reason, it felt really damn good to laugh about it.

Chapter Thirty-Nine

JAXON

December 2021

The last time I made a grilled cheese sandwich, it was for Evie. She went through a phase where peanut butter and jelly were unacceptable, and I didn't have the unicorn-shaped macaroni and cheese. I was never a fan of grilled cheese, but as I sat across from Maci working my way through sandwich number three, it was the best damn thing I ever had.

Since the wine wasn't pairing well, we switched to bottled water. I was grateful when she made the suggestion. The last few times we were together, there was alcohol involved. I wanted a fair shot at having a good conversation with her without the safety net of Moscato or bottled beer.

I'd had that version of Maci—the carefree girl from college who made impulsive decisions and served me uncooked lasagna. I wanted this one. It allowed me to look at her with fresh eyes, rather than searching for the girl I used to know.

"Not bad for a frying pan of seven years," she teased. Her smile reached the corners of her eyes, accentuating the baby blues that could make me drop to my knees. The shocked expression on my face prompted her into another fit of giggles. "It works just fine!"

Fuck, I loved to make her laugh.

"I'm gonna start pouring the paint," I said. "Do you want a roller or a brush?"

She scrunched her nose. "Which one is faster?"

Her question shouldn't have shocked me. Still, I sweetly answered her question with, "The roller."

"Gimme." She waved me forward with her hand. I handed her the roller, and she sprinted into the living room to turn up the music, returning just in time to watch me pour the dark green paint into the tray. "Ugh, it's gorgeous!"

I couldn't have agreed more. The color would pop against the white cabinets. It was just bold enough for a kitchen and dining room, and it wouldn't overpower the space.

I faced the wall and looked over my shoulder. "Ready?"

We settled into a comfortable pattern. Every time the songs changed on Maci's playlist, we'd steal glances at each other, and she'd smile or roll her eyes based on my reaction. It didn't take me long to realize that this was the playlist she shared with Katie in college. They filled it with new hits, throwbacks, and songs that reminded me of Bowling Green.

A song came on that I didn't recognize. "What song is this?"

She gasped. "Did we stumble across one you don't know?"

I coated my brush with more paint. "Taylor Swift?"

"Yes," she said with a chuckle. Her hand brushed against my forearm when she reached for a towel.

We locked eyes. A simple touch was all it took to light a fire under my skin—to pull me back to a time when I trailed my fingers over her hips and brushed my thumbs along her panty line.

She cleared her throat, using the towel to remove the paint streaks from her hand. No matter what I tried to distract myself with, I couldn't break free. A few seconds passed before a specific lyric drew her attention back to me.

I held her gaze, giving her another chance to look away if she wanted me to let go.

"'Out of the Woods,'" she said, forcing the sentence between us.

"What?"

"The song," she explained. "It's 'Out of the Woods' by Taylor Swift."

"Huh." I stifled a grin. I'd forgotten what we were talking about. I gestured to the can of paint on the table. "Did you need more in the tray?"

"Actually, I just need a second." Maci retreated to the other side of the kitchen, putting the breakfast counter between us.

I'd watched her run before. Fuck, I even chased her when she did. But this was different. There was a back-and-forth going on in her head that I couldn't hear.

"You okay?" I prompted softly. When she didn't answer, I started walking toward her. "Mace?"

Through dark lashes, she pleaded with me to be the one to cross the line. That look told me everything she wasn't saying, but I refused to keep guessing. I couldn't. After everything that had happened, I wouldn't fill in the blanks for her.

"I just need a second," she repeated.

"For what?"

She shook her head. "You know what."

Say it, I willed her. *Talk to me, pretty girl.*

"Let's pretend like I don't," I said. As much as my body willed me forward, I forced myself to stay put. I'd been here before. We'd already played this game. Whatever happened next was up to her.

"I lied to you before," she admitted, "about not wanting to hate you."

My heart hammered in my chest. There was still something there. *We* were still there. If this was my shot, I wasn't going to throw it away. "Would you be pissed if I kissed you?"

"Fuck yeah."

The small quirk of her lip pushed me to take another step forward. "Do you feel like forgiving me tomorrow?"

Her lips parted slightly, and a heavy silence hung between us as we waited for her answer. She rolled her eyes, growing frustrated with her inner dialogue. "Fuck yeah."

Everything around us blurred together, shifting in slow motion when her mouth collided with mine. We moved as if we'd never hit pause—blending in a sweet sensation that I didn't want to turn off. A song that never stopped playing. The heat of a summer night that never faded away. A fire that never went out.

I spent hundreds of hours trying to picture what it would feel like to have her in my arms again. I tried to convince myself that she wasn't mine to miss, that everything happened the way that it needed to because I couldn't be what I promised her. It was unthinkable—the idea that I could survive without this feeling for the rest of my life. Her touch was everything. *She* was everything, and I was kidding myself if I thought happiness was attainable without Maci Lawson.

My thumbs skimmed the soft skin of her hips, and when my teeth grazed her bottom lip, she groaned into my mouth. That sound sent a pull to my groin. Any attention I'd gotten over the years was enough to keep me from going dormant. There was no comparison to the real thing. As soon as she pressed her body against me, my cock woke the fuck up.

I swept my fingers across her lower back, teasing the band on her panties and tracing imaginary lines on her sensitive skin. She dug her nails into my neck, pleading with me to take it one step further.

My hands gripped her ass, moving to cup the backs of her thighs so I could set her on the counter.

"There isn't much to these counters," she said, her frustrated sigh turning into a satisfied moan. The harder she tried to fight it, the more her body betrayed her. It made it that much harder to keep my hands to myself.

I smiled into the crook of her neck. "I built these counters, baby." My lips traveled down the side of her throat, trailing soft kisses to her collarbone. "They're not going anywhere."

Chapter Forty

MACI

December 2021

Baby.

As quickly as the high came from kissing Jaxon Hayes, it threw me back down to the fucking ground. It was all so simple when it lived inside my head. I could forgive him for kissing me, even though my clit throbbed through my shorts, begging for the hands that pushed me over the edge more times than I could remember to ruin me.

It made sense in the silence when our bodies did the talking. Hearing the words out loud made it real, and I wasn't sure if I could handle it.

The terms of endearment—the way he used to talk to me when I was his—that's where he threatened to cross the line. I willed myself to push it aside, to be the type of girl who lived in the moment and forgot about the past.

I tugged softly on his curls, angling his mouth to mine. "Kiss me again."

His nose skimmed against my jawline as he straightened up, his hands shifting to the counter on either side of me. He was studying me, searching my face for any signs of hesitation or indications that he should stop. If I let him look any longer, he'd find one.

He traced my bottom lip with his thumb, the heat in his green gaze growing more intense with each passing moment. The right side of his mouth lifted into a cocky grin. He wasn't naive to the thoughts going on inside my head. He'd had enough practice.

"You gotta let me know what we're doing here, Mace," he whispered.

I kissed him gently, ignoring his plea. He leaned into it at first, slowing me down with the sweet guidance of his tongue.

Fuck, I missed him.

He cupped my chin with his hand, forcing me to look at him. "I don't wanna mess this up. Talk to me."

Words. What were words? Suddenly, I had none.

I swallowed, nodding my head as if it would toss some letters into a sentence. "Yeah."

"Yeah," Jaxon echoed my unhelpful response.

"I think we should stop."

"I think I should go," he offered, sounding more like a painful suggestion.

My fingers traced the stubble along his jawline. "Yeah."

A soft laugh fell from his lips. "You're not helping."

My hand recoiled back to the safe zone. "Sorry."

He stepped back, running both of his hands through his hair. "Fuck."

Yeah, that's one way to say it.

This would hit me like a fucking freight train tomorrow morning. I didn't know where to go from here. Shit, half of my kitchen still needed its first coat of paint.

Jaxon walked back over to the dining table, unable to look at me as he picked up his brush and dipped it into the paint. I drummed my fingers quietly against the countertop, unsure of what to say next as I processed the last fifteen minutes. Contrary to what I thought I'd feel, one thing was sure.

I wasn't pissed that he kissed me. There would be no apologies for something I thought I'd only experience again when I was alone and closed my eyes. For three years, I craved his touch. I yearned to have his hands on my body, exploring territory I was afraid he might forget.

He remembered everything.

One kiss was enough to bury anything I ever had with anyone else. A placeholder, as Katie called it, was putting it lightly. No one else ever stood a chance.

I slid off the counter, ignoring the throbbing between my legs. We could move past this. We could finish out the night and go on as if nothing happened. As I picked up the roller, I realized I wasn't sure if I was including Jaxon in that "we" or if it was just me and my unsatisfied clit.

I pressed the roller into the tray, only to realize Jaxon still hadn't added more paint.

Jaxon stifled a grin, pressing his lips into a firm line so he wouldn't make any other suggestions.

I tried to sound convincing when I said, "You don't have to go."

He averted his gaze to the green wall behind him. "I probably should. If I don't go now, there might be too much snow on the roads when I try to leave later."

Just the thought of him staying over set off sirens in my head.

He rested his hands on the table. "What do you have going on this week?"

"Just some running around with Katie. I'm going over there tomorrow to help bake cookies."

We exchanged an amused grin, both of us knowing that I'd only be there to taste test and offer moral support.

"I'll swing by tomorrow while you're out." His warm gaze said the rest out loud. He'd come back when I was out, so this wouldn't happen again. "It's pretty much just paint and finishing touches at this point."

"Counters are good?" I asked.

His heated gaze dared me to keep dancing around what just happened. "I just need to put the doors on a few of them. But they aren't going anywhere. They're screwed in."

I leaned against the doorway to the living room, watching him slip his hoodie over his head.

Jaxon teased the idea of closing the space between us. Instead, he reached for his hat and covered his curls. "Thank you for the grilled cheese."

I answered with a slight nod.

"I'm going to Charlotte for Christmas," he added.

Maybe that's how we moved past this, with random points of conversation.

"Not California?" I asked.

"My mom wants to be home for a little while. Things tend to slow down between Christmas and the New Year, so we're all going there."

I knew that. It was the only time of year Jaxon could see me in New York.

As he lingered near the front door, I longed for the days when I wasn't stuck in my head about how to be around him. I ached to rest my hands on his chest—press myself into the warmth of his hoodie like I used to before he'd leave my apartment. His cologne would thread into my shirt one last time while his lips brushed near my temple. It was just him and me.

"Thank you for the paint," I said, trying to put an end to this roundabout farewell. I needed to sort through my sober thoughts. I couldn't even blame tonight's choice on the wine. "I'm sure I'll see you before you leave for Charlotte."

Jaxon looked me up and down once more before he stepped out into the cold. "Good night, Mace."

For the next hour, I finished the first coat of paint in the kitchen. I thought I'd want some wine to accompany me, but when the songs on my playlist spoke where I couldn't find the words, I realized I wanted to take in everything about tonight the way it actually happened. No fluff or dramatized rendi-tions, just the butterflies in my stomach and the fireworks in my chest.

When I crawled into bed and closed my eyes, I replayed it all again until I fell asleep. I dreamed of kissing Jaxon Hayes on my kitchen counter, and for the first time in three years, I woke up, only to remember it hadn't been a dream at all.

Chapter Forty-One

MACI

December 2021

It was humbling how two completely different scenarios could exist in the same time frame. This morning, when I woke up, I eased any thoughts of regret by reading a good-night text from Jaxon. He'd sent it around two o'clock in the morning, which meant he left my house, went back to Bryson's, and was still thinking of me.

I hesitated to send a good-morning text. Should I invite the idea of continuing the conversation throughout the day?

Right above Jaxon's text was a fresh text from Spencer to Katie and me. While I waited for my Keurig to heat up, I opened the thread.

Spencer

> So I know I said I'd be staying in town for Christmas, but I don't think I can do it.

> I'm thinking of booking a trip somewhere.

> I just don't want to be here.

> Like in Chicago.

I felt Katie's panic through the phone screen. She was probably pacing around her kitchen, talking through a possible response with the butter softening on the counter. My thumbs hovered above the keyboard, unable to form a coherent sentence that would validate what Spencer was saying.

We had a week and a half until Christmas, and she was trying to run from a date that was quickly approaching. She didn't need to be talked out of it. She needed support from the people who knew how hard this day would be without Jared.

Katie's photo replaced our text thread, and I swiped up to answer. "Hello?"

"Hold on!" she screamed, her voice diminishing into the background.

"Did you just call me to walk away from the phone? I hate when you do that."

"Don't get grumpy with me because of Spencer's text," she snapped, making it clear that she was in front of the speaker.

"I'm not grumpy," I muttered. I pressed my right hand to my forehead while my left turned off the Keurig. I wasn't having coffee at home today. This phone call was a cry for early assistance.

"We should've seen this coming," Katie said. "What kind of trip do you think she's going for?"

I slipped on my moccasins and grabbed my car keys. "She probably doesn't know. I don't think I would. I just wouldn't want to be *here*."

"Hmm," Katie murmured.

"I can offer to go with her," I blurted, the words leaving a sour taste in my mouth. I looked over my shoulder as I walked out into the cold. I pictured hosting a Christmas here. Fuck, Jaxon was putting in the work to make sure I had the option.

Jaxon. My ex-boyfriend, who kissed me last night.

In slow motion, I watched the fog disappear from my windshield, running back the events of last night and remembering one glaring detail. It wasn't him who kissed me—I kissed him. I stepped forward and pulled him in.

"What?" Katie exclaimed. "No! You were so excited to have Christmas. Your parents—"

"Still haven't booked their flights," I admitted weakly, channeling my frustration into the gas pedal as I took off down the street. "I think it's time that I accept that they aren't interested."

"That's so shitty. I'm sorry."

"Maybe that's what I get for thinking we could all be together for Christmas."

"What about Chase?"

My older brother loved his new life in Europe for two reasons—it made Trey happy and put over 3,000 miles between him and our parents. Sometimes I found myself jealous of the distance. It wasn't shocking to me that Spencer wanted to retreat for a little while.

"Chase was at least honest with me and said he wouldn't be able to swing a trip until February," I added. "Do I need to stop and grab coffee?"

"What about our condo in Port Clinton?" Katie suggested. "It's not super far, and that way she isn't booking something last minute."

The Port Clinton condo—the place where Jaxon and I officially started. I rolled my eyes to the sky, blaming Jared for Katie's throwback offer. It was hard not to think he had something to do with this.

Tears sprang to my eyes. If he were here, I would've called him in a panic this morning about what happened last night. He would've eaten up the drama, eager to have my latest slice of nonsense with his morning coffee. He was my goofy and down-to-earth backboard for the chaos. His boyish grin and infectious laugh constantly shed some light on whatever darkness I was navigating.

I blinked a few times, regaining my composure. "So that's a no for the coffee?"

"No to the coffee," Katie stammered impatiently. "Did you hear me? What about the condo?"

"I heard you. Yes, the condo."

"I could probably swing a few days too—"

"You have Connor's parents coming into town." I chuckled at Katie's apparent hesitation as I pulled into her driveway. Once I stepped into her house, I hung up the phone. "I'll bring up the idea to her and offer it as a girls' trip. Maybe Elle can come too."

Katie's smile tapered off into a giant pout. "Well, now I just feel left out."

I reached into the fridge for the creamer and the jug of cold brew. I couldn't hold off on the caffeine any longer. "Why?"

"You and Bryson have done Christmas together the past two years," she noted sadly. "Once he catches wind of a trip, he's going to want to go. Elle being there will just be a bonus."

I rolled my eyes. "Don't speak that curse into a possibility."

Katie scoffed. "Please. Don't act like Bryson has *ever* been a curse to you. If Jaxon is going home for Christmas, Bryson will tag along."

Katie's lingering gaze indicated that she knew there was something I wasn't telling her. It was annoying how spot on her hunches were. I couldn't have anything for myself when I was in her presence.

"Should I text that to her, then?" I pulled out my phone. "I don't want to keep her on read much longer."

Katie's eyes narrowed, giving me my answer. I sent the text offering Port Clinton as an option, and before I could place my phone back on the counter, Spencer answered.

Spencer

Perfect.

"Alright then!" I rubbed my hands together, peering over the recipes that Katie had spread out near the mixer. "What are we baking first?"

"Why don't you start with the chocolate chip dough and tell me why Jaxon is texting you?" she instructed casually.

A follow-up text. Did Jaxon send the text that I talked myself out of this morning?

I opened my mouth to answer, and it betrayed me by falling into a satisfied grin. "He's just following up."

She blew out an exasperated laugh. "On?"

With one quick tug, I decided to rip open the conversation like the bag of chocolate chips in my hand. "He kissed me last night."

Katie's eyes burrowed holes into the part of me that dared to keep this from her for a few hours.

"Technically, I kissed him," I added.

"Holy fuck," Katie whispered, as if her response might alert the rest of the neighborhood. "Start from the beginning."

Chapter Forty-Two

JAXON

December 2021

A loud beeping came from the kitchen, making my third attempt to get some sleep seem impossible. Was it the fire alarm? I didn't fucking know. I'd been wide awake since I returned from Maci's last night, and I was still waiting to come down from the high.

Every time I closed my eyes, I saw her. I felt her hips in my hands and the ache in my groin from being pressed against her. It was like waking up with an agonizing hangover. It wasn't until the next morning that you dealt with the aftermath.

I teased an addiction, and it would take more than a solo shower session to get me through the withdrawal.

A round of high-pitched cackling accompanied the alarm. It was time to give up on the idea of sleep and face whatever nonsense was happening on the other side of my bedroom door.

I threw on some basketball shorts and wandered downstairs to find Elle and Bryson at the stove, fanning whatever was burning in the skillet. On the counter, there was a spread of bacon, sausage, and what looked like pieces of chocolate chip pancakes. Eggs had to be the culprit. They always were in this group.

"Good morning!" I yelled over the alarm.

Elle spun around on her heels, leaving the cleanup to Bryson. "I'm surprised you're up! I heard you out here at like three."

I took a seat at one of the barstools. "You're *surprised* I'm up? How the fuck does one sleep through all of this?" I gestured vaguely to the mess in front of me, sending her into a burst of hysterics.

Bryson grabbed a broom from the closet, using the handle to turn off the alarm. I didn't think there could be a downfall to having such high ceilings—until an unwanted trigger was out of reach.

"Happy?" Bryson teased with an annoying grin. Having Elle around always put him in a good mood, and it wasn't fair of me to spoil their morning because I was exhausted.

"Extremely," I murmured, biting into a piece of bacon.

Elle passed me a plate so I could help myself to some food. So I didn't feel like a complete mooch, I offered to make the coffee. With some time and practice, I mastered the iced vanilla latte that Bryson started his day with. I even added an extra shot to mine, hoping the boost would hold me over until I could get a nap in later this afternoon.

The bacon was crispy, the sausage was greasy, and the pancakes were delicious. Overall, Elle and Bryson provided the perfect distraction to my quiet text thread with Maci. It was almost ten, and I knew she had to be at Katie's by now.

Had the good morning text been too much? Was she dissecting it as I powered through my second pancake? I wasn't used to having to guess, and it was maddening being in the dark.

I also wasn't prepared for Elle's nosy stream of follow-up questions. Bryson never had questions—only cocky commentary and witty remarks.

"So, what time did you get in last night?" Elle mimicked the playful grin Jared wore whenever he dipped his toe into business that wasn't his. "Three sounds kind of late for a kitchen paint job."

Bryson stifled a laugh.

"I didn't get in at three," I countered. "I left before the weather got too bad to leave."

Elle pouted. "Yes, that would've been tragic if you had to stay."

"Tragic's one way to put it," I said, excusing myself from the table. They weren't getting any hints from me about last night.

"What day are you leaving for Charlotte?" Bryson asked, his question earning a scowl from Elle.

"Wait," Elle said, turning her attention to me. "Charlotte?"

"We're doing Christmas at my parents' house," I explained.

Her shoulders fell. "Oh."

"Oh?" I echoed playfully as I closed the dishwasher. "What's, oh?"

"We're going to Port Clinton now for Christmas."

"Port Clinton?" I asked, looking at Bryson for confirmation. "Connor's condo?"

Bryson answered with a quick nod.

"Spencer didn't want to be here for the holiday." Elle softened her gaze. "So we're doing a trip instead."

I pressed my hands against the counter, unsure of what to say. Of course, Spencer didn't want to be here for Christmas. Why would she? The reminders weighed on her every day that she woke up in that house. A day like Christmas would make it even heavier to carry.

I should've asked her to come with me to Charlotte. My parents would've been more than happy to host her. Instead,

Bryson was filling me in on the plans to leave for Port Clinton two days before Christmas. He'd meet Maci out there in the morning after work, and Elle and Spencer would leave later that afternoon.

That also meant that Maci wasn't hosting Christmas. After all the planning and excitement that surrounded her favorite holiday, there was only one thing that would change her plans. Her parents were still putting their own shit before hers, and they probably never planned on coming. It pushed me even more to finish everything in her house before she returned from her trip.

Elle pulled her knees to her chest, staring blankly at the ice in her vanilla latte. It was easy to think about Spencer whenever someone brought up Jared's name in conversation. I had to remind myself that Elle's world fell apart that day, too.

Bryson noticed her silent shift and ran his fingers down her leg. She smiled weakly at his attempt to pull her back.

"How are you doing, Foster?" I asked. "Are you okay with going somewhere instead of staying here?"

Elle shrugged. "The day is going to be hard no matter where I am."

"It will be good for you guys to get away," I reassured her with a smile. "You know Katie and Maci won't let you have a shitty trip."

Elle chuckled. "Katie isn't coming."

Bryson sucked his teeth while I rolled my eyes. Katie inserted herself into every possible monumental moment. There was no way she was missing that trip.

Chapter Forty-Three

JAXON

December 2021

Traveling during the holidays was not for the faint of heart. It was miserable on a typical day, without the added traffic from last-minute shoppers and out-of-town travelers. My flight wasn't leaving for another three hours, and I was already on my way to the airport.

When I left Bryson's, he was finishing up a conference call. All of the extra hours we put in at Jared's workshop had paid off, and we were finally ready to start looking at the calendar for next year. Bryson had exceeded Spencer's expectations, and I was excited for everything that would come to him in this next chapter.

Slowly and quietly, I slipped into an optional extra hand for help rather than a requirement for success. I was ready to take on more at Hayes Sports and Entertainment, and Christmas with my parents offered the perfect segue into a conversation I'd been putting off since October.

There were pros and cons of stepping back into the role of CEO. A monthly agenda would restrict my free time. Without realizing what I was doing, I rolled to a stop in front of a place where I wanted to spend most of it.

Maci's car was in the driveway. The light was on in the living room. And I was out of my mind.

I hadn't heard from her since the night of our kiss. There was no text back—no phone call that assured me that I hadn't completely fucked this up after the last time we saw each other. I had to see her again, and she was leaving me on read.

Before I could change my mind, I cut the engine and stepped out into the cold. I shut the car door as quietly as I could, buying me some time before she looked out the window and saw me approaching the porch.

The loud chime of her doorbell warned me that there was no going back. I was on camera. There would be footage. Maci could be looking at me right now through her phone, debating whether she should come and answer the door or act like she wasn't home.

The deadbolt clicked, and suddenly she was in front of me, standing there in a loose black T-shirt that showed her stomach and sweatpants that hung off her hips. Her head fell slightly to her shoulder, and a small smile crept into her right cheek. She wasn't upset to see me. She didn't even look surprised.

"You stalking my house now?" she teased.

I chuckled. "Can I come in?"

She stepped aside and closed the door behind me. Before I could even get my shoes off, she returned to whatever she was doing in the kitchen. A Kindle was on the counter, and a hot cup of coffee sat next to a pair of thick-rimmed glasses.

Glasses. When did my girl get glasses?

"Did you want coffee?" Maci tucked her hair behind her ears and spun unevenly on her heels. "Or, wait, did you need something?" She put her hands on her hips to steady herself, reminding me how adorable she was when she was flustered. "Why are you here, exactly?"

"I wanna talk about the other night."

A dark pink flooded her cheeks. "And you drove all the way over here for that?"

"You won't answer my texts," I stated, taking a few steps toward her. "I leave in a few hours for Charlotte, and I couldn't go any longer without hearing from you."

She seemed surprised. "There's nothing to say."

"There's nothing to *say*." I knew she'd do this. If she could avoid having to talk about it, she didn't have to admit what she was feeling. "You haven't thought about it? I haven't crossed your mind since we—"

"Yes!" Maci's arms shot out in front of her. "How could I not think about it? It happened and it was—" She returned her hands to her hips, glaring at me with piercing blue eyes. It was an equal balance of fire and ice—one threatened to put everything out while the other craved the heat. "It happened. We had a moment, but this"—she gestured to the space between us—"cannot be anything more than a friendship."

"Friendship?"

The pleasantry in my voice threatened to throw her even more off balance. "Yeah?"

"So, when you *didn't* want to hate me, we were acquaintances. Now that you *do* want to hate me . . . and then there was the kiss . . . now I get to be friends with you?"

She narrowed her gaze. "Are you mocking me?"

I quickly shook my head. "No."

"You are!"

I burst into hysterics.

"Don't be fucking weird!" she warned through a breathy laugh.

I stared longingly from the other side of the kitchen, tempted to grab her chin and silence her in a way I knew worked every time. Back when I made it my mission to make her smile.

I'd used these counters once. I could do it again. I imagined the view was better when I was on my knees.

Maci's laughter tapered off into a comfortable sigh.

"Fuck, I missed that," I murmured.

She furrowed her brow. "What?"

"Your laugh." I quickly changed the subject so she didn't have to. "Now that we're friends, can I ask about Christmas?"

"I'll probably leave around noon—"

"Not Port Clinton," I coaxed gently. "Christmas. Here. With your parents."

Maci shrugged. "Are you surprised?"

Surprised didn't begin to cover what I felt. Maci's parents had been on the rocks since we started dating. It wasn't until they finalized their divorce that I noticed the toll it had on her. They were never there when they said they would be. All they delivered were excuses and rainchecks that never came.

Since I didn't know what else to say, I said, "I'm sorry."

She surveyed the space around us. "I'm sorry for the rushed timeline."

I scoffed. "You have nothing to be sorry for. It's their loss."

"Yeah." She tilted her head, her gaze drifting to my mouth. "So, is that all? Now that you've heard from me, are we good?"

Unbelievable. Her ability to jump from one thing to the next was almost impressive. It seemed impossible to leave her like this when her eyes said something completely different. She wanted me to come closer. She wanted to see if I would test the newly drawn lines of our friendship.

How did that work, exactly? Did we pick up where we left off, or were we starting over?

"We're good," I stated, backing away slowly toward the front door. "Just checking in on you."

Maci rolled her eyes, matching the tempo of my steps as she followed me out. "Thanks for your concern."

"What are friends for?" I shot her a cocky grin. "Merry Christmas, Mace."

Chapter Forty-Four

MACI

December 2021

It was as if the Ghost of Christmas Past had shown up on my doorstep and offered me a chance to redeem myself after my foolish mistake. Only this ghost looked a lot like Jaxon Hayes. By ignoring him via phone, I caused him to come in person. It was an unexpected twist in this holiday nightmare.

But was it a mistake? How could it be a mistake when I craved to do it again?

Because he broke your fucking heart.

Okay, well, it was hard to be positive about anything when I channeled Krampus instead of Buddy the Elf. One saw the magic in every opportunity, while the other was a shadowy folklore creature. It wasn't a very holly-jolly attitude to have as I arrived at Connor and Katie's condo—a refreshing piece of the past that provided the secluded scene we were looking for.

It was also the place where Jaxon and I began. Memory strands from five years ago shuffled in behind me when I opened the front door. I saw Jaxon setting our luggage down in the hallway while we picked our rooms. Stepping into the kitchen, I heard old country songs and Jaxon's laugh. He was everywhere—sprinkled throughout the living space, slowly digging a hole in the center of my chest.

It felt like someone was missing. Everyone I cared about would surround me in a few hours, and all I could focus on was the person who wouldn't be present.

"I lied to you before, about not wanting to hate you."

Not hating Jaxon might have been easier, but hating him was so much more fun.

He missed my *laugh*? Where were these comments when we spent most of our relationship over the phone? Suddenly, he was full of all the words. There wasn't a lack in his vocabulary whatsoever now that he was trying to get under my skin.

You could just let him.

I dropped my duffel bag on the ground with a loud *thump*. Nothing about Jaxon felt unnatural. If anything, being with him was the easiest thing I'd done in a long time.

Like singing the lyrics to a throwback song—you never lost the words. Every time it came around, it threatened to be better than the first listen. I could hit rewind. I could play it again. But then what? Would we just be thrown back into the shuffle?

Staring out at the lake, I remembered a conversation I had with Jared—his boyish grin greeting me on the beach and cutting into my moment of solitude. When I told him that Jaxon's family would always be his first love, Jared just smiled and told me I was wrong.

"First obligation, maybe, but first love? Nah. You guys are on the endgame track."

Tears rolled down my cheeks, and I let them fall. There was no one to hide from—no mask to put on. I'd do anything for Jared to come back and prove me wrong again.

For the next hour, I moved in silence, setting up the tree Katie gave me and making sure I decorated the mantel with stockings and garland. Lights twinkled along the kitchen counters, giving the space a homey cabin glow instead of a bright lakeside retreat. When I added the evergreen candle and clicked on the gas fireplace, I knew it was enough to get us started. Everyone would trickle in and make the space their own. All I had to do was provide the base.

The door opened behind me, and I didn't turn around. Bryson called my name, and I heard him place his keys on the counter.

I turned to face him, greeting him with the blotchy evidence of my breakdown. He furrowed his brow, closing the space between us so he could pull me into his chest.

"Hey, hey," Bryson murmured. He tightened his grip around my shoulders and rested his chin on top of my head. "It's okay."

I nodded, squeezing him harder as I sobbed into his hoodie.

"You're okay," he assured me. "I'm right here."

Last time I was with Bryson in this condo, we ended things. I was never sure what we used to have, and I didn't think he knew either. We said goodbye to the end of a beginning—a beginning that I never knew I needed until someone with a firearm threatened to take it all away.

Chapter Forty-Five

MACI

December 2021

When Katie showed up the morning of Christmas Eve with Max in one arm and a bin of homemade gingerbread cookies in another, I shouldn't have been surprised.

"What happened to your dinner plans?" Spencer exclaimed, jumping up from the barstool to snag Max.

"We switched from dinner to brunch," Katie glanced over her shoulder at Connor. "It worked out better for everyone anyway!"

Connor gestured vaguely to the decorated space in front of him. "And of course we couldn't miss this."

"Told you," Bryson murmured to Elle. Since he never grasped the concept of whispering, we all looked at him, waiting for some sort of context for his comment. Flabbergasted, he offered an innocent shrug. "I just knew she'd find some way to come!"

Katie rolled her eyes, making room for herself in the kitchen. While Connor got them set up in their bedroom, Spencer kept Max busy with the twinkling lights and dangling ornaments on the Christmas tree. "Last Christmas" by Wham! played softly in the background, and the snow was picking up outside. We could've been a submission for a holiday card.

"The place looks great." Katie gleamed as she set out her bakery spread.

"It's been nice," I admitted softly, slightly nodding toward Spencer. "It's been very low-key."

"Low-key is good."

I took a sip of my coffee, trying to nurse the afternoon crash.

Katie gave my hand a gentle squeeze. "We'll make the best of it. Together."

I excused myself to my room so I wouldn't destroy the picture-perfect setting with more tears. I reminded myself why we were all here in the first place. We'd cook a cozy dinner tonight and wake up tomorrow morning with hot chocolate and pancakes. Max would open a few presents, and we'd get to experience Christmas through his eyes, rather than the ones we used in real life.

Even though everything had changed, it all looked the same. The soft bedspread, the fluffy towels in the bathroom, the patterned dishes in the kitchen—all left untouched since the last time we were here. Dragging my hands across the duvet, I pictured both of them—Jared making everyone laugh and Jaxon backing me into the bedroom.

"She said your name kind of sweet there, Jax," Jared teased.

I remembered the look on Jaxon's face—serious and un-apologetic, tangled in a cocky grin.

"Believe me," he stated. "She's said my name sweeter than that."

After that, it all plummeted. There was screaming and tears. I told Jaxon I loved him right before we crossed the line. It seemed so simple back then—catch feelings, fall for each other, work through the distance, and live happily ever after.

I was so quick to feed into the optimism that I hadn't considered the possibility of it falling apart.

Tomorrow morning would come, and we'd all make the best of it. Maybe one day it wouldn't feel like pretend.

Pretend.
And then it hit me.

Chapter Forty-Six

Jaxon

December 2021

We'd spent the last three hours watching *Frozen* and *Frozen 2,* and I was starting to think I was the only one left with some sanity. After opening her presents from my parents, Evie declared she needed the movies to play while she wore her new Elsa costume. Sure, the music was well-written and the beats were catchy, but I was over the snow witch and her frosted powers.

I clapped along with the rest of the room as Evie did a bow. Once the credits started, she went right to Alex for a rewind.

"Elsa again, Daddy!" Evie squealed, getting an excited Peyton to join in. She was only two years old, but she backed her sister up whenever it came to anything important—like the only TV in the living room.

If I had to endure another family rendition of "Let It Go," I was going to need another whiskey on the rocks.

"The game," I begged, gesturing toward the TV screen. "The game? *A* game. Any kind of sport, please, I beg you. What time does Santa usually get to Charlotte?"

"Let the girls have their fun, Jax." Mom swatted my forearm, taking it upon herself to grab my glass for a refill. She'd been spending more time on her feet lately, trying to convince the room that she wasn't out of commission. Cancer or no cancer, nothing would stop her from being the host of a holiday gathering, especially when everyone in the family was in the same place at the same time.

Home. It felt great to be home.

Mom placed my full glass of whiskey on the end table, squeezing my hand before she returned to her seat next to Dad.

"I don't think you realize how much you'll disrupt the peace if you turn this off," Bella warned me. In other words, the TV was off-limits until the girls went to bed.

"We choose peace every time," Alex added.

Bella assured me that I'd understand one day. Her assumption that I wanted kids didn't start until I brought Maci home. Out of all of the shitty things I'd done in the past, breaking up with Maci hit her the hardest. She didn't talk to me for weeks after she found out, but I knew she never let go of the hope.

When I arrived for Christmas, I chose to leave my life in Chicago out of the conversations. I wasn't ready for the questions. There would be no such thing as a silent night, and I would be the one who didn't know peace.

Things were safer in my head. *Maci* was safe. I didn't care how she labeled us. I wanted her back regardless of how she would have me.

But that kiss. *Fuck*, that kiss. I couldn't get it out of my head.

"Uncle Jaxon is right, girls," Bella warned, eyeing me over the brim of her wine glass. "Santa Claus won't come if you're still awake when he gets here!"

Evie's eyes went wide, as if Bella told her that the great Elsa would never sing again. Peyton looked at her sister, and we all laughed when she did her best to mimic Evie's expression. It didn't take much convincing after that. Everyone got their rounds of hugs and kisses before Bella carried them up to bed.

"Did they set out cookies?" Alex asked.

Mom nodded reassuringly.

"Thank goodness, too," Dad added. "If they had waited until now, Peyton would still be in there picking out a cookie."

"They are good, though," Alex noted. "You're making those for the gala, right?"

The First Quarter Gala for Hayes Sports and Entertainment. Fuck. How could I forget? My parents hosted it every January.

Dad read me from across the room. "It's been a difficult year. If you can't make it—"

"No!" I forced a smile. I couldn't miss another event—not one that would include investors and potential partners. "I'll be there."

Mom thought she was slick when she added, "You can bring someone, you know."

Maybe she was on to something. Because the first person that came to my mind was the last person I stopped to check on before I flew out here.

It would be ridiculous. Unheard of. *Insanity*. I couldn't ask Maci to come with me to something like that, no matter how much I wanted to.

"I'll think about it." I averted my gaze to the TV. "Dad, really?"

The cheerful opening of *National Lampoon's Christmas Vacation* played softly through the surround sound.

"It's tradition," Dad stated, clinking glasses with my mom. "We'll wait until Bella is back—"

"Oh, I'm back," Bella said with a hefty sigh. She crashed into the couch next to Alex, reaching over him for her glass of wine. She patted his thigh. "We'll be Santa after this is over."

When Cousin Eddy arrived with his RV, my phone rang from the pocket of my sweatpants. I pulled it out and saw Spencer's name on the screen.

I made a silent exit from the living room so I could take the call from my dad's office. "Spencer? Is everything okay?"

There was a loud burst of laughter in the background, and she had to shout over the noise. "Merry Christmas! Yes, everything is fine. I just wanted to call and tell you that I sold the house!"

"Are you serious?" I said through a breathy laugh. "That's amazing!"

"Someone went by for a showing yesterday, and they must've loved what they saw! My realtor wanted to let me know before Christmas."

"Just another gift from Jared," I teased, knowing that it made her smile.

"Right!" she exclaimed. It was already an exciting moment, but I knew the joy was heightened by whatever fruity drink Katie had given her.

"I'm happy for you, Foster. How are things going? You guys having a good time?"

"Yeah, we—" Bryson's screaming cut her off, and she said something in the background that I couldn't make out. "Bryson's calling me for Mario Kart."

Mario Kart. Now *that* was a throwback. We spent most of our time pregaming in college with those characters. Drunk driving on race tracks until we could stumble out the front door and make it to the bars.

When I walked back into the living room, Bella and Mom were staring at me. Dad and Alex could at least pretend like they weren't nosy.

"Spencer sold their house," I said, getting a round of applause and cheering.

"That is fantastic news," Mom swooned. "Ugh, I was hoping that it would happen soon."

"We'll need her new address," Dad added.

"Oh yes." Mom widened her gaze. "The subscriptions—"

I chuckled. "You guys *did not* set her up with more food."

Dad sipped his whiskey so he wouldn't have to answer.

Before I went up to my room, I helped Alex and Bella place presents under and around the tree. I took a picture and sent it to Katie, commenting on how parents didn't get enough credit for Christmas morning. She responded with a photo of everyone gathered in the living room. Dark red drinks were in their hands, and I assumed Katie was responsible for the greenery that stuck out of them.

When Connor called me about Jared's passing, I thought there would be no recovering, no stepping forward and finding peace where only chaos seemed to exist. Yet, somehow it happened. New beginnings had started.

Spencer sold the house, and Katie was following a dream.

Maci had her home, and Bryson was finding peace.

Connor's light was slowly coming back, and Elle returned to Chicago, no longer fighting the chemistry between her and Bryson.

What else would I be willing to sacrifice to find my peace? Since I had it once before, I feared I might be too late.

Chapter Forty-Seven

Jaxon

December 2021

When my phone rang around eleven, I wasn't sure what to expect when I looked at the screen. Bryson, maybe, or Vince after he learned I was home for Christmas. But when I saw her name, I hesitated to answer, assuring myself that it had to be a mistake. It had to be a butt dial situation.

Great. Now you're thinking about her ass.

I swiped right before I could change my mind. "Mace?"

"Hey," she said, her voice barely above a whisper.

I smiled sleepily. "Hey."

"I—" She let out a staggered breath. "Why did you come up to my room that night?"

The night of Friendsgiving. She didn't need to clarify. It was only a matter of time before something sparked her memory. "I just wanted to make sure you were okay."

"But you stayed?"

"Yeah," I admitted. "I stayed."

"I asked you to pretend."

My stomach dropped. "You might have asked me to do that," I hinted cautiously.

"I remember, Jaxon."

I rolled over on my back and rested my arm above my head. "And what exactly do you remember?"

"You know—" Maci sighed, and the rustling of her sheets told me she was getting comfortable too. "I went months without being myself. *Months* after we broke up and again after Jared died. Katie was concerned about me from time to time, and Bryson was too. But honestly, no one noticed. No one knew that when I was alone, I became a completely different person."

So much of what she was saying made sense. When I was in California, no one saw how I was barely hanging on.

"But you would've," she added softly. The snag in her voice broke my heart.

We were supposed to be there for the bad and the ugly. Every struggle Maci had when we were apart, I wasn't there. There were so many times I ached to call her about my mom. We'd lost so much more than a title when we broke up.

"My mom is sick," I whispered.

A small gasp fell into the speaker. "Evelyn?"

She couldn't see me, but I nodded. I clutched my temples with my fingers, trying to relieve some of the pressure in my head.

Maci sensed that I needed her to speak next. "What kind of sick?"

I swallowed around the lump in my throat. "Cancer. She was diagnosed a few months before my dad made me CEO. They kept it quiet since they were still getting answers to everything."

"That's why your dad left LA. The summer we—"

"Yeah," I murmured, not wanting to hear the end of that sentence. I didn't want her to have to say the words.

"Jaxon, I'm—" She caught herself slipping. "I'm so sorry."

I resorted to changing the subject. People turned to humor to cope. Sometimes it seemed like the only way to get by the parts of you past that hurt the most.

"You know you never told me," I prompted casually.

"Told you what?"

"What you remember." I closed my eyes, trying not to think about what oversized T-shirt she was wearing or what boyshorts were underneath. "The question you called about?"

"Oh, that." She chuckled. "It's nothing."

I shoved my disappointment to the side. Maci was giving me her time, and I refused to come off as ungrateful. "How was your Christmas Eve?"

"It was good!" she said, sounding more like herself. "It's a little weird, though. I'm in that room."

That room. The first place where she was mine. I'll never forget how she said my name.

As soon as the words left my mouth, I knew there was a chance I'd regret it. "I had some good times in that room." I couldn't explain how, but I knew she was smiling. "Why did you call, Mace? Is everything okay?"

"Everything is fine," she assured me, her laugh tapering toward the end. "I was just stuck in my head a little bit."

Regardless of how much time passed, I still heard it in her voice. The longing to have company in the room, even if it meant there was silence. They were the phone calls I'd get the nights before she had a big test. She wanted to hear whatever was happening on the other end of the call.

She didn't want to be alone.

"I'm not sure if I'm allowed to say this—" A nervous chuckle escaped me as I hesitated to continue. "If you ever just want someone to talk to, or someone to be on the other end of the line, you can call me."

"You understand how ironic that offer is, right?" she snapped, the playfulness still heavy in her voice. "All of the times I called when—"

"Yes, yes, I know," I blurted. "But now it's . . . I don't know. I just want you to know that, okay?"

"Hmm." She sighed, probably sinking into her pillows and clutching one tightly in her arms. "Well, thank you so much for that offer."

"Of course."

"What are friends for, right?" she teased.

The word lingered around me like smoke.

Friends.

It took me a while to fall asleep. Every time I closed my eyes, I remembered us in that bedroom at Port Clinton.

Was she thinking about me? Did she want me there as much as I *thought* she did?

The next morning, I watched Evie and Peyton open their presents with stars dancing in their bright blue eyes. After Mom served her breakfast buffet style and we exchanged stockings, I double-checked that there was still a seat available on the route I looked up last night.

When I told everyone that I was heading back early, no one commented on the last-minute decision. Bella and Alex shared a playful exchange, and I could have sworn my parents smiled. I didn't linger to study their reactions. I had a plane to catch, and I hoped with everything that I wouldn't regret it.

Chapter Forty-Eight

MACI

December 2021

"Santa came!" Katie yelled from the kitchen, followed by a banging of cookware and a loud cheer from Connor.

I pulled the comforter over my head. You had to appreciate the effort some parents put into Christmas morning. They genuinely looked forward to watching their kids open gifts they wrapped the night before.

My hands skimmed the empty side of the bed. Last night, I pictured it—Jaxon and I talking in person as old friends, not over a late-night phone call. What the fuck was I thinking?

I wish he were here.

Jaxon slowly integrated himself back into the flow of our lives. Shit, when Jaxon was in the room, he was the first person Max wanted to show his toys to. Katie never said anything—probably to spare any foul feelings I might have—but I knew she loved having Jaxon back.

"Maci!" Spencer sang, bursting into the bedroom without even a knock. She looked adorable in her matching red reindeer pajamas. "Good! You're up!"

The open door offered me a peek at the chaos happening in the living room. While Connor and Katie were giving Max instructions on how to sit in front of the tree, Bryson and Elle exchanged a few yawns in the kitchen. It was no secret that Bryson and Elle had a late evening. Everyone would do their best today to try to ignore the giant hickey on Bryson's neck. It was juvenile and tacky, but I found myself loving it.

Spencer chuckled. "I would pay to see Jared's face if he saw that."

"I might actually have a picture of that expression," I offered, sending us both into a fit of laughter.

When Spencer and I emerged from the bedroom, I made a beeline for the coffee. I already saw a nap in my future, but I needed to get through the rush of presents, breakfast, and cleanup.

"Merry Christmas!" I announced, helping myself to the creamer in the fridge.

"Merry Christ—wait, Max, one more, okay?" Katie shoved a red bow into Max's hands. "Can you smile big for me?"

"Oh, for fuck's sake." Bryson groaned, sending Elle and me into a burst of hysterics. We hid our faces in the fridge so Katie wouldn't see. "Would you just give the kid his presents? You're torturing the little guy!"

Katie narrowed her eyes. "Simmer down, Mr. Love Bite."

Bryson dragged his hands down his face, trying to pull the sleepiness from his cheeks. It wasn't working. I slid a cup of coffee in front of him and patted his shoulder.

The morning went more smoothly than I anticipated. Max took his time analyzing each present, carefully peeling away the paper as if it were more fun than the gifts themselves. Spencer and I helped Katie prepare breakfast, setting out plates and trays so we could eat family style at the dining table. We kept Christmas movies on repeat, everyone rotating shifts between napping and spending time with Max. The wind outside was starting to subside, and a light snowfall slowly took its place. It was the Christmas that Spencer wished for and the holiday that the rest of us needed.

Around seven o'clock, everyone was ready to call it a night. Before anyone could retire to their bedrooms, Spencer insisted on topping off the evening with a cup of hot chocolate—Jared's staple since he didn't favor coffee. I went crazy adding marshmallows, whipped cream, a candy cane, and chocolate chips as toppings. I had no regrets; I only hoped that my stomach would understand later.

One by one, people trickled off into their bedrooms until eventually, it was just Katie and me in the kitchen.

"It was a good day," Katie whispered.

I nodded, keeping my voice low. "It was a *great* day."

Katie's eyes glistened with the flames from the fireplace. "Do you think it was great for Spencer, too?"

I held her gaze so she knew I was telling the truth. "I think this was exactly what she needed. I think we all did."

Katie twirled a curl from her ponytail around her finger. "Have you thought about him?"

I knew this question was coming as soon as she touched her hair. She raised a brow, daring me to lie.

I stifled a grin. "Yes."

She pulled a candy cane slowly from her mouth.

"See, if I were Connor, that distraction from your question would work."

Katie hopped off the couch to put her mug in the sink. She spun on her heel, innocently keeping her hands behind her back as she gave a little shrug. "Act like it didn't work just a little bit."

I rolled my eyes. My mug barely made it to the counter before she peeked her head back around the corner.

"In about five minutes, get the door," she blurted, taking three giant steps down the hall and closing her bedroom door.

"What?" I whisper-yelled so I wouldn't wake up the rest of the house.

Katie would never lead me astray, but still I drummed my fingers nervously across the countertop, staring aimlessly into the gas fireplace. Before my mind wandered any further, I turned off the flames.

Only there was one spark in my chest that wouldn't go out. No matter how many times I tried to smother it or pretend it wasn't there, the heat was too hard to ignore, like the coals of a fire that's burned to the core. You couldn't always see it, but the intensity of the heat drew you in.

There was a soft knock at the door, and when I unlocked the deadbolt, a pair of dark green eyes stared back at me.

"I don't know if we were ever friends," Jaxon said, his voice raspy.

My mouth was drier than the winter air outside. No amount of hot chocolate could save me. I might as well have been housing the Sahara Desert.

"The day I met you, you had me," he added. His mouth curved into a cocky grin, threatening to make me collapse in the doorway. "I was yours."

I just hoped that I didn't get burned.

Chapter Forty-Nine

JAXON

IT WAS THE MOMENT that made me question what the fuck I was doing here. Maci could shut the door in my face, tell me to fuck off, and have my sorry ass looking for a hotel. She could laugh or tell me I was an idiot for saying the words I just muttered between us.

Muttered. Who was I kidding?

I said those words with my chest because they were the truth. I'd always been hers. I was just the idiot who thought there was a chance I could move on. As soon as I saw her at Jared's service, I knew it wasn't possible. Maybe I had been right all along in my plan.

I might not have stayed for her, but for a reason entirely different. I stayed for myself, and that somehow felt even more dangerous.

Maci rested a hand on her popped hip, the gesture pulling up on the plaid shorts that covered her ass. She was in a plain gray hoodie and fluffy black crew socks. The last thing she expected to end her Christmas with was me standing on the other side of the front door.

"Katie knew you were coming here, didn't she?" she probed casually.

Of course, she wouldn't bring up anything I just said. Her goal over the past few weeks was to completely ignore anything I admitted to her.

My smile grew. "Of course she did."

Maci rolled her eyes, but I knew she was glad to see me. She'd shifted slightly to the left, a telltale sign that she was preparing to let me pass her. In the past, whenever she was annoyed to see me, she would stand her ground right in the middle.

She started walking down the hall and looked over her shoulder. "We just had some hot chocolate. I can make you some if you'd like?"

I closed the door quietly behind me, looking around the space as if it were my first time. The decor, the furniture, the smell of clean laundry, and lemon—I might as well have been the twenty-two-year-old kid who was pining for the girl down the hallway.

"Jaxon, why are you here?" she prompted softly.

Apparently, I wasn't getting the hot chocolate she offered me. I wouldn't be able to stomach it anyway. I was already riding a high from traveling all day, and the last thing I needed was more sugar.

"You called me," I stated. Maci let me keep coming closer until there were only a few inches between us. "And I wanted to see you."

She narrowed her bright blue eyes. "So you flew all the way from Charlotte on Christmas?"

I traced her jawline with my finger, quickly drawing back my misbehaved hand. Her breath caught in her throat, tempting me to continue with the gentle touch.

"Yeah," I said. "It doesn't make up for all of the times that I should've come to see you, but—"

"Stop." Her hands flew to her head, and she closed her eyes.

I froze, my mind failing on every level to come up with a response. When Maci opened her eyes again, I knew it was safe to continue.

"Is this okay?" I noted the lack of space between us and figured I should specify. "That I'm here?"

She sighed, her smile showing no signs of diminishing. "Yeah, it's fine."

I looked her up and down. "You were heading to bed, weren't you?"

She nodded.

"Feel like staying up for a little while longer?"

Maci pursed her lips, taking a step back and putting the counter between us. She was debating where to put me. If I offered to stay out here on the couch so she could retreat to her bedroom, she might not stay. If she went to lie down and invited me in there—

"Hey," I said, ensuring her focus was in the room with us. I held her gaze, repeating her warning from before, "Don't make it weird."

With a quick nod of her head, she gestured toward her bedroom. I threw my duffle over my shoulder and grabbed a water from the fridge. I didn't want to have a single reason for leaving once she closed that door behind us.

She turned on the bedside lamp and stepped inside the bathroom. I turned around, pretending to search my bag for something. I heard her come back in the room, and when I looked over my shoulder, she returned wearing a baggy shirt, her plaid shorts from before, and glasses.

Glasses, and she looked fucking adorable in them.

"When did you get those?" I teased, stripping off my hoodie. It had to be Katie in charge of the thermostat.

She flipped on the ceiling fan. "Right before I graduated from my Master's program."

"They look cute."

She scrunched her nose and fell onto the right side of the bed.

"What?" I chuckled. "They look sexy as fuck, but I can't say that."

Maci shook her head, her grin digging deeper into her cheeks as she slid under the comforter. She was nervous. *I* made her nervous, and the last time she put me in that position was when we were in this room.

"Can I say that?" I challenged.

"I mean, it's better than cute," she murmured. "Can you sit down, please? You're making me nervous."

At least we were admitting *something* in this conversation.

I lowered myself onto the corner of the mattress, keeping my distance until she gave me more direction. "Did Max enjoy his Christmas?"

That got her shoulders to relax. "Yeah, but I think he had more fun playing with the boxes and bags."

"That's not shocking. Evie did the same thing when she was that age."

"Evie." Her eyes softened. "Evelyn?"

The assumption caught me by surprise, but I loved how my niece's name sounded coming from her. "Bella wanted to name her after my mom. Evie's always fit her better."

She held my gaze, but she was kidding herself if she thought I'd ever look away. "I love that. And Peyton, right? Did it make you think of—"

"*One Tree Hill*," I exclaimed, keeping my voice down. Her hand flew to her mouth to smother her laugh. "Every damn day since they called me from the hospital."

Maci fell back into her pillow and pulled her knees to her chest. "Do you have any pictures of them?"

"Do I have *pictures*?" I pulled my phone from the pocket of my sweatpants. Even with the ceiling fan, these would have to go, too. Fortunately, I had basketball shorts underneath. "I have so many that I just made them an album."

Before I could hand her my phone, she patted the mattress. "Can I see them?"

I shifted so I was sitting next to her, using the spare pillow as a cushion against the headboard. She leaned into me. Our shoulders barely touched, but it was enough to start the pounding in my chest. I pulled up the album of photos and gave her the phone, eager for something to distract me from the erection resting on my thigh.

Nevermind. The sweatpants would be staying on. I wasn't ruining this with my careless cock.

Maci swiped through the photos, smiling and aww'ing at the ones that stuck out to her. I watched, mesmerized by the gentle expression that came over her the moment she laid eyes on those two little girls.

"I can't get over how precious they are." Her mouth fell open as she ogled over a picture of Evie in her Halloween costume. "I'll never forget the day I realized your socials were gone."

I furrowed my brow. "Why is that?"

Maci lowered the phone into her lap, as if she didn't mean to admit that out loud. "It just felt a little more . . . permanent, I guess?" She gestured to the phone. "Missing out on moments like this, even though they were no longer mine to be a part of."

"It was too hard," I admitted. "I was afraid of what I might see or go looking for."

I felt her staring at me as my head fell against the headboard. My focus drifted to the spinning fan blades above us, drawing out the words I struggled to say.

"On nights I drank too much, I pictured you married—married to someone who wasn't me." I chuckled nervously, running a hand through my hair. "It was enough to knock me out. I started spiraling. That's when I deleted my social media accounts. I had to cut everything off. Anyone who could tell me something about you was a threat. You were like smoke. I was trying to catch something that I couldn't have."

The silence that fell between us made me look at her. Maci studied me closely, as if part of her didn't believe anything that I just said. "You did have me."

I shook my head, ashamed that I ever let her go. "Not in the way you deserved."

Chapter Fifty

MACI

December 2021

When I told Jaxon that I loved him for the first time, I knew I was gambling. I tossed my heart on the table, hoping it would be enough to make him go all in. I'll never forget the way he looked at me, with hooded dark green eyes, a sly smile, and a calm exterior that would shock most people who knew him.

He was the fuckboy who never caught feelings, and I was daring him to push his boundaries. For months, I worried that I had admitted it too soon. People didn't go falling in love with someone they weren't even dating.

Did they?

The road to my happily ever after seemed so linear before. Then, I turned over the ignition and started driving, and staying in one lane wasn't as easy as I thought.

My route turned into a winding reality check. There were moments when I wasn't sure if I wanted to refill the gas. Through the uphill battles and the uneven terrain, I kept going. I bet on myself, and right now, I wanted to gamble on whatever tension was still holding me upright.

I remembered everything Jaxon said to me the night of Friendsgiving. When I asked him to pretend, he said he never stopped. At first, they simmered, and then, without warning, they reached a rapid boil. The same feelings from the first night we slept together resurfaced. Only this time, it wasn't me who said the words out loud that they couldn't take back.

Jaxon's eyes traced the outline of my mouth, completely unaware that he was drawing me in with every second they chose to linger.

Kiss me, I willed him. *Please.*

As if he read my mind, his fingers found my jawline, finishing the gentle stroke that he had robbed me of earlier. He leaned in, his nose barely skimming mine as he tilted my chin.

I shuddered against his touch, but that was all he needed. He drew me the rest of the way in, pressing his mouth to mine. His lips were soft and patient, as if he needed to wait and see if I would pull away. I turned into him, gripping his shoulders and teasing the muscles in his upper back. Strong and warm, I melted into his arms as his mouth grew more eager.

My hands found their way under his shirt, admiring the sculpted definition of his chest. Every mark and every feature, I remembered them all. His body might have changed a little over the years, but the foundation remained the same. The way he kissed and how his hands caressed my lower back. It was exactly what I needed and everything that I missed.

A groan vibrated from the back of my throat, my body betraying me as I pushed myself into him. Jaxon shifted us over, testing his ability to remain in control as he tried not to pin me underneath him. It was so easy, crawling over me and taking complete control. He drove me crazy in the most delicious way, calling the shots as I submitted willingly to him.

He rested his forehead against mine, using his arms to keep our chests from touching. His eyes held my gaze, pleading with me to give him some sort of direction on where to go next.

I wanted to. I *could*. But I knew we shouldn't.

"Jaxon, I can't." My body begged me to change my mind as the throbbing picked up between my legs. He was right there. If I lifted my hips, I knew exactly what I'd feel.

"I'm not asking you to." Jaxon crawled slowly on his hands and knees toward the edge of the bed. His eyes flickered to the drawstring on my shorts. "I wanna touch you like I used to." His thumbs teased the waistband. "Can I?"

I let out a shaky breath. "Can you what?"

"Touch you," he prompted softly, his fingers grazing my inner thigh. "Like I used to."

Since I didn't trust myself to speak, I nodded, sending his grin into overdrive as he tugged off my shorts.

"Socks," I reminded him, earning me a chuckle. He pulled them from my feet and tossed them over his shoulder.

"Heaven forbid," he growled, his fingers riding the sensitive skin of my thigh to the heat of my core. Seeing how eager he was turned me on even more. "*Fuck*, Mace."

My name on his lips channeled another groan from the back of my throat. I gripped the pillow on either side of my head and closed my eyes. The curling of his fingers and the teasing strokes of his thumb on my clit threatened to make me combust. It was like everything in my body woke up all at once, willing him to keep going and begging him not to stop.

I bucked my hips, and Jaxon used his free hand to pin me back down on the mattress.

A playful spark ignited in his green eyes. "If it gets to be too much, just say the word, and I'll stop."

"Don't stop," I begged through a breathy laugh.

Keeping his fingers at work, he leaned up to kiss me. His tongue moved slowly against mine, but he became hungry when my sighs turned to moans in his mouth.

"Come for me, pretty girl," he said, moving his hand from my hip. The shift allowed me to chase the pleasure building under my navel, riding his fingers toward my release. With one last arch of my back, I crumbled, shaking underneath him as I groaned his name into the crook of his neck.

Jaxon pressed his mouth to my forehead, trickling soft kisses down the side of my face until he landed on my mouth. I continued to take from his hand, moving slowly as the lightheadedness subsided and the stars disappeared from my vision. When I opened my eyes, he was staring back at me, his cocky grin from before replaced with a sweet smile.

"Are you okay?" he asked, sliding his fingers from my slick entrance. I couldn't bear to look at the sheets. I knew exactly what I'd find. Jaxon, however, couldn't have been happier to see the evidence of my arousal.

"Yeah," I breathed. "I'm okay." But I wasn't done. I didn't *want* to be done. "I want to see you."

My statement came across as more of a demand. Without warning, Jaxon pulled off his shirt, revealing a smooth chest and arms that I craved to be wrapped in. My mouth parted slightly, and I wanted to run my tongue up the side of his throat. Before I could formulate another direction, he stepped out of his sweatpants.

It was hot. Was it hot?

No shit. You're still in a hoodie.

I was trapped. I couldn't possibly take my sweatshirt off now. It would be an open invitation to the R-rated version of this film.

"You can watch me," he offered, lowering his voice as he crawled to the edge of the bed again, "and while I do the tasting, I'll make sure you can see."

"Jax—" But it was too late. His tongue flicked across my clit, picking me up right where he left me.

I sat up on my elbows, and he stared back at me through dark lashes. He held me there, holding me, and I had no idea how much time had passed. With every suck and stroke, I ached to throw my head back and give in to another release. But I couldn't. The thought of breaking this connection felt worse than never crossing the finish line.

His hand disappeared between his legs, and I knew he was touching himself. He closed his eyes for only a second, but it was enough to tell me that he was close. Fuck, I wanted him. I pictured him inside me instead of his fingers. His tongue picked up the pace, feeding off the moans that floated from the deepest parts of my chest.

"Jaxon." I groaned, running my hand through his hair and gripping his curls between my fingers. I pulled a pillow over my face, unable to keep it together as the sound of his release followed quickly after mine. His breath was warm against my clit, threatening to start me up again if he didn't lift his head.

I heard him cross the room, but I kept my head under the pillow. I needed a moment alone with the pathetic grin that was digging into my cheeks.

"Mace?"

I fixed my face so I could look at him without a barrier between us.

Jaxon smiled, stroking himself with the towel and standing completely on display. "You good?"

At this point, I had no shame. I stared longingly at the body I had tried to reimagine in my head so many times. He was gorgeous, and like the cocky asshole he still was, he knew it.

I held out my hand for the towel, and he stepped forward to close the space between us. He placed it in my hands, his eyes following the fabric as I reached in between my legs to wipe away any evidence of my release.

Jaxon ran a hand through his hair and sighed. "Can I sleep in here?"

I tried not to smirk at his question, but I couldn't help it. He was nervous.

"I can go on the couch," he offered. "It's not a problem. Just let me—"

I shoved a finger into his bare chest. "You have to sleep in shorts." I grabbed my own and pulled them on for emphasis. "Clothes. Now."

Jaxon rolled his eyes, quickly shifting back into the confident man who was between my legs a moment ago. He stepped into his shorts, and when he turned to throw the towel into the hamper, I stripped off my sweatshirt. I figured I was in the safe zone now.

His fingers had already been inside me. His tongue had gone to work. What more could happen?

Bitch, don't ask stupid questions.

I reached for the bedside lamp and clicked it off as Jaxon slid into the bed. The tension between us slowly fizzled into something I realized I hadn't felt in a long time. An effortless contentment—the kind of peace that came from silent exchanges that didn't require words to fill the lingering void.

"Good night, Mace," Jaxon murmured through the dark. He planted a kiss on my forehead and rested his hand on my hip so he could get a little closer. He didn't pull away, and I didn't want him to.

I relaxed into the mattress, submitting to the sweet wave of exhaustion that carried me to the other side.

Chapter Fifty-One

MACI

December 2021

By some miracle, I woke up before Jaxon. With the heat that was radiating from him underneath the blanket, there was no question that he was still here.

In my room. After he flew in last night because of . . . a *phone call?*

When I called Jaxon, I despised the part of me that wished he were here. It was hard to ignore the craving even though I knew he could be bad for me. It was like my unhealthy habit with ice cream after dinner. No matter how many times I tried to set a boundary, my impulsive decision-making won.

I stared at the aftermath of that decision, breathtakingly good-looking and innocent as he drew in deep breaths. His bare chest looked smooth to the touch under the light that snuck in between the blinds. Hell, I knew it was smooth. Soft, even. My hands were all over it last night and in my sleep.

We'd cloaked the room in his cologne and my post-orgasm bliss. If I didn't get some space now, I feared I might over-think everything that happened. The image of him between my legs would stick with me long after this very Merry Christmas.

When I stepped into the hall, I heard someone in the kitchen. It took one crack of my ankle to alert them that I was emerging from the bedroom, and Katie's head peered around the corner. She stood on her toes, trying to sneak a peek at what was behind the door. The giant grin she met me with when I plopped into a barstool told me that she had been successful in her snooping.

"Oh my god," Katie murmured gleefully as she stirred the pancake mixture. She favored pancakes when feeding a crowd.

I raised a brow. "Oh my god."

"Oh my *god*," she swooned, sliding the bowl to the side so she could lean her elbows on the counter.

"Can we not?" The way my voice decided to jump up two octaves made it difficult not to smile.

Katie widened her eyes. "Oh, but we are."

"Do you *like* having your coffee unbothered? Because I'll go wake up your kid," I threatened, forcing her to step off the path of endless goggling. Last night seemed like foreplay for whatever else was about to happen. I wasn't ready to be drilled about it just yet.

How diabolical. I'd already labeled this as something to hold space for in the future.

"Ugh, fuck me." I groaned, resting my face in my hands. "Fuck me, fuck me."

"Oh, but honey, he *did*." Katie struggled to keep her tone casual.

My hands flew from my face to the counter. "No, he didn't."

"No?"

Last time I checked, a finger didn't count as a body. It wasn't a total lie.

Great. Now I was back to channeling my inner Bryson.

"No cock fucking." I held up my hands to emphasize my answer. "Swear."

Katie rolled her eyes. "Nice cover."

"Nice planning on your part," I snapped back, stealing a chocolate chip from the bag. She added a few shakes to the bowl before she started ladling batter onto the skillet.

Since my head was throbbing, I wandered over to the coffee maker. If I didn't get caffeine soon, no amount of ibuprofen could save me. I was used to nursing a hangover after I made most of my questionable decisions. It was incredibly different processing them with a clear head.

A door opened in the hall, and I waited to see who would make an appearance first. Jaxon turned the corner, shooting Katie a broad grin before he pulled her into a side hug.

"Mornin'," he mumbled, giving her one last squeeze before he let her go. It was kind of him to hug his partner in crime first. Making his way around the counter, he came up behind me, wrapping his arms around my shoulders and dipping his mouth to my ear. "Mornin', Mace."

His breath on my neck sent shivers down my spine. I was thankful for the hot coffee instead of my usual iced latte. His lips brushed my temple, and Katie pretended not to see. I knew her inner hopeless romantic was on the verge of combustion.

The sound of someone sucking their teeth echoed in the living room. "No way," I heard Bryson say before he slid into the seat beside me.

He rested his head in his hand, looking between Jaxon and me. I wanted to dunk his smug smirk into Katie's bowl of unused pancake batter. If I weren't starving, I might have.

I hadn't noticed Jaxon's arms still around me until Bryson smacked his bicep. Jaxon pulled away, making me wish I had thrown on my hoodie before I left the room. One of my favorite things about Jaxon's morning hugs was the heat.

He'd always greet me with a warm-up, staying there until he thought I was okay.

Bryson muttered something about Christmas and how Jaxon was here instead of Charlotte. I was halfway paying attention because of Max's giant grin coming down the hallway.

Max scrambled to get out of Connor's arms. As soon as his little onesie-covered feet landed on the floor, he took off toward Jaxon's leg. Spencer and Elle came up from downstairs just in time to see Max reach his target. Jaxon pulled Max into his arms, partaking in an adorable conversation with the toddler.

While Jaxon received greetings from the remainder of the group, Max's innocent little eyes locked with mine. He gave me a toothy grin and a tiny wave to mock me.

Traitor, I joked, using my free hand to squeeze his toes.

Chapter Fifty-Two

JAXON

December 2021

Somehow, I convinced Maci to let me ride back to Chicago with her. Being trapped in a car with someone for five hours was a lot, and I took it as a step in the right direction—a positive mark on the scoreboard I had going in my head.

Last night was, *fuck*, better than I could have ever imagined. The way her pussy squeezed my fingers and how her hips begged me to go faster.

I reached forward and hit next on her playlist, desperate to distract myself for the thirtieth time this ride so I wouldn't get a hard-on in her passenger seat.

"That's like the fifth good song you've skipped in a row," Maci snapped. She hit the back arrow, and "STAY" by The Kid LAROI started playing. "Is this your way of telling me you want your music?"

"No." I chuckled and offered her my phone anyway. "But you mix it up if you want."

She scrunched up her nose. "I'm not gonna find anything disgusting on here, am I?"

"Nah." The idea of it was comical. I forced myself to delete pictures of her a long time ago. No one else even came close to being saved.

"Pull up your music," she instructed, tilting the screen toward me. She kept her eyes on the road as I did a few taps.

"The *Frozen* soundtrack is for Evie and Peyton," I noted, imagining her eyes hyper-focused on the Disney playlist. Maci kept scrolling, and I had no idea what she was looking for.

Finally, she said, "You kept it." She sounded conflicted, yet sentimental. "My playlist . . . why did you keep it?"

There was one thing on my phone I couldn't part with, and she was staring at the evidence. The Mace Playlist. Every song that made me think of her—think of *us*. So many memories strung together with music that gave me the words when I couldn't find them. I couldn't get rid of it, because part of me never wanted to forget.

"I couldn't delete it," I said. "Too many bangers."

Maci let out a soft chuckle. "Makes sense."

I ran a hand through my hair, letting it fall lazily in my lap. "I just couldn't do it. I made it for you. It reminded me too much of—"

"Us," she added quietly, stealing a glance at me. "I get it."

"Mace—"

"This one." Maci placed my phone in the cup holder and turned up the volume. "Promiscuous" by Nelly Furtado exploded from the speakers. She moved her body to the beat, as if she had practiced this routine from the driver's seat hundreds of times. She probably had. It was one of the many things I loved about her when we were together.

It was also one of the things I loved about her now.

"Can we stop by my place before I drop you off?" she asked.

That was unexpected. "Sure."

I had about seven songs until we pulled into Maci's driveway, plenty of time for me to muster up the confidence to *not* fuck this up.

When we walked into Maci's place, I let her get a few steps in front of me. I gave Bryson one task before he left for Port Clinton, and her high-pitched, "Oh my god!" told me that he succeeded.

I stood in the doorway of her kitchen, smitten with the way she was doing a five-point examination on the packaging. On the counter was a brand new set of emerald pots and pans. She plucked the giant red bow from the top of the box, searching it for evidence of the sender.

"They're from my mom," I offered.

She furrowed her brow. "How?"

"I had Bryson drop them off on the way to Port Clinton."

"He just walked in the house—"

"Because you don't check the fucking camera I installed for you," I snapped playfully.

She stifled a laugh, running her hands over the box and gripping the corners.

"I promised that by Christmas, you'd have *everything*," I said. "My mom tried not to judge you too harshly when I told her about the grilled cheese."

Maci rolled her eyes before they softened into a deep appreciation for what was in front of her. I knew she loved that they came from my mom.

I started to sweat under my hoodie, practically blurting my next question across the counter, "What are you doing two Saturdays from now?"

An adorable grin curved into her cheek as she waited for me to provide context.

"There's this—" Nah, that wasn't a good delivery. I was already fucking this up. "In two weeks I have—"

"For fuck's sake. Spit it out, Jaxon."

I smirked, letting her have her moment since my name was still fresh on her lips. "There's this gala I have to attend for Hayes Sports and Entertainment. It will be flashy with good food and warmer weather." I gestured to the snow falling outside her windows. "Would you wanna get away for a weekend?"

"A weekend?" Her eyebrows shot to the top of her forehead. "In LA?"

"It doesn't have to be a thing," I added quickly. "I'm asking as your friend."

She popped her hip. "I thought you said we were never friends."

"Last night I also said I was yours." I mimicked her stance, my face only inches from hers. "Friends is what you choose to focus on?"

"I'm choosing to overlook a few things."

"Why?" I challenged, pushing a little closer.

She didn't fight me on the lack of space. In fact, what she did next made me weak in the knees. She kissed me, gently at first, before she dragged her teeth down my bottom lip and sucked.

When she pulled away, she left me with an agonizing pull in my groin. My cock was going into panic mode. That was two days in a row I'd had my mouth on this girl, and he wasn't joining the party.

She knew exactly what she was doing to me. "I'll think about it. Now, let's get you back to Bryson's."

Chapter Fifty-Three

MACI

January 2022

No matter how many times I had been left alone with Max, it always seemed like my first time with a toddler. He was unhinged, tempting fate with every sharp corner and bad idea his little human mind could come up with. As soon as Katie left for her first culinary class, my confident smile dwindled, and I was elated when Spencer knocked at my front door, happy to help with the babysitting duties.

"They sense fear, you know," Spencer insisted, pulling Max into her lap before he could run off again.

"It's just so diabolical." I narrowed my gaze when Max looked in my direction. "Like, he senses my stress and just doesn't give an eff."

Spencer laughed. "That's usually how it goes."

Spencer always looked so confident in what she was doing. I envied that about her.

I waited until we had hot cups of tea in front of us to ask my next question. "How are you doing with everything? Do you need any help with packing?"

"Honestly." She drummed her nails against the side of her mug. "It's like a breath of fresh air, knowing I get to . . . try again? Pick up the pieces somewhere else? I'm not really sure what to call it. That probably doesn't even make sense."

"It does," I assured her. "Where is *somewhere else*?"

Her hesitation made me nervous, and I tried to drown my stress with another sip of tea. I'd been putting off the idea of Spencer leaving Chicago since the house sold. I'd also been too afraid to ask to confirm it.

Her smile tapered at the idea of disappointing me, and she said, "I think I wanna go back to New York."

I softened my gaze and smiled. "New York?"

She nodded.

"That sounds—"

Incredible? Amazing? Right up your alley to pursue writing opportunities? Any answer was better than the dreaded silence I was offering.

"It's a big change," she noted.

"But it will be *great*," I said, unsure of who I was trying to convince. "Imagine the writing inspiration—the stories you can come up with being surrounded by the city!"

"I just don't want to let a chance pass me by. I need this—the uncomfortable push to stand on my own and try something different. I can't do that here."

"Are you going to keep Jared's workshop?"

Spencer pursed her lips, as if she was still deciding whether or not her decision was a good one. "I made Bryson a co-owner of the business. Whatever happens to Jared's workshop is up to him. He's earned it, and I know he'll do a good job."

Both of us chuckled at the idea of Bryson handling anything on his own. It wasn't because we doubted him; it was actually the opposite. It was unbelievable how much he'd changed since college.

"I think it's exactly what he needs," I said. "It's a chance for him, too."

"Speaking of chances—"

"Wait, when do you have to be out by?" I blurted through a laugh. She wasn't transitioning that easily away from her and her big news. "Have you even looked at apartments?"

"I have! I contacted our old landlord, and he sent me some properties. I have to be out by January twenty-fifth. They close on the twenty-sixth."

My stomach dropped. A few weeks. Less than a month. If Max hadn't interrupted my spiral with an empty sippy cup, I might have gotten lost in the whirlwind.

"Juice!" he chirped.

I obeyed his tiny demand, giving him half apple juice and half water in his Spiderman tumbler. Once he had his drink, he took off back to his racecars.

"Have you told anyone else?" I asked.

She gave a quick nod. "Just you. Well, and Jaxon. His parents were asking about an address."

Ah, yes. Reed and Evelyn Hayes wouldn't stop with their food deliveries that easily.

Spencer gestured to me with a dramatic eyeroll. "*Speaking* of chances, how are you and him?"

"Who?" I teased.

She smacked my forearm. "You know who."

It was my turn to give an eyeroll.

"Girl, he came to *Christmas*. You really don't expect any follow-up questions after that?"

"I don't know what is going on," I stated matter-of-factly. "Scout's honor. But he did invite me to LA next weekend."

Spencer almost dropped her mug on the coffee table. "Are you going to go?"

"It depends on which Maci you're asking. The twenty-four-year-old in me is already packing."

She leaned forward, like she was watching a riveting episode of a TV show unraveling in real time. "What does this Maci say?"

I blew out an exaggerated breath. "Don't be an idiot."

"Can I say something really unfair?"

I shrugged in defeat.

"I was humbled really fucking quickly when Jared passed. I thought I had all the time, all the things figured out—you name it, I thought I had it. Jaxon isn't perfect. He's made mistakes. He's done shitty things. He broke your heart."

Unless Spencer wanted me to wither away on the couch with all the reminders, she'd need to shift her focus soon.

She must've felt my tension, because the side of her mouth lifted into a small smile. "If there is even the *slightest* chance that this *could be* another chance for you . . . take it. Don't ask questions and don't get in your own way."

"You think I should go," I muttered softly.

"I see the way he looks at you, and you try to hold back when he's around. You try, but you can't. You want to give in to him, but there's part of you that is waiting for someone to tell you it's okay, like it won't be your fault if it doesn't work out."

I willed myself to argue back, but I couldn't.

Spencer wrapped her hand around my wrist. "It's okay to try again," she reassured me. Her voice was so soft and comforting that I felt the pressure building behind my eyes.

"Okay," I said, my voice raspy.

Before I could prepare for the intrusion, Spencer shoved my phone into my chest. "Tell him before you can change your mind."

Fuck, she knew me well. I tapped on Jaxon's contact and started a video chat. My pulse quickened with every ring, as if my body had this moment confused with a life-or-death situation. When he picked up, it was clear he was at the gym. He wore a dark blue sleeveless compression shirt, and I remembered my nails digging into the back of his shoulders.

He smiled when he saw me, wiping the sweat from his forehead with the back of his hand. "Hey, Mace."

I swallowed to clear my throat. "I have to be back by Monday."

Jaxon licked the center of his bottom lip, and his smile grew. He knew exactly what I was referring to when he said, "Okay."

Spencer giggled across from me like a middle school gal pal.

"I have class on Tuesday morning, and I watch Max for Katie in the evenings," I added sternly.

He gave me a quick nod. "You'll be back Monday morning. I promise."

There was something in the way he responded, as if everything weighed heavily on his ability to fulfill my requests. We'd had a similar conversation before, only he was inviting me to Charlotte to meet his family, and I had a statistics class I had to pass to graduate. He'd planned for that trip, and part of me was too curious not to ask about this one.

"You bought my ticket already, didn't you?" I challenged playfully.

He lolled his head to the side, sending me into a nervous chuckle.

Or was I flattered? A flattered chuckle?

His boyish grin told me all I needed to know.

Chapter Fifty-Four

JAXON

WHEN I INSTRUCTED ALEX to pick Maci and me up from the airport in my Jeep, I thought I was doing myself a favor. The goal was simple—make sure Maci didn't regret coming with me to California. She knew my Jeep. She knew the ride. I didn't want Alex's rental of some glamorous sports car tipping us out of balance.

Our flight went by quickly, thanks to Maci's quick thinking of downloading a few movies for us to watch together on the flight. We shared her headphones and watched some classics from the vault that she insisted were necessary. After we finished *She's the Man, Easy A* was next. It honestly didn't matter what was playing on the screen in front of me. She included me in her plans to pass the time, and that was more than enough.

Sunshine and an unforgiving breeze greeted us when we stepped outside. It was much warmer here than it was in Chicago, but the wind still had Maci shoving her hands into the pocket of her sweatshirt. I was about to offer her mine for an extra layer of support, but when I caught a glimpse of dark gray rounding the corner, I knew it was Alex with our ride.

Alex practically hung out the window as he swung into the pickup lane. A loud stream of honking announced his arrival as he slowed to a stop in front of us.

His mouth fell open as he slowly removed his sunglasses. "Holy shit."

Don't make it a big deal. Don't make it a big deal.

As if repeating the plea in my brain would stop my older brother from pointing out the obvious.

"Maci?" Alex prompted, unable to wipe the shit-eating grin from his face. Fortunately for me, when I looked over at Maci, she was mimicking his excited expression. They embraced in a quick hug, as if years hadn't passed since they last saw each other.

I stood there, trying not to make it awkward, as if I hadn't been the reason why.

Alex shifted his attention to me and pulled me in for a side hug. "Good to see you, man." He patted me hard on the back, informing me that while he was stunned that I hid my guest from him, he was happy that it was her.

"Thanks for the ride," I said, loading my luggage into the trunk.

Maci lingered next to me, hesitant to get into the back seat.

"Hey," I murmured, waiting until her blue eyes met mine to continue. "You okay?"

"Yeah!" she exclaimed, a little too brightly for someone who had just traveled all morning.

I saw right through her exaggerated smile, but I didn't push. She wouldn't confide in me with Alex standing so close. I guided her to the passenger side of the car and opened her door, making sure she slid inside before I climbed in after her.

When she realized what was happening, she asked, "You're not sitting in front?"

I shrugged. "Nah."

As if he knew what was good for him, Alex didn't comment on the seating arrangements. Instead, he asked if we had enough air coming through the vents and turned on the same station he had been listening to before.

While Alex and I got caught up in conversation about our parents and the company, Maci looked out the window. Her shoulders were tense, and since I had no idea what was going on in that gorgeous head of hers, I slid a little closer so I could grab her hand. She didn't pull away, and when I stroked the top of her wrist with my thumb, she relaxed into the seat.

My fingers were on fire, tingling with the sensation of touching her again. It wasn't lost on me that I was starting from square one with Maci in the trust department, but I loved that I could still calm her. It was so easy back then, reassuring her that she was safe with me.

Loved. Taken care of. *Mine.*

"I'll have to tell Bella that you're here, Maci." Alex caught her attention in the rearview mirror. "Maybe you guys could get lunch or something?"

Listening to Alex beat around the bush was enough to make me chuckle. Maci looked from me to him, as if she were missing out on some inside joke between us.

"I'm not sure how long you're in town for—"

I interjected before Alex could dig a bigger hole. "She's coming to the gala tomorrow."

Alex did his best to sound surprised. "Oh!"

Maci leaned forward and rested her free hand on Alex's shoulder. I noted how she didn't let go of mine. "Tell Bella I'm excited to see her," she offered sweetly.

We'd pulled up to my parking lot, and I had to remind myself that Maci had been here before. It was the same place I lived in while we were together. The home that she visited all of those times when she was at school in New York.

Alex tossed me my keys and pulled his own from his pocket. "You guys need a ride tomorrow?"

"I got it covered," I answered, slamming the trunk closed. "We'll see you tomorrow."

Alex furrowed his brow, quickly smoothing out his forehead before Maci looked up from her phone. He could read a room, or in this case, a parking lot, and he wouldn't overstay his welcome.

Maci was here—*actually* fucking here in my parking lot. She was going to spend the night at my place.

Once I entered my apartment, I knew my mom had been here. It smelled incredibly clean for a place that hadn't seen life for a few weeks.

Maci lingered near the front door, unsure if she should go any further. There was something she wasn't saying, and since she wasn't going to unravel willingly, I knew I'd have to do a little poking.

"Mace," I prompted softly. "What's going on?"

There was a slight gloss to her eyes. "Seeing your family again didn't cross my mind," she said through a breathy laugh.

"You don't have to see them. Shit, we don't have to go at all tomorrow. We can just stay here and—"

"I just—" She closed her eyes, and her mouth curved into a crooked smile. "I just didn't prepare myself, that's all."

"You won't see anyone else until tomorrow night," I assured her. "Alex might bother me later about getting together because he's . . . well . . . Alex, but—"

Her tongue grazed her bottom lip.

What *was* I saying?

Any mischievous intentions she had got lost in the innocence of her blue eyes. They looked around the room, wandering down the hall until they landed on the door of my bedroom. "So it's just us here?"

My heart raced in my chest, and I ran a hand through my hair. "I can see if Bryson can swing a late flight if you want," I joked, hoping that the drop of his name would send my hard-on running in the opposite direction.

Maci burst out laughing. "No, that is totally okay."

For some reason I couldn't explain, it relaxed me to hear her say that. Maybe it boosted my ego a little bit to hear that in this exact moment, she preferred me over Bryson. It sounded dumb, given everything I knew about their past and their friendship. It reassured me of one terrifying fact.

I was scared. What if I fucked this up again?

What if I were still so deeply in love with this girl and she had no intentions of taking a step forward?

What if a hookup here and there was it?

I cleared my throat. "My mom set up the guest room so you can have your own space. I wasn't playing around when I said I was asking you to come as a friend."

The minor quirk of her lip eliminated the remaining tension from her shoulders. "Do you have any ramen?"

Half an hour later, I removed two steaming cups of ramen noodles from the microwave. I offered Maci a fork, and she propped herself up on my counter. She twirled her fork in her cup, eyeing me playfully as I came up beside her.

Since she was fucking with me about our countertop kiss, I asked, "Feel sturdy?"

"Mine are sturdier," she teased. "Nice to see you still eat the delicacies."

My eyes trailed down to the apex of her thighs, working their way back up again.

Her mouth parted slightly, waiting to see what I would do next. As much as it tormented me inside, I decided not to push my luck. I wanted her to know that I was serious about hosting her as a friend first. I didn't bring her here to persuade her. Her limits came first.

I mimicked her shrug. "I've got a thing for delicacies, baby. Always have."

Chapter Fifty-Five

MACI

January 2022

I had a dream about noodles.

Fucking noodles.

I had no idea something could even dream about pasta until I was wrapped up in it, twirling around until Jaxon reached his hand into the cup and pulled me out. Freeze-dried vegetables danced around us, bouncing back and forth from the giant fork overhead to the styrofoam cup.

And the worst part about this dream? It made me *horny*—horny enough where I had to tiptoe over to my bedroom door and double-check the lock so I could knock out a solo session. Every time I slid my fingers inside myself, I pictured Jaxon. The way his cock knew exactly how to hit my most sensitive spot and his mouth would work up the side of my neck as I tangled my fingers into his hair.

I lied. The worst part about this dream wasn't that it made me horny. The worst part was that I had the very real, very *attractive* Jaxon Hayes across the hall, and I was depriving myself of him. Suddenly, my reality seemed sadder than the ramen noodles.

The first time I got off, I came so hard I had to bite down on my pillow. The second time, I fell into a lightheaded bliss, sinking deeper into the mattress only to be rattled awake by the smell of bacon and syrup that floated in underneath the door.

After a pit stop in the bathroom to make it look like I wasn't some sex-crazed ramen freak, I made my way to the kitchen, where a shirtless Jaxon in gray sweatpants was plating two servings of bacon and pancakes.

Fucking gray sweatpants and a smooth six-pack. Jaxon planned on playing dirty this weekend. I'd have to step up my game if I were going to survive.

"Good morning." A boyish grin curved into his dimple. "Hungry?"

Very, I thought, my eyes shamelessly trailing his chest. "It smells good."

"That's the one thing I got going for me is breakfast." He slid my plate to the edge of the counter. "Want something to drink?"

I took a seat at the barstool and bit into a piece of bacon. It was heavenly. "Coffee? With cream if you—"

Jaxon placed two bottles of creamer on the counter, one hazelnut and one vanilla.

"Have it," I finished lamely.

Jaxon took a bite of his pancakes, slipping his fork slowly from his mouth and licking his lips to catch some syrup. I took another bite of bacon to keep myself from drooling.

"I have to go into the office for a few hours this afternoon to prep a few things for tonight. Nothing crazy, but it will be a few meetings that even I don't want to sit through." He reached behind him, grabbed my coffee, and placed it next to my plate. "Will you be okay here by yourself for a little while?"

"Are you kidding?" I exclaimed, sneaking in a sip. I was so desperate for caffeine, I decided the creamer could wait. "I have no work to do and—is that sushi place still down the street?"

Jaxon stifled a grin. "Yeah."

I swatted the air in front of me. "Oh, yeah. I'll be fine. What time do I need to be ready?"

"Five thirty?" Jaxon weighed his answer in his head. "Let's say five. It takes about half an hour to get to the venue, and I'm anticipating traffic."

"Five," I stated, pouring a little bit of creamer into my coffee. I willed my clit to stop throbbing while the colors swirled together. "I can do that."

⁂

Jaxon texted me the entire time he was in the office. He sent me a video of him pouting adorably at his desk during my rewatch of *Pirates of the Caribbean*. When my sushi arrived, he sent me a selfie of him and Helen, the woman I spoke to just as often as him when we were dating during my master's program. Still, it made me laugh, and it made me embarrassingly giddy inside to know that he was thinking of me while he was at the office.

Don't get it twisted. He's bored.

"Okay, bitch," I murmured, sticking a piece of spicy tuna roll in my mouth. I was in his apartment—*Jaxon's* apartment, eating takeout sushi on his dollar and renting movies. He wanted me here. He asked me to come.

He told me he didn't have a choice but to love me.

Love. As in the present. As in not past. As in currently.

I wasn't sure how much longer I could pretend like I hadn't heard it. How much longer could I dance around the fact that what was happening right now was real?

This rabbit hole was way too deep to crawl in with sushi and Johnny Depp. As if he sensed my internal panic, Jaxon's name appeared on my phone screen.

"Hey!" he said, some muffling in the speaker taking up the space between us. "Can you hear me?"

"Yup," I said, sliding another piece of sushi into my mouth.

"I forgot I have to get my tux from the dry cleaners, so I'm going to be a little late. I'm so sorry, baby—fuck . . . I didn't mean that. I take that back. I'm—"

I chuckled. "Jaxon, please shut up. I'll be ready when you get here. Five, right?"

"Yeah." He sighed, his voice growing husky. "Five. I'll see you in a few hours, Mace."

Baby. Fucking baby. It was embarrassing how quickly a word could burrow its way deep into my core.

When the credits rolled for *Pirates of the Caribbean: Dead Man's Chest*, I decided I needed to unattach myself from the couch before the third film began. I had pretty much perfected my routine of getting ready, but something about this seemed different. There was added pressure not only to look good for Jaxon, but also to see his family—people I had considered an extension of my own since the first time I met them.

Like any girl with an undecided motive for the evening, I brought two options. While my dark green dress had a flattering scoop neck and made my boobs look amazing, my burgundy dress had a slit going up the right leg and hugged my curves in all the right places, providing a high neckline to balance out the coverage.

I slipped into my first choice, and my reflection in the full-length mirror made it clear that there was no question.

We'd be going with the red tonight, and I'd pair it with a low black heel to make sure I didn't fall on my face.

I'd just secured my last curl when I felt him enter the apartment. There was no knock or no warning text. I knew from the goosebumps on my arms and the flutter in my stomach. I only had a few moments to apply my mascara before he joined me in the bathroom.

He appeared in the corner of the mirror, leaning against the doorframe in a dress shirt that hugged his shoulders. I was confident with my dress choice, but the following words out of his mouth made the simmering pot in my chest start to boil.

"Fuck me," he murmured, turning his back to me. He ran a hand through his hair, tousling his loose curls before he faced me again. "You're playing dirty."

He meant it as a joke, and part of me took it that way. But when a girl was feeling herself, it was hard not to let the wild thoughts run rampant.

"Funny," I stated, dropping my lipstick in my clutch. "I said the same thing about you."

Chapter Fifty-Six

JAXON

January 2022

When the limo arrived right at five, I led Maci downstairs by the hand and helped load her dress into the backseat.

That fucking dress. Red and tight and teasing me with a slit that rested right at her mid-thigh. I might combust before we even arrived at the venue.

What happened to Jaxon Hayes, the CEO of Hayes Sports and Entertainment? He never made it to the gala. He couldn't get past his ex-girlfriend and love of his life with the bright blue eyes. My parents wouldn't be surprised, and Alex and Bella would laugh. Bella's wide eyes and cheerful smile when Maci stepped out of the limo confirmed that fact.

It was painful, having her this close to me within arm's reach and unable to claim her. I couldn't touch her without putting some intentional thought behind it. It was no longer my place to pull her close to me and remind her how much I wanted her in a room full of people. I didn't know how to exist like this—finding the balance between having her as a friend and stepping back into what we used to have.

What we used to be.

The sheer blue fabric of Bella's dress draped over her arms. "Can I please hug you?"

Since she wasn't talking to me, Maci stepped toward her. "Of course you can."

While they exchanged a hug that was beyond the male understanding, Alex pulled me aside.

"Mom's not feeling well," he explained softly so Bella and Maci wouldn't hear. "I guess she got really sick on the plane."

My shoulders tensed. "What? Where is she now?"

"She's inside already. I wanted to let you know in case you noticed anything. You know her. She's going to try and hide it as best as she can."

I sighed, trying to slow my heart rate.

"Hey, you." Bella pulled me in for a hug, whispering, "I don't know how you did it, but *do not* fuck this up."

I chuckled. "Good to see you too, sis."

Bella rolled her eyes, looping her arm into Alex's as they made their way to the main hall.

I steadied myself, willing the pounding behind my ears to subside before I entered a room full of people I was supposed to impress. Wear a smile, roll your shoulders back, and steady your handshake. They were easy steps to miss when your mind was on other things, like your mom's health and flashbacks of a doctor's office.

I felt Maci's fingers lace with mine. "Jax?" She pulled me closer and rested her hands on my shoulders. "Hey, are you okay?"

"Yeah." I cupped her chin to try to prove my point. "I'm okay."

Even though she wasn't convinced, she let me lead her inside, where reporters and eager guests soon surrounded us. The greeting wasn't anything new to me, but as I watched people surround Maci, I stepped in to put myself between her and the crowd.

"I'll take questions after I see my parents," I announced, grabbing Maci by the hand and leaving the masses at the doorway.

"That seems a little . . . intense," Maci muttered once we were alone. "Is it like that all the time?"

"Only when my family is all in one place," I said, keeping my voice steady. The last thing I wanted was to sound ungrateful. "Which lately hasn't been often. I've been gone for a while. People—especially people with money—like to notice changes and shifts within the company."

Maci tightened her grip on my hand. "It's kind of amazing, you know."

I slowed our pace to buy myself a few extra minutes of uninterrupted time with her. "What?"

"Watching it all unfold in real time." She gestured to the ballroom on our left. Lights danced on the walls behind her, and a soft, romantic instrumental coaxed people to their seats. "You really did it. Everything you had planned."

"Not everything," I admitted. My eyes trailed down the fabric of her dress, admiring how it cinched at her hips and teased a peek with the slit up her leg. I reached out and brushed her curls over her shoulders, letting my fingers linger along her soft skin.

An adorable flush of pink flooded her cheeks as she softened her gaze. A comfortable silence passed between us, and for a moment, it was just me and her.

"There you are! I was just about to call you—"

I looked over my shoulder, and my mom stood in the entrance of the ballroom. Her hair was pulled up into a bun, and the cream color of her dress popped against her brown skin. She looked absolutely stunning.

Mom drew in a shaky breath, placing her hand on her heart as she stepped forward.

Maci pressed her lips together in a tight smile, wrapping herself in Evelyn's embrace. A warmth filled my chest at the sight of them together in the same room. When they pulled apart, they kept each other at arm's length to get a full view of the other's dress.

"Absolutely beautiful," Mom said, wiping a loose tear from her cheek.

Maci snuck a glance at the ceiling to avoid any tears of her own. "Thank you. It's . . . It's really good to see you."

Mom shot me a glance, warning me that I better not have any other surprises up my sleeve. I prepared myself for the stream of threats that she was about to whisper in my ear.

Only they never came. There were no words except for, "You did good, J."

Mom rested a hand on my cheek, stealing one more look at Maci before she returned to the ballroom.

"She looks incredible," Maci noted, slipping her fingers through mine.

The lump in my throat started to form. "Yeah, she does." I kissed her quickly on the top of her head and pulled her forward. "Let's find our seats."

The beginning of the gala went exactly as it had in the previous years. Investors were announced and brought on stage, emphasizing the crucial role their support played in making all of this possible. Three of our top clients were introduced to the crowd, generating more interest from potential partners and reassuring them that we were expected to grow even larger next year. Sponsors of the gala insisted that everyone grab more food and take advantage of the open bar, earning them a few laughs from the crowd. It was the same routine, only this year, I had one hand wrapped around my drink glass while the other teased the slit on Maci Lawson's dress.

A tornado could rip through this room, and I wouldn't notice the chaos. While I knew it was important, it took a back seat to who I had next to me. Maci had agreed to come, and that mattered more to me than any speech I gave or the number of handshakes I received because of who I was and what my father built.

My dad greeted Maci with the same amount of excitement as Bella and my mom. There were no tears or endless hugging, but he couldn't hide the enormous grin on his face when he squeezed her tiny shoulders. He told her how nice it was to see her and how excited he was that she was here. My dad had always been good at saying a lot with a few choice words. He had a way with people. He made them feel valued and cared for.

Reed Hayes unintentionally took up space in whatever room he stepped into. It was a trait I dreamed of inheriting from him when I stepped into the role of CEO.

Our table was small and near the front with just enough seats for the family. Alex and Bella took up one side, while Mom and Dad took another, leaving Maci and me with our backs to the rest of the room. I was grateful for the arrangement, as it let me drown out the noise for a little while. It was like having a family dinner at our house in Charlotte, only everyone was dressed in suits and formal gowns.

Conversation flowed comfortably around the table. Alex and Bella provided a few stories about the girls, and my parents took turns asking Maci questions that weren't too invasive. They asked about her job and if she liked Chicago. I paid attention to how Maci responded, whether her shoulders tensed or her hands searched for something to fidget with as she got too antsy. Nothing indicated that I should suggest getting another drink from the bar. She wasn't looking for an escape, and when she noticed me staring at her too long, she rested her hand on the back of my neck, dragging her nails in a relaxing motion against my skin.

Maci chuckled, and I realized I had missed my mom's comment.

"And if the pots and pans are too much, Maci, I can have them shipped back," Mom added. "I went back and forth about sending them, but I got such a good deal!"

"Please don't make me send them back," Maci begged, laughing along with my parents. "I'm sure Jaxon made my cooking skills sound worse than they were."

I shook my head. "I've never said anything bad about your cooking. Your lasagna, your chicken parm—"

Maci smacked my forearm before I could continue with the endless list of dishes she'd attempted over the years. They always ended the same way, with me requesting seconds no matter how the food turned out, and me thanking her by using my mouth in an entirely different way.

She held my gaze, enticing me with the slight glimmer in her eyes. She lowered her voice so only I could hear her, "You'll make the lasagna."

And you'll help the kids with their English homework.

I remembered exactly what I said to her back in her college apartment. But instead, I repeated my part of the promise back to her, "I'll make the lasagna."

Chapter Fifty-Seven

JAXON

January 2022

Nothing ever prepared me for speaking in front of a crowd. Most people liked knowing their audience and even encouraged their friends and family to attend. It had the opposite effect on me. Knowing my parents, Alex, Bella, and now Maci were in the room, I second-guessed everything I had tried to memorize. It was a quick two-paragraph thank-you, but my brain convinced me that the fate of the world rested in whatever words I was about to say.

I stood at the podium, my fingers wrapped tightly around the microphone as I mindlessly repeated the speech I prepared last week. I'd rehearsed it so many times, it almost felt like I wasn't speaking at all. It was like arriving at a destination after you'd zoned out during the drive. You didn't know how you got yourself there, but you trusted your body to do the work.

"Thank you for your endless support and the love that you've shown to me and my family," I emphasized, looking over at my parents. "I'm honored to be standing on this stage, and I'm excited to see what we accomplish this year. Enjoy your night, grab a drink, make sure you do some dancing, and thank you for being part of Hayes Sports and Entertainment."

When the room erupted into applause, that was my cue to return to my table. Maci reached for my hand when I got close enough. Her cheeks were flushed, and her eyes had a slight shine to them from the lights that dimmed above us. She looked . . . *proud* of me.

"You did great," she said, her voice catching near the end. She rubbed her hand up and down my bicep, and I grabbed it before she could snatch it away.

I kissed her fingers, holding her gaze as the sound of a piano played softly in the background. People swarmed the dance floor behind her, drawing her focus to the couples joining hands in the middle of the room.

"Dance with me, pretty girl," I said over the music.

She didn't fight me; instead, she followed my lead, resting her arms around my neck as my hands found her hips. The silkiness of her dress prompted my hands closer to her ass, until I remembered where we were and adjusted my grip.

"Nice save," she teased.

"I can't help myself," I admitted. Fuck, I missed the way she looked at me when I had my arms around her. "It's like I'm back in that kitchen."

Maci cocked her head, urging me to continue.

"Spring break in Port Clinton. You were dancing next to the stove, singing some country song I didn't know at the time, only now I do, because it makes me think of you—it's even on your playlist."

My rambling made her chuckle, but when her smile tapered, I knew the memory entered her headspace.

"As much as I wanted to—no matter how natural it felt to me—I couldn't touch you. I couldn't kiss you or pull you close because of a decision I made. I had to pretend."

That drew her eyes back to me. That word she left me with the night of Friendsgiving. I knew she remembered some of our conversation. It didn't occur to me until now just how much.

The music transitioned into a song I recognized right away.

"One more song?" I prompted.

Her mouth curved into a playful grin. "Only if you can tell me the name of it."

"Fair enough. 'Beautiful Crazy' by Luke Combs." I drew her closer to me, reveling in my correct answer.

She was impressed. "You know a country song?"

I rested my forehead on hers and whispered, "I listened to a lot of country songs after I ended things."

Maci's mouth was inches away from mine. With her lips parted slightly, it was hard to keep my composure. If I leaned in just a little, I could kiss her—kiss her in front of everyone in this room and not give a fuck about who saw or who captured it.

Everything around us was a blur, and when her tongue teased the center of her bottom lip, I almost missed it when she asked, "How long do we have to stay?"

An exasperated laugh escaped my chest. "My parts over, sweetheart. You say the word, and I'm yours for the rest of the evening."

"Good." Her eyes glistened with a newfound excitement. "Can you take me home?"

***

The back seat of the limo wasn't big enough. We were hands and skin and kisses and everywhere all at the same time. As soon as the divider went up to separate us from the driver, she straddled me, spreading her legs and pushing against the erection that was fighting against my dress pants. Her hands were in my hair, tilting my head so she had the perfect angle to trail her lips down my jawline and tease my neck. When she bit into my collarbone, I almost begged to take her right there in the limo.

"Mace," I pleaded, but not wanting her to stop.

"Touch me," she demanded.

With a mischievous grin, she rocked her hips. I groaned, throwing my head back against the seat so I could steady myself. I was not about to lose it when we were only ten minutes away from the house. She was punishing me in the best way that she knew how. She was right there with only a few layers of clothing separating her sweet pussy from my cock. And I couldn't have her. Not yet.

Fuck, I wasn't even sure if she'd *let me* have her.

My fingers cupped her ass, digging into the flesh as if my life depended on it. Her soft moans were warm on my neck, and she kissed me again—eager and hungry and—

The pull in my groin subsided when I realized we pulled into the parking lot of my apartment. I reached for the door handle, shifting Maci off my lap so she could adjust her dress. The driver was no idiot, and when I yelled a thank you through the window and handed him a tip, his suggestive grin solidified that assumption.

Maci grabbed my hand so she could shove me into the elevator. I backed her up against the wall, not bothering to wait until the doors closed behind us to continue what we started in the limo. My hands slipped under her dress, teasing the apex of her thighs until my thumb found her clit. She was slick and wet, and I couldn't wait any longer. I thrust two fingers inside her, kissing and nipping the sensitive skin behind her ear. She arched her back, pulling at my hair and grinding her hips.

The elevator dinged, and we didn't stop. I picked her up and walked us down the hallway. Without looking down, I typed in my lock code, pushing open the door of my apartment and shutting it behind us.

Chapter Fifty-Eight

MACI

January 2022

"Jaxon," I pleaded, his name falling from my lips for the third time since we reached his bedroom. We hadn't even made it to the bed, both of us tangled up with one another in the doorframe.

Fuck, I wanted him.

Fuck, what was I *doing*?

Jaxon was in front of me, with half the buttons on his shirt already undone. His pants fell halfway down his thighs. My dress bunched around my hips, my bare pussy free and exposed to his empty living room.

We were passed logic. What I needed now was to fuck.

"Jaxon," I said, repeating his name more sternly.

A cocky grin settled deep into his dimple. He planted another soft kiss on my lips, his hand tugging gently at the curls near the nape of my neck. "What do you need, baby? Talk to me."

I needed a lot of things. So many things, actually. But right now, I could only think of one thing that would allow me to clear my head.

"Can we pretend?" I prompted.

Jaxon's smile tapered. He pulled back, putting significantly more space between us. "It won't be pretend. Not for me."

Alarm bells rang loudly in my head. Not the feelings. I couldn't do the feelings. I was still taking this one step at a time.

"I've waited three years to have you again, Mace. I couldn't pretend even if I wanted to."

There was a tenderness in his dark green eyes that hadn't been there before. This was more than just physical for him. We meant something, and I had a feeling we always would.

"Okay." I reached for him, and he leaned in closer so I could kiss him. "No pretending."

As if those words triggered something inside him, Jaxon cupped my face, backing me up until my legs hit what I assumed was his mattress. It felt like I was in foreign lands, navigating territory that seemed forbidden to those who spent so much time away. Why couldn't we have done this in his living room? A bedroom was so personal.

But wasn't that what this was? What *we* were? Personal.

Jaxon slowed the tempo of our kiss, working his way up the bed as he crawled over me. With strong hands on either side of my face, I was trapped, wrapped up in him like I had been all those years ago. Using his knee, he spread my legs wider, allowing himself to work the angle and tease my clit.

I gasped, the friction igniting what he left me with in the elevator. My body responded immediately, my hips bucking at the familiar rhythm of his fingers.

"You tell me to stop, I stop." He lifted his head, leaving my lips swollen and begging for more. "Understand?"

I nodded.

"Mace." His voice was demanding and delicious—exactly how I remembered it when he wanted to be in control.

"I understand," I stated, whimpering as he pulled back his fingers.

Jaxon worked the clasp at the back of my neck as he said, "That's my girl."

The top of my dress fell forward at the waist, leaving me completely exposed. Jaxon paused, taking a moment to let his eyes dance down my bare chest. They lingered, taking their time as if they were memorizing a new landscape. He'd mapped it all before, but with the time that passed between us, I imagined it looked a little different.

I'd gone up a jean size since college, and softer skin covered my once-toned abdomen. My hips were wider, and my thighs were fuller. I'd never felt self-conscious before about my body. I loved my body. But this was the first man I'd been naked in front of who had an older version to compare it to.

"You're fucking beautiful, Mace," Jaxon said with a boyish grin. He stripped off his shirt and stepped out of his pants. "Fucking perfect."

Before I knew it, he tossed my dress to the side along with his boxer briefs. His mouth was on mine, eager and hungry as he backed me up to the headboard.

I trailed my fingers down his chest, following the lines of his V until my hand wrapped around his cock. A groan vibrated in the back of his throat, the sound egging me on as I gripped him harder. His warm, silky skin felt like heaven in my hand. I wanted nothing more than to feel him—all of him. His hands cupped my hips. My breasts. My face. Until he broke our kiss and forced me to look at him, drawing in heavy breaths as he met me with a pleading gaze.

"I don't expect anything," he said, his voice almost a whisper. "This can be enough."

The thought of stopping made my heart race in the most devastating way. The words flew from my mouth before I could stop them. "I want you." I leaned forward and kissed him, tugging on his bottom lip with my teeth. "Now."

Jaxon reached behind him. There was some ruffling, and he muttered something before he presented a condom between us. The gold glint of the foil taunted me as he opened the package, his hand disappearing under the blankets so he could put it on.

He rolled on top of me, his elbows pinning me to the mattress as he lowered himself between my legs.

"You say stop, I stop," he reminded me, his mouth millimeters from mine.

"Yeah," I breathed, lifting my head so I could kiss him.

There was no wanting to stop. That thought never crossed my mind. When Jaxon eased himself inside me, he set my world on fire. It was a delicious burn, left over from a flame that never went out. With every thrust, he fed it, stoking it until it consumed me whole.

I threaded my fingers through his hair, pulling him closer, needing to feel his weight on top of me to assure me that this was real. *He* was real, and he was mine.

"Fuck, I missed you," he murmured against my lips. "You feel so good, baby."

The pressure began to build in my core, my sighs turning to whimpers as Jaxon bucked his hips harder and hit the sweet spot between my thighs.

I groaned, my nails digging into his back. "Don't stop," I begged. "Fuck—"

The fire exploded, corrupting everything and everyone who came before or after it. My body shook, struggling to ground itself as Jaxon chased his release. I screamed his name before his mouth crashed into mine, slowly guiding me back down to earth. There was a tenderness to Jaxon's touch that wasn't there before. Hungry kisses were replaced with soft and patient lips, embracing the moment for as long as we could before reality checked us in place again.

There were no more words. We'd said everything we could tonight. I didn't go across the hall to the guestroom, and I didn't crave my space. Jaxon left my side so he could return with a towel and some clothes for me to sleep in.

I chose not to get dressed, snuggling into him as close as I could. Skin on skin, he wrapped his arms around me, planting kisses in my hair while he pressed me against his chest.

"Good night, pretty girl," Jaxon whispered, lulling me to sleep with the warmth of his touch and the sound of his heartbeat.

Chapter Fifty-Nine

MACI

January 2022

A change of scenery was warranted after the weekend I had with Jaxon. Hell, a change of scenery was *necessary* if I was going to make it through the next few days without falling victim to my draining method of overthinking. Every time I sat down in the kitchen to try to get some lesson planning done, I was reminded of him. I figured I'd be safe in my bedroom, but he'd left his mark there, too.

He was everywhere, and I hated how much I loved that feeling.

Stepping into Katie's living room felt like a breath of fresh air. Smells of cinnamon and coffee enveloped me in a comforting hug. The TV was loud and Max was singing a song that I didn't recognize. It was the complete opposite of my quaint, quiet home.

Katie eyed me from across the counter as she filled her travel mug with coffee. "You're early."

I stretched my legs, sinking into the back of my barstool. "I missed you guys."

With an accusatory glance, she challenged me to come up with a better reason.

A low chuckle stumbled out of my mouth. "Why are you looking at me like that?"

"Because it's Tuesday."

I cocked my head. "So . . ."

"Well, every Tuesday I get an update." Her voice climbed a few octaves. "You're like a podcast episode I don't have to download." She sipped her coffee. "So what happened this week?"

My smile tapered. "I slept with him."

Katie almost spat her hot drink across the counter. "What?"

"After the gala," I admitted weakly.

"Oh my god!"

Max squealed from the living room, mimicking the sounds coming from the kitchen.

I looked over my shoulder and murmured, "My thoughts exactly."

"Talk it out," Katie prompted, gesturing to me with her hand. "What's in your head?"

Fuck if I knew. I'd been trying to figure that out since Monday morning when I boarded the plane back to Chicago. Everything about being with him felt right. It felt natural. But did it feel safe? It would never be what it was between us. Too much had happened and too much had changed.

Jaxon made a choice three years ago. Was I supposed to just forget about how easily he tossed me aside?

"I'm an idiot, Katie," I said, lowering my voice. Suddenly, I was ashamed of Max hearing me admit defeat. "I honestly don't have an excuse other than that."

Katie looked at me with kind eyes and a patient smile. "Maybe you don't need an excuse. I hate to say this to you, but do you think—"

"Then don't say it," I begged.

She ignored my plea. "Do you still love him?"

The dreaded question. I sucked my teeth. "Love is a strong word."

Katie smirked. "Is it, though? This isn't a new match we're striking. The flame was already lit."

The hopeless romantic side of her made it sound so simple.

"What is the endgame here, Katie?" I spat, letting my hands fall to the counter. "This is no different than last time."

"I could argue that Jaxon's here and not across the country."

"Yeah, he's here *now*." I heard myself growing more frustrated the longer this topic went on. It was a horrible habit I had with things that I didn't want to talk about. "This will run its course."

Katie tapped her nails on the counter, the clickity rhythm threatening to toss me off the edge. Between the TV, Max's song, and the fresh gel manicure in front of me, I was incredibly overstimulated.

I was also anxious because I didn't know what to do. My emotional and logical arguments weren't lining up, and no matter what I decided or how I moved forward, someone would get hurt.

A scene from *Sex and the City* entered my head. "Remember when Big comes back from Paris and Carrie throws the McDonald's?"

Katie smiled reassuringly. "This is not the same thing."

"Just call me fucking Carrie," I teased, lolling my head in her direction. "She walks right into getting herself hurt again, and I might as well be holding her hand.

"Let's stop with the dramatics, please. Other than the obvious, what is stopping you?"

Ah, yes. The one thing I wouldn't let Jaxon talk about when he tried.

"The why," I stated. "*Why* did he do it? Part of me doesn't want to know. I have guesses, but—"

"And that's all they will be until you have that conversation," Katie said, as if I were one of her young patients trying to refuse medical advice. "If you had to rate it, though . . ." She widened her gaze, begging me not to make her ask out loud in front of her son.

I sighed. "It exceeded all of my expectations."

"I love this for you." Katie threw her arms out to the side. "I love this for *us*. I'm starting a new career path and throwing my medical degree out the window, and you're reuniting with the man who broke your heart."

"We're basically poster children for the next generation," I joked.

Katie kissed Max on the top of his head. "I'll be back soon. Practice your questioning on Max. He's a tough critic."

I met the toddler's eyes as he placed another block on his tower. The final piece touched the top, and the entire structure came tumbling down. While his listening skills might have been questionable, he somehow put into words what I was most afraid of.

After all the work I'd done to build myself up, would Jaxon Hayes be the reason I came tumbling down again?

Chapter Sixty

MACI

February 2022

The last week of January went by fast. The new semester tossed me out on my ass, questioning my ability to shift lessons and merge material to adjust for snow days. Cold weather had already cancelled two of our sessions. I wasn't opposed to working from home, but it was hard to get a handle on a schedule when it kept changing.

I couldn't be the teacher who assigned work on snow days. Regardless of whether they were adults, I wouldn't rob them of that natural high. I considered it an early Valentine's Day surprise.

No in-person class? No homework. Enjoy the day and recover from whatever battles you were fighting behind closed doors. Or maybe it was just me with my hands on a sword. I was the one who managed to avoid being alone in a room with my ex-boyfriend after we slept together, yet somehow agreed to hang out on Valentine's Day.

It had been almost a month since the gala, and we'd managed to act like nothing happened. There were small touches and occasional comments, but for the most part, we were both driven to keep the tension high. If we didn't speak about that weekend, we could hide it from the rest of the world. Something about keeping it a secret made it much more exciting.

It also excused us from talking about it.

When the doorbell rang, my heart dropped to my stomach. To avoid overthinking my outfit, I settled on leggings and a cropped hoodie. We were two friends staying in and hiding from the cold. It just happened to be Valentine's Day, and Jaxon just happened to be holding flowers when I opened the door.

"Jaxon . . ." I shot him a warning glance and snatched the flowers from his hand.

He smirked at my aggressive greeting. "Don't make it weird. It's just flowers."

"On Valentine's Day," I argued, leading us into the kitchen. Whatever he was hiding in the takeout bags smelled spicy. Was it garlic? The aroma made my stomach growl.

While I dug out the only vase I owned from the back of the pantry, Jaxon stood with his back to me, trying to keep as much of the table from my view as possible. The gesture made me giggle, and heat rushed to my cheeks.

Goddamnit, Maci. Get it together.

He looked over his shoulder, unable to hide the excitement on his face as he added the final touches to the table. I continued arranging the flowers aimlessly, buying him more time. I couldn't rob him of whatever he was about to hit me with.

Jaxon moved to the side so I could take in his delivery. It was a replica of our Valentine's Day from 2016. We were two college kids sharing cheap beer and wings, both of us unaware of how things would end. Yet here we were, using that memory as a crutch to try to begin again.

A platter of wings sat in the center of the table, surrounded by various dipping sauces. He filled two tall glasses from Carl's Corner with beer, and giant red takeout baskets took the place of plates. There was no cutlery, but the stack of wet wipes made it clear that we wouldn't need those.

Jaxon pulled out a chair and gestured for me to sit down. When I didn't move from the other side of the counter, his smile faltered. "Is this too much?"

Tears sprang to my eyes. "No. It's not too much."

It was suddenly hot in here, too hot for my arms to have goosebumps. My heart pounded in my chest, sending a high-pitched ringing to my ears that made me lightheaded. The explosion was barreling toward Jaxon, and before I had any time to prep the battlefield, it ignited between us.

"Why did you do it?" I prompted softly.

"Why did I—" Jaxon's eyes danced between me and the food. "Why did I do what?"

"Why did you do it?" I repeated angrily. "*It.* Not the food. Not the flowers." Pain resurfaced in my chest as he registered what I was talking about. I needed him to say something—*anything*—that would segue us into this conversation. Years' worth of tears threatened to spill out if I uttered another word.

"It's not that simple, Mace," he whispered.

"I gave you *everything*, every single part of me." The pain in my chest subsided with every syllable, yearning for me to keep going, writing all of the words I had wanted to say since he hung up the phone that night. I was yelling now, unable to bottle myself back up after I permitted myself to combust. "I *loved* you. I would have followed you anywhere you wanted to go. I would have waited for you. *Why did you do it?*"

"It's not that simple, Mace," Jaxon pleaded with a pained expression. His green eyes were glossy, almost desperate, like he would lose it if I kept going.

"I would've forgiven you for how you ended it. I would've gone back to you." I shook my head, and a few tears slipped down my cheeks. "Why did you say you loved me if you were just going to throw it all away?"

Jaxon took a few steps toward me, and I stepped back. If he touched me, everything I built to keep him out would collapse.

I drew in a staggering breath. "You cut me off like I was nothing. You gave up on us. You gave up on *me.*"

He dragged a hand down his face, wiping his tears away as he tried to regain his composure.

I needed to see him hurt. I needed him to feel the pain he left me with.

"You completely destroyed me." I struggled to get the words out. "I loved you, and you broke my heart. You *cannot* come back into my life and do this to me again, Jaxon. I *cannot* do this again."

He searched for any signs of weakness in my confession, weaknesses that would invite him to come and touch me. To say he was sorry. To say he loved me. But if that happened, he would ruin me. He would destroy me all over again.

"You need to leave," I demanded. "You can't be here."

Jaxon rested his hands behind his head. My feet stayed planted on the floor; the only confirmation of his movement was the front door opening and closing behind him.

At least, I thought it was behind him. Before I could register what just happened, heavy footsteps brought him back into the kitchen.

Jaxon was out of breath, his eyes zeroed in on me from the other side of the counter. His nostrils flared, anger permeating through him at an alarming rate. He kept his voice steady, making it clear that his rage wasn't directed toward me. "I couldn't let you choose me when I wouldn't have chosen you. It wasn't fair. I was too consumed with everything else, and you didn't deserve it. Look at everything you've done—"

"So I'm supposed to thank you for all of my accomplishments?" I asked through a condescending laugh.

"What?" he spat. "No!"

His anger fueled mine, unknowingly pulling me closer as I tried to decipher his answers. "I'm supposed to be *grateful* that you ended it because I might not be where I am today?"

"I didn't want to be a reason why everything you deserved didn't work out. You were making room for me, and I was taking advantage of the space. I didn't want you waiting for me, Mace."

"I knew—I *know* how much your work means to you." My voice began to climb, and there was no turning back. "But I wanted you to put me first. I wanted you to choose me."

Jaxon's mouth formed a hard line, a sign that I should recoil and let him explain. Instead, I kept pushing.

"You expect me to see you as the good guy because you chose for me instead of choosing me? You did it because you're selfish."

"I did it because I love you!" he yelled, pushing against the counter so he could gain some space. He ran his hands through his hair, craving movement as he worked through whatever was going on in his head. His shoulders tensed, and the heat drained from my cheeks.

Suddenly, I was cold. The word hit me just like it did in November—just like it did the first time he said it after Alex and Bella's wedding.

Love. Present tense, still in the room with us, *love.*

We locked eyes, tempting me toward him.

"Ending things with you—" A breathy laugh fell from his lips, and he shook his head. "It had nothing to do with not loving you."

I hung on his words, pleading with him to continue. I thought my heart was going to fumble onto the floor. I'd waited so long for an answer, but I never imagined it would cause him so much pain to deliver it.

His voice was softer now, but it didn't lack the urgency. "I looked for you in everyone I met. In every partner and every friend. I listened for your laugh in a room full of people, just hoping to catch a glimpse of you, even though I knew you weren't there. I never found what you gave me in anyone else. I never stopped looking for you. I never *stopped* loving you."

I hadn't realized Jaxon closed the space between us. He tucked my hair behind my ears, his thumbs grazing my jawline as he tilted my head so I could look at him.

His eyes pleaded with me to consider what he was about to say next. "I missed you, Mace."

"No," I said weakly. "You're not allowed to say that. You can't just choose me now because you didn't back then—"

"I chose you over everything else the moment I let you go. I couldn't have given you all this." He gestured to the space around us. "Look at my life, Mace. Look at yours!"

"And everything I felt for you, it was just supposed to go away when you ended things?"

He raised a brow. "Has it?"

No, I screamed. *Kiss me, now, before I change my mind.*

Chapter Sixty-One

Jaxon

February 2022

Silence hung between us, and I never knew it could be so heavy. The answer sat in her eyes, but I had to hear it. I had to know that there was still something there for me that she wasn't saying.

I leaned closer, brushing my lips against hers. "Tell me to stop."

Her mouth parted as I slipped my hands around her waist. "Maci—"

"Stop talking," she muttered before she crashed into me, coaxing my tongue into her mouth, and slipping her fingers into my hair as she pulled me closer. Eager and wanting, we were both gasping for breath as I tried to get a word in.

"Bedroom?"

"Couch." She slid her hands under my shirt and kissed me again. I let her back me into the living room, guiding me to the couch before she pushed me down onto the cushion.

I gasped, struggling to pick up my jaw from the floor.

Maci pinned me there with a heated gaze. "I'll be right back," she promised before she ran upstairs. When she returned, she was in a red lacey bra and matching panties. I barely noticed the condom she tossed on my lap.

I guided her hips closer, immediately letting my hands glide along the fabric. I ran my fingers under the hem, cupping her ass and kneading my thumbs into her flesh. The curves on this girl made my mouth water, and I sent up a thank you to any higher power that had anything to do with placing me here.

A satisfied groan fell from her parted lips. It was all I needed to make up my mind on what to do next. I tossed the condom on the end table and spread my legs.

She eyed the gold foil. "What are you doing?"

"If you're gonna be mine again, I'm gonna take my time." I kicked off my jeans and took my cock in my hands. I stroked myself, chuckling in defeat when her tongue grazed her bottom lip. Fuck, she was gorgeous, and I was completely gone.

"Don't do that," she threatened playfully, unclipping her bra and letting it fall to the floor. Her bare chest taunted me as she kept her distance. I ran my free hand through my hair to avoid pulling her on top of me.

I swallowed, struggling to keep my voice steady. If I weren't careful, I'd make myself come right in front of her. "Do what?"

"Call me yours"—she stepped out of her panties and knelt between my legs—"and act like you mean it."

I tipped up her chin with my finger so I could hold her gaze. "You're a little pissed at me, aren't you?"

She ran her hands up and down my thighs. "Just a tad."

My jaw went slack. "You're gonna tease me, aren't you?"

"Just a tad," she repeated, her mouth hovering over the head of my cock. I tightened my grip on her throat as she took me into her mouth.

"That's my girl," I murmured proudly, throwing my head back as her tongue swirled around my shaft. "Fuck, baby."

Without warning, she took me all the way in, letting me hit the back of her throat as I matched her rhythm. When I heard her gag, I hesitated, but she urged me to keep going, using her hand to stroke whatever couldn't fit in her mouth. She groaned, the vibration from the back of her throat threatening to push me over the edge.

Her eyes flickered up to mine when she noticed me staring, and I brushed my fingers down her jawline.

"You look so fucking beautiful with my cock in your mouth," I growled, slowly rolling my hips. She sucked harder, and before I could tell her I was close to coming, she rose slowly, letting me drop from her mouth.

Maci licked her lips, satisfied with the taste. "Fuck me," she said, half panting, half pleading. "Show me I'm yours."

I wasn't sure if the taunting was only to get what she wanted, but I didn't care. In that moment, I would've done anything she asked me to. I gripped her hips, pulling her on top of me and kissing her, my tongue sweeping her mouth as I plunged two fingers inside of her. Wet and ready—so ready that I had to remind myself that the condom was still sitting on the end table.

"You want me to show you?" I teased, reaching for the condom.

Maci snatched it from me so I wouldn't pull my hand back. She tore open the foil packet and rolled it on, all while grinding her hips and teasing my erection.

"Come for me, pretty girl." I gripped the back of her neck, holding her in place as I swiped my thumb across her clit. "Come for me, and then I'll fuck you."

Her sighs turned to whimpers as she shuddered against me, pushing against my arm as she tried to arch her back. I kept her steady, teasing the soft spot inside her that I knew would cause her to lose control.

"You're mine, you hear me?" I growled, tugging on her earlobe with my teeth. "Say it."

"I'm yours." She groaned, and I let her throw her head back. Her walls clenched around my fingers, squeezing them as she found her release. Her orgasm dripped down her thighs and coated my hand.

Fuck me.

I kissed her again, harder as I lined myself up with her entrance. Before I could ease myself inside her, she spread her legs and sank on top of me. We exchanged a groan, pausing so she could adjust to the position. She rocked her hips, and I kissed her slowly as she took me all the way in, grinding against me in a motion that let me know I was hitting her sweet spot.

"You always have been," I said in between soft kisses. She was letting me talk to her, and I took advantage of the space. "Fuck, I missed you, Mace."

"I missed you, too," she whispered.

Maci slowed our rhythm, and I followed her lead. I kept waiting for her to speed up, to beg me to go harder so I could fuck her the way she wanted me to. But the pleading never came. She let me shower her in soft kisses and gentle touches until she was moaning into my mouth, calling my name, and pulling me against her as she shuddered into my chest.

Chapter Sixty-Two

JAXON

February 2022

No matter how many times I tried to stay focused at the workshop, all I could think about was Maci. Her mouth, her body, the way she felt on my lap when she rode my cock. She'd completely corrupted my ability to focus on anything else but her.

My mind revolved around the girl that my heart never gave up on three years ago. She was the constant, and I loved it. She made me feel like I was home.

Over time, without me ever realizing it, that's what Chicago became to me. Home. I never saw myself coming to the Midwest and getting sick over the thought of leaving. Yet, here I was, unable to get through the rest of an email because one date kept taunting me through the computer screen.

March 31st.

"Jaxon?" My dad's voice boomed throughout Jared's office.

I thought Bryson was going to fall out of his desk chair. He'd had a late evening last night, keeping Elle preoccupied from the madness she was dealing with at work. While I was grateful for the hospitality, he really needed to consider getting a place with thicker walls.

"Yeah?" I asked, running a tired hand through my hair.

At the same time, I'd spent half the night talking with Maci on the phone, learning all about the next set of lectures she'd been preparing for her courses this semester. It didn't matter if she was talking to me about her job, the weather, or reading to me from the dictionary. As long as she felt that I was worthy of her time, I'd listen to everything and anything she had to say.

"Boy, you're really about to make me repeat myself again, aren't you?" Dad threatened with a hefty chuckle. "Why do you look like that? Are you sick?"

Bryson cackled from his chair, and I rolled my eyes.

"Long night," I stated. "Just repeat your last sentence."

Another screen appeared in the video chat, and my mom's eager smile took up a corner of the window. "Hi, baby!"

I battled harder against the exhaustion and forced a smile. "Hey, Ma."

After Christmas, Mom decided to stay in Charlotte while my dad took weekend trips out to California. I offered to be the one to hop on a plane, but he insisted. While it was good for me to be here right now, it was also good for my dad to be there. My mom was starting to do events again for her business, and she was back in the kitchen.

Change didn't have to be a negative thing, but it was hard to get your brain to believe that after you'd conditioned it to feel safe with specific outcomes.

"The email," Dad said before my mom could get another word in. "Did you get the email?"

"Yes, I got the email."

My eyes avoided it like the plague as it stayed put in the center of my screen. March 31st marked the end of quarter one and marked the start of the time of year when most of my traveling would begin. This conversation was a long time coming, and I knew what question my dad was putting off.

"Have you thought about what you're going to do?" Dad prompted gently. "I don't need an answer now, but the board will want to know who will be leading—"

"I know," I unintentionally snapped. "I'll be there for the meeting."

Even through video chat, I felt the weight of his gaze. "You can take more time, J."

"I have a few things I wanna discuss with the board," I noted. The truth was, I'd been working on a few items in the background since November. I was just waiting on a few loose ends before I presented the entire product.

"Is anyone there with you?" Mom craned her neck as if she could turn my monitor.

I shifted the camera so Bryson could wave. His smile lifted to the corners of his eyes, and before he could say something, I turned the camera back to me.

"Guys, I gotta go," I lied. "A customer just walked in." I shot a warning glance to Bryson so he could read the room. Mom was the last to hang up, and I waited until she left the chat before I closed my laptop.

"You good?" Bryson asked, resting his feet on the desk.

I nodded. An uncomfortable pot of guilt, shame, and frustration simmered on my chest.

"Why the imaginary customer?" he prompted.

I didn't answer him. He'd heard enough to know what the conversation with my dad was about. Still, he gave me the chance to explain from my perspective, and when I continued to choose silence, he answered with an exaggerated sigh.

Bryson lolled his head in my direction. "Look, uhm—" He dragged his hand over his mouth, irritated that he even had to have this conversation. He chose his following words carefully, making them sound more like a warning than advice. "You don't get to do this to her again."

Since nothing was certain yet, I couldn't reassure him that it wasn't even an option. I had no right.

"I know," I stated plainly. "I don't plan to."

Chapter Sixty-Three

MACI

March 2022

I knew it was stupid. I knew it was a bad idea. I just wanted Jaxon to love me one more time—one more time before he shattered me again.

It was pathetic. But I called myself pathetic the next morning when the hurt sank in. We did the flirty late-night phone calls, the movie marathons, and all the little things we used to do back when we fell for each other. It was easy then. There was no choppy past to work around or future to worry about when it came to timelines.

Whether I wanted to accept it or not, Jaxon would have to go back. He'd return to the life he left behind before Jared was killed. Before Spencer moved to New York, and before Katie was halfway through her first semester in culinary school.

I knew it would end. I knew it would fucking hurt. And for that, I was stupid.

I scrubbed harder at the dark green non-stick pan that had come in Evelyn's gift set. My breakfast this morning flipped flawlessly, and it was hard to sit in my feelings when I'd just inhaled the most perfect mountain of chocolate chip pancakes.

The reason for my indecisive emotions was about to arrive at any minute. Last night, Jaxon asked if he could come over for a "work brunch."

A *fucking* work brunch—where we made coffee and hung out in a comfortable silence. It was the perfect introverted activity, and he'd become my favorite person to do it with.

The sound of chimes echoed around the house, and I yelled for Jaxon to come in. If there was anything that ruined the aura of a work brunch, it was a sink full of dirty dishes. I had a few more left until the kitchen was clear of any evidence that someone lived here.

"Hey," Jaxon said, placing his laptop on the table. He leaned over the counter to kiss me. His lips were soft and all over mine, and when he tried to push his tongue past my teeth, I backed away.

His eyes narrowed, but I recognized the pattern. The eager greeting, the cocky grin, the grey sweatpants—

I blew a frustrated breath from my nose. "Just tell me."

His smile faltered, but he didn't argue. There were parts of him I still knew—parts of him that I hated knowing. My hands began to tingle. In a few moments, my arms would feel numb, and the ringing would start in my ears. It was my classic fight or flight mode, and right now, I was panicking in between.

His voice was barely above a whisper when he said, "I have to go back."

"When do you leave?"

He studied me, making note of any twitch in my expression or new line in my face. "March twenty-fifth."

Only I didn't give him any. Not this time. "The day after your birthday."

"It won't be forever." He slowly rounded the counter. "I will come back—"

I moved before his hands could run down my arms. My reaction sent soap suds into the air as the pan dropped into the sink. Droplets of water splashed onto the floor around us.

I placed my hands on my hips. "When?"

His silence triggered something in me that I didn't even know was there.

"*When?*" I demanded, unwilling to look away from him. I didn't want this to be easy. I didn't want him to have an out.

"Soon." He meant it as a promise, but I heard it as a lie. I'd spent too much time in a world where Jaxon Hayes was the CEO of Hayes Sports and Entertainment. I knew what the role required of him. There was no way this ended differently from last time. The only difference was that I walked right into the flames, knowing I would get burned.

I *asked* for it. I was okay with it. Everything was fine until Jaxon threw the endgame in my face. It wouldn't break me this time.

Instead of proposing an argument or hinting at disbelief, I gave him a small smile. He helped me clean up the kitchen before we sat down in the living room. He worked on spreadsheets while I typed up notes for this week's lecture. He'd stroke my thigh with his hand as he thought through numbers in his head, and I would trail my fingers across the back of his neck while I scrolled through old lessons.

Sex and the City played in the background, and as I fought the pressure building behind my eyes, there was one phrase I couldn't get out of my head.

Call me Carrie, I thought, willing the words to settle into a space where I wouldn't have to hear them for a while.

Chapter Sixty-Four

JAXON

March 2022

There was one day from my childhood that I would never forget. Regardless of how much time had gone by, I remembered the day of my adoption like it was yesterday. There was a judge, and we dressed up for court. Evelyn cried most of the time, keeping her tears to herself so I wouldn't think she was sad. Reed stood proudly beside me, squeezing my shoulders every few minutes. Back then, I thought it was to keep me calm. I learned later that it was because he didn't know how to handle his excitement.

My dad and I still shared this trait, unable to handle anxious energy that came with excitement or nerves. It was the reason I paced around my desk all afternoon. If there were permanent markings on the floor when Robert Arlidge, our company's top investor, arrived to see me, I wouldn't be surprised.

Dad's skeptical gaze followed me throughout my mindless wandering, until he finally said, "J, you're making *me* nervous, and I'm not the one asking for more money."

"He could back out," I blurted.

"He won't."

I turned to face him. "But he *could*."

"And he won't," Dad assured me, placing a steady hand on my shoulder. "Rob might say no, but he won't back out."

I spent most of last night picturing Robert Arlidge looking me in the eye and telling me that he was pulling his funding. People would lose jobs, and contracts would fall through. All I could hear was Helen pleading with me not to let her go. It was a very dramatized version of what could happen, but my imagination didn't care. My mind loved to twist shit, so I prepared for the worst; that way, if it actually happened, I couldn't be surprised.

Gotta love a good trauma response.

The phone on my desk rang, and I knew it was Helen. Robert was here.

Dad nudged me toward the phone. "I'll be right here, but you won't need me. You know what you're doing, J. You're the boss now."

I gave a quick nod before I answered. "Hello?"

"You ready?" Helen asked.

Her cheerful grin on the other line shifted the weight on my chest. "Yeah. I'm ready."

Robert Arlidge was the definition of a man who could rock a salt-and-pepper look. Even in his sixties, he'd managed smooth skin, bright eyes, and a smile that still made him seem young at heart. His voice took up space when he entered the room, but not in an intimidating way. It boomed with purpose, inviting everyone and everything to step into his inner circle.

"It's good to see you with that skyline in the background," Robert said, offering me his hand. "Glad to have you back, Jaxon."

"I appreciate that," I said. "Thank you for coming."

After Robert and my dad shook hands, I gestured for them to have a seat. While I sat on one side of the desk—my Jared

Foster Original—they sat on the other, and I reminded myself of who I was.

I was the fucking CEO of Hayes Sports and Entertainment. I had no reason to be nervous. "A few years back, I mentioned opening another branch for the company."

"The East Coast branch." Robert smiled proudly, as if he already knew what was coming next. "I think with Reed heading back to Charlotte permanently now that you're back, it sounds like a perfect transition."

Three years ago, I would've been elated with that answer. I never imagined I'd be changing the narrative on a story I sold Robert before my mom got sick.

"I'd like to change the location," I stated. "To the Midwest."

Robert scowled. "The Midwest?"

Dad chuckled, earning him a few laughs from Robert.

When he didn't pick up any indication that I was joking, Robert shot me a sideways glance. "And I suppose there is more?"

Butterflies erupted in my stomach, and I stifled a grin. "I'll be running Hayes Sports and Entertainment from that location."

Robert's eyebrows shot to the top of his forehead, revealing wrinkles I didn't even know he had. "As in . . . you won't be in California?" He looked at my dad, then back at me. "You're the face of the company."

"And I can travel here when needed," I explained. "Robert, I spent most of 2020 working from my apartment. Do you remember our numbers for that year?"

Robert gave a slight nod. "Better than 2019."

"Better than 2019," I echoed proudly. "I'm not stepping down. I'm only asking for your continued support when you receive an email that states that I'm living in Chicago."

"And let me guess." Robert leaned forward. "That girl from the gala lives in Chicago?"

To my surprise, he wasn't mocking me. In fact, the slight upward turn of his smile said the opposite.

"She does," I confirmed, "and I made her wait too fucking long for me to go to her."

Robert leaned back in his chair. "Sounds like you've already made up your mind."

"Most of the Big Ten schools are in the Midwest." I mimicked his posture. "Think of all of that opportunity to invite prospects to my office in person. And since I won't be in *this* office, there is no reason for us to have it."

"And what exactly does that mean for everyone on the other side of this wall? The money we put in here just goes to your new office, and people don't have jobs?"

I knew how ridiculous I was about to sound to a man who kept his wallet under lock and key. "The people who work here—people who have stuck by my family ever since my dad started this company—will have the option to work from home or relocate to a new office."

"To the Midwest."

I shrugged. "Or the East Coast."

Robert dragged his hands down his face. "So no California, but Chicago, and what, I'm assuming Charlotte?"

I shrugged again. "The cost of what we're paying for our office here would equate to two others in those locations. But, I wouldn't want to use all of that money for those renovations."

Robert's jaw was practically on the floor.

"I want a monthly donation from our proceeds to go to various organizations that are fighting for gun reform. I had Helen print out a list this morning so we can reach out to the organizers." I placed the list on my desk and slid it toward Robert. "What brought me to Chicago in the first place was my friend, Jared Foster, who was shot and killed during a school shooting."

Robert scanned the document with a curious gaze.

"We claim to help people achieve their dreams—to take giant steps toward their goals as if other things aren't going on in the world around us." I tapped the list with my finger. "*This* is important. This is the shit that matters. And I want our clients to know more about the values of who they are choosing to sign with. Family has always been one of them. That's why my dad will oversee the office in Charlotte."

Dad's easygoing grin was the cherry on top of the conversation. There was some paperwork and additional commentary to ensure that I had the details in order. Still, after a few signatures and a drink to celebrate, Robert Arlidge said, "Enjoy the snow in Chicago."

Chapter Sixty-Five

MACI

It was the Monday after Easter, arguably the worst day of the week for college students. Fortunately for me, my lectures on Mondays were in the afternoon, so I wasn't a total buzzkill when students greeted me for a lecture on the ADDIE model. Analysis, design, development, implementation, and evaluation were exactly what everyone wanted to chat about after a holiday. At least, that's what I told myself when they were all staring at me with blank faces and tired eyes. It was precisely how I felt when I fell into my office chair a few hours later, eager to call it a day and aching to curl up on my couch with some ramen and a comfort TV show.

My eyes fell on the bamboo plant in the corner of my desk. The greenery was a gift from Jared. He reassured me that I couldn't kill it and that every new office needed a plant to look official. I remembered how excited he was to give it to me. He was so proud when I told him that I got the job at the university, and he was the first person to call me that night to ask how my first day went.

Tears sprang to my eyes. Fuck, grief was weird. It showed up when we least expected it and took hold of everything around us.

My phone vibrated in my bag, and as much as I wished that it were Katie or Spencer, I knew who it was. It was Jaxon, and he was adding to the endless stream of text messages that I wasn't replying to. I had nothing to say.

Please come back.

I miss you.

Fuck, I still love you?

None of those options was helping. I wasn't doing that again—waiting for Jaxon to want me in his life as much as I wanted him.

Ever since my parents divorced, I've never been sure whether I'm meant to be happy. I was convinced that I was better off as a side character who supported her friends in their endeavors as they found their way.

I gave a promising opinion on Spencer's apartment before she signed the lease in New York. I encouraged Bryson to see things through with Elle, arguing that she was the only person who could ever deal with him in the way I failed to in college. I applauded Katie for being brave enough to follow her passions and planned to be in the audience when she graduated from culinary school.

When my plans with Jaxon fell through, it taught me something. It was easier to be in the background—to focus on myself without requiring too much of the people who were living their own lives.

I uncapped my water bottle and poured a steady stream into the bamboo plant's basin. It coated the rocks, trickling down to the bottom and settling into the soil. The sun was starting to shine again, so I moved it to the window for some much-needed light. It would be fine overnight, and when I returned tomorrow morning, I'd rotate it back to my desk, where it belonged.

I gathered up my things and turned off the light, humming Redbone's "Come and Get Your Love" until I got to my car.

Chapter Sixty-Six

JAXON

April 2022

One month. It had been one month since I had seen or heard from Maci, and I was driving myself crazy with my theories.

She was seeing someone else. She blocked my number. She was screenshotting all my text messages and sharing them with Katie and Spencer to get feedback. Nothing was off limits. Part of me even wondered if she decided to keep her house after I worked on it.

Maybe she followed Spencer to New York City. Perhaps she wasn't the only one who needed a change after everything that had happened.

My Jeep arrived in Chicago a few hours before I did, along with a moving truck that housed most of my apartment. While I had plans for my office space, I had no idea where I would unpack. I used Bryson's address as the drop-off point, and he didn't look surprised to see me when he walked downstairs to head to the office.

"I can honestly say I'm happy to see you." He eyed the moving truck and shot me a cocky grin. "We'll find a place for it."

"Were you not happy to see me all those other times?" I spun my keys around my finger, toying with them as the movers worked to unhitch my Jeep.

He patted my shoulder as he crossed the parking lot. "You nervous?"

"Should I be?"

Bryson hesitated near his car door. "Honestly? I'm not sure. Good luck to you, though." He gave me a supportive honk before taking off down the road.

His answer left an unsettling pit in my stomach. There was a very real chance that Maci wouldn't take me back. She'd slam the door in my face and make me feel like an idiot for shifting my life halfway across the country. At least it wouldn't be a total loss if she denied me. Sure, I'd never find happiness with another human being, but at least I'd have Bryson and Connor back in my life.

Maci would claim Katie. Spencer wouldn't be around enough to have to pick a side.

"You're all set, man!" One of the movers patted the top of my Jeep and gave me a nod.

I thanked him not only for getting everything here safely, but also for keeping me from mentally dividing my friends as if Maci had already given me an answer.

My confidence must have climbed as I turned down Maci's street, because instead of parking on the curb like I intended to, I decided to take up the last spot in her driveway. There was no going back. This was it. The words were still working themselves out in my head, but I trusted that they would surface when it mattered.

Taking a deep breath, I cut the engine. In about thirty seconds, her camera would alert her that someone had stepped in front of her door. I rang the doorbell, running a nervous hand through my hair and tapping anxiously against the side of my jeans.

Maci answered the door, looking me up and down as if she was surprised to see me. Fuck, I missed her. Even with the tiny angry scowl that settled into her brow, she looked gorgeous. Her hair was down, slightly curling over her shoulders in a way that told me she'd recently gotten out of the shower.

"What are you doing here?" she demanded softly.

As much as I wanted to take a step forward, my feet stayed planted on her floral welcome mat. "You didn't leave me much of a choice," I joked. "You won't answer my calls or my texts, and I refused to let an entire month go by without us speaking."

"Technically, tomorrow will be one month."

My smile grew. "You kept track?"

She crossed her arms in front of her chest. "Your birthday made it easy. Don't think too much into it."

I chuckled, dragging a hand over my mouth so I wouldn't pull her into my chest and kiss her. She hadn't given me the green light yet, and I still hadn't asked for it. "I'm back, Mace."

Her expression didn't change. "For how long?"

"For good," I assured her.

Part of me expected tears. The other part of me braced for a slap in the face. The silence was unbearable.

Since I was anxious and impatient, I muttered, "Still nothing, huh? I'll say it if you need me to."

"And what is that?"

"That I know I fucked up." I took a small step forward. "That I know I'm three years too late."

"Jaxon—"

"But I've always been yours, pretty girl. I will spend the rest of my life making sure you know that. Please be mine, Mace. Be with me—"

"I can't do this right now." Maci spun on her heels and walked into the kitchen. I wasn't sure if it was the most brilliant move on my part, but I panicked. I followed her inside, keeping a small distance between us as she took safety behind the counter.

"Do you still love me?" I blurted.

She looked over her shoulder, meeting me with flushed cheeks and bright eyes. Suddenly, I couldn't catch my breath. I wasn't sure which one of us was more surprised by that question.

Her mouth parted slightly, and neither of us could look away. We were locked in, both of us waiting for the other to say something. *Anything* that would break the tension that ignited as soon as we locked eyes over brownies on the kitchen floor.

I repeated the question, slower this time, so it didn't seem like I was yelling at her. "Do you still love me?"

"I don't know," she said quickly.

"When you picture your life five years from now, is it me who's in it?" I prompted. She let me within arm's length, and I decided to keep pushing. I raised my hands, allowing her to strike them down before I cupped her face, stroking a few tears from her cheekbones. "Marriage, babies, everything we talked about when we were together . . . is it still me?"

She blinked a few times, drawing in a shaky breath. I knew she was trying to remain guarded for as long as she could, refusing to touch me back. All the time she spent trying to keep me out reminded her to think about this. I was competing with a version of myself that hurt her, one that I handed her over the phone while I was on the other side of the country.

I'd broken promises, and I'd broken her heart. I'd never stop hating myself for it.

"I love you, Maci," I stressed, pressing my forehead to hers. "I never stopped loving you. If it isn't me that you see, then I'll walk away. Just tell me what you want, baby."

"Stop!" she screamed, wiggling out of my grasp. She turned her back to me and let her head fall into her hands.

Everything inside me wanted to go to her, to tell her it was okay and hold her until she was calm enough to talk to me. While this moment propelled me forward, the last three years held me back. They wouldn't let me reach out because I was the cause of everything in the first place.

I opened my mouth to speak, but nothing came. I'd said it all—leaving nothing but apologies, regrets, and broken promises between us. There was nothing else I could say to try to fix this.

And maybe that's how it was supposed to be.

Chapter Sixty-Seven

MACI

April 2022

I heard the door, but I knew the moment he turned and left the room. It was a slight pull to my chest, an indication that Jaxon Hayes was missing from my personal space.

The dialogue in my head was incessant, and it wasn't long before I was hearing everyone else's voices over my own. There were too many tabs open—too many conversations going on while I tried to focus on the argument that mattered most.

"Do you still love me?"

I'd lied right to his face. Did I still love him? Of course I did. I spent the last three years willing myself to fall out of love with the man I pictured as my final destination.

Endgame, Jared's voice raised above all the others.

Maybe the path wasn't perfect. Our journey wasn't the one most people chose once they thought they'd found their person. But no matter how much I tried to deny it, Jaxon Hayes was mine. He'd always been mine, and I'd always been his.

I sprinted to the front door, not bothering to close it behind me when I stepped onto the porch. Jaxon lingered near his Jeep, waiting to see what I did next before he chose to act.

More tears unwillingly fell from the corners of my eyes. I'd never been so happy to see that goddamn Jeep in my entire life. "It's always you," I whimpered.

Relief washed over him as he ran to me.

I struggled to catch my breath. "It's always you that I see, and I hate you for it."

"Yeah," Jaxon said, pulling me into his arms. "I hate me for it too."

Jaxon leaned down and kissed me, slow at first, inviting himself in before he was consuming and there all at once. I tugged at the hair at the nape of his neck, warning him that he wasn't going anywhere else today but here. My teeth nipped his bottom lip, and right as I was about to suck, he murmured, "Marry me."

That halted everything: every voice, every passing car—even the throbbing between my legs.

I blinked. "What?"

He smiled, kissing me softly again before he said, "You heard me right. Marry me."

"We don't even know what this is yet—"

"Then tell me no," he challenged, his heated gaze threatening to rob me of my willpower.

Words, Maci. Say the word.

No. *No.*

But I couldn't say it. Even the thought of it tasted wrong in my mouth. When I pictured Jaxon asking me this question, that wasn't the word that came to mind. There was no hesitation or questioning it.

"I'm not the hookup type, Maci Lawson." Jaxon ran his hands over my hips. "I'm on the endgame track. I know what I want. I know *who* I want, and if you let me, I'd love to be your husband."

I feared that my mouth was watering. Just in case, I snapped it closed and shook my head. "It's not that simple."

"It is," Jaxon pressed. "Marry me, Mace."

I wasn't striking a new match. The flame was already lit. The heat rose into my chest until the desire was so unbearable, I couldn't keep fighting against the word I really wanted to say.

"Yes," I whispered, neither one of us believing it.

With a quick quirk of his lip, he said, "Yes, what? Please say it. I won't believe it's real unless you say it."

I took his face in my hands, chuckling as more tears streamed down my face. A montage of memories played across his dark green eyes.

A Cotton Candy Blizzard. A journalism class. My oil change on College Drive. Our first kiss. Waking up next to him. Port Clinton. His face when I told him I loved him. One Tree Hill. The Red Bullet. His brother's wedding. Hearing that he loved me for the first time.

A counter kiss. Ramen noodles.

Mine.

He didn't rush me; in fact, it was the opposite.

"Yes, I will marry you."

And before I could mutter anything else, he kissed me again.

EPILOGUE

JAXON

JUNE 2023

Every weekend, I had the same routine—gym, shower, wedding ring, and coffee. I'd start my Saturday at the dining room table with my calendar pulled up on the laptop. Light would hit parts of the dark green paint that could probably use another coat. The countertop usually displayed evidence of our dinner from the night before, and the shoes near the front door made it look like five people lived here.

Only it wasn't five at all. It was just us, and this home was *ours*.

There were moments when I missed having a city skyline outside my window, but over time, the view of our quiet and charming neighborhood became exactly what I wanted to wake up to. I had unashamedly fallen into the pattern of a suburban husband, and nothing made me happier than listening to my wife getting ready upstairs. There was always a song blasting from our bathroom, and her footsteps were loud. My office at the new branch was quieter, but nothing beat the moment when Maci joined me in the kitchen and greeted me with a kiss.

"Morning," I murmured against her mouth. I admired how her leggings hugged her ass when she turned around for coffee. The sight almost distracted me from my next question. "Any news?"

She spun on her heels slowly, meeting me with a curious gaze. "Nope."

I rolled my eyes, earning me a giggle from her gorgeous mouth as she slid into the seat beside me. I took her hand in mine, pulling it closer so I could brush my lips along her fingers. She tried not to smile as I eyed her over her knuckles, willing her to give me something other than a stagnant, "Nope."

The sun bounced off her wedding ring as she placed her mug on the table. "It's only been a day."

"And you won't test?" I challenged, lowering her hand to the table. I sucked my teeth, daring her to verbalize a reason for her silent torture. "You're as regular as they come, Mace."

She laughed. "And how would you know?"

"I've been planning getaways and dates around it since college." I stood so I could wrap my arms around her shoulders, letting my words hit the sensitive spot on her neck. "Let's just say I know your body pretty damn well."

Maci shuddered, brushing me off in an effort to regain her focus. "I told you I wanted a dog."

"Yeah," I spat, earning me another laugh. "You even told my *mother* you wanted a dog."

"Evelyn thought it was funny."

Of course, my mom thought it was funny. Maci captured her attention the moment they met. Maci was the girl who stole my heart and the first person my mom watched me fall in love with.

"Don't bring Evelyn into this," I warned her playfully. "I offered to go to the shelter that day, and you didn't want to."

"Because getting a dog is a big deal!"

"And this isn't!?" I exclaimed, extending my hand over the counter.

Maci smothered another laugh with her hand. I hated how much I loved watching her enjoy this—fucking with me since I was at the mercy of her choices. She rested her head on her shoulder, her mouth curving into a sleepy smile that could only be turned up by another cup of coffee. I gestured for her to hand me her cup.

She leaned across the counter to slide me her mug, her mouth landing a few inches from mine. Her voice was soft, almost as if she were afraid to say the wrong thing. "We said we'd wait."

It wasn't disappointment that I heard. It was fear, and she was scared. It seemed like only yesterday that we were getting married on a beautiful fall afternoon in September. Our friends and families were there, and the wedding was small. It was the perfect day that led into the perfect night, when I reminded Maci, over and over again, how much it turned me on to call her my *wife*.

Our wedding night was also the first time we threw any family planning out the window. While we weren't in a rush to step into parenthood, we didn't see any logic in trying to prevent something we both wanted anyway. Maci wanted kids, and so did I. I hadn't realized how much until I watched Maci become an aunt to Evie and Peyton. It came so naturally to her, loving tiny humans who were reflections of Alex and Bella. It was impossible not to picture her with ours.

I'd never forget the look on Maci's face when I offered the idea of turning our third bedroom into a nursery. I'd also never forget her telling me how much she'd always wanted a dog. It became a running joke for us—getting a dog. Honestly, if a dog were what completed our family, I'd be okay with that. Only somewhere in between all our joking and lack of planning, we forgot that all of our newlywed fucking might actually result in something else.

I relaxed my shoulders, ignoring the feral beating of my heart as I caressed her cheek with my hand. "I'm afraid there's no going back now, pretty girl."

An adorable pink flushed her cheeks. "We haven't even been married a year."

Married. Sometimes the word still sounded surreal.

"Why do I feel like I'm on *Teen Mom*?" She shook her head. "I'm in my twenties. I have a house and a good job and—"

"You're my wife," I added gently, reaching for her hand out of habit.

Heat ignited behind her glossy blue eyes. "Don't do that."

"Do what?"

She rounded the counter and slipped her arms around my neck. "Call me your *wife* and expect me not to want you."

I took her face in my hands and kissed her, making it clear that, regardless of her eager tongue, she wasn't flirting her way out of this conversation. It was hard not to get distracted. There was a chance that the woman who I loved more than anything in the world was carrying my child—*our* child.

I pressed my forehead to hers and held her gaze. "We won't know anything until you want to know anything, okay?"

Maci exhaled slowly, drawing back a few steps to clear her head. "Okay."

"I have a few more contracts I have to send out to vendors, but did you wanna get lunch before we head downtown?"

That perked her up. It was almost as if she forgot about Spencer's book signing. Our friend had officially dived into the world of paranormal romance, and I wasn't going to act like I knew what that all meant. Vampires were doing it while trying to avenge the fall of their species, and that was enough to snag my attention.

"Katie wanted to meet us at Brooks Books at one. Do you think we'll have enough time?"

I stifled a grin, unable to ignore the way she nervously played with her hands behind her back. "We can make the time."

Maci glanced up at the microwave. "Could we leave by eleven?"

"Eleven," I promised. She was already pivoting toward the stairs when I added, "I love you, Maci Hayes."

She got two steps up before she halted, letting her chest fall against the railing so she could look at me. "I love you, too."

***

Brooks Books was a bookstore in downtown Chicago, nestled among restaurants, coffee shops, and other local businesses that thrived amid the city's hustle and bustle. It was owned by two fellow Bowling Green State University graduates. When they found out Spencer was a local author who also graduated from BGSU, they practically dragged her in for an author signing.

"Spencer's, like, famous," Katie exclaimed, noting the line of eager readers forming behind the VIP section. Spencer requested a small sitting area for her friends and family on the outskirts of the crowd. "Look at all these people!"

"Who knew so many girls liked books with fangs, blood, and dicks," Bryson murmured. Since he still hadn't mastered the art of whispering, we all turned our heads to see Elle deliver a soft smack to his bicep.

"Only you could make that all sound so disgusting," Maci snapped, sending Katie into a fit of laughter.

I chuckled too, running a nervous hand through my hair since I couldn't keep still. My leg bounced all through lunch, and the inside of my mouth was begging for me to stop chewing. I couldn't help it. I dug my grave the moment I told Maci we could wait, and I might as well lower myself down now. My mind was running in circles around the idea that I could be okay without knowing, bouncing between images of deciding on a nursery theme or how we'd tell our parents.

"Just checking in!" An eager brunette stepped between our tables, her green eyes piercing right through the mental block I was struggling to get over. "I wanted to introduce myself and see if anyone needed anything. A water or lemonade, maybe? My name is Lyla Brooks, and I'm the owner."

"Your store is absolutely adorable," Katie said, taking the reins on the introductions. "The rose garlands along the ceiling might be my favorite part of the decor."

Lyla shrugged, sending her soft curls over her shoulders. "I actually can't take credit for that. My husband has a thing for roses." She turned and pointed to the register near the front of the store. "That's him with our son, Dominic. They help me navigate this craziness."

I didn't have to hear the connection to know that it was a father and son. Dominic was a mini version of the man who was helping him sort through coins in the register.

"Before Spencer gets started, did anyone want a water or something?" Lyla prompted again.

Maci steadied my bouncing leg. "Did I hear you mention lemonade?"

Lyla smiled. "I'll bring out a pitcher and some water. Thank you so much again for coming."

"She looks familiar," Bryson noted once Lyla disappeared into the back.

"Spencer said the owners went to BG," Connor said.

Elle rolled her eyes toward Bryson. "Did you sleep with her?"

Bryson gasped, drawing the wandering eyes of some people around us. He looked like a deer in headlights. "No!"

We laughed as they fell into a playful banter. A few minutes after Lyla brought out some drinks, Spencer stepped out from behind a curtain, embracing the applause that followed throughout the store. Lyla came over the microphone, introducing Spencer and encouraging people to come forward so they could start the signing. While readers readied their novels, Spencer did a quick jog over to our tables, where she exchanged a round of hugs and a few tears.

"I'm so proud of you," Maci gushed. "I know Jared is loving how he gets to read about vampire sex."

Spencer chuckled softly as she wiped away a tear. "You think he gets to read it?"

"Jared was probably reading over your shoulder as you wrote it," I assured her, pulling her into my chest. "You're amazing, Foster."

For the next hour, we watched Spencer indulge in the aftermath of her hard work. She signed copies of her book, posed for photos, and gave away various items available only at an in-store signing. I had no idea how much work went into the behind-the-scenes process, but Spencer somehow made it look like this had been her tenth event this afternoon.

She was a natural at embracing the creative journey. Her new chapter in New York City had reflected on her, pulling out parts that had gotten lost in Chicago.

Parts of Jared still lingered, and there were times when the pain resurfaced. But for the most part, the traces felt like a glimmering memory. They flowed whimsically through gatherings, friends, and items he left behind.

The desk in my office.

The home I shared with Maci.

The smile on Spencer's face when another round of applause declared the end of her first successful book signing. We all parted ways, offering our final congratulations to Spencer and promising to see her in August for our next Fostering Safety Fundraiser, the organization that Hayes Sports and Entertainment funded in honor of Jared. While my name was on the donor list, I couldn't take the credit. It was Spencer and Helen who made the event as big as it was, spreading awareness about gun reform and school safety procedures in a world that refused to take accountability.

It was a way to promote change—to give a voice to those who couldn't speak because they were no longer here.

"I think I wanna do something," Maci said as we crossed into our neighborhood. "Is there a Dairy Queen around here?"

I furrowed my brow, unable to formulate a good reason as to why she wanted that information. "Uhm, I don't know? We can look?"

"I think I want to test."

That admission almost made me slam to a stop in the middle of the intersection. I looked from the road to her and then back again. "You *think*? Are you sure?"

Maci shrugged, a soft chuckle falling from her gorgeous mouth. "If I am, I am, right? And if you keep bouncing your leg like that, you'll need another pair of shoes."

I smirked, letting her laugh even harder at the dig. She reached into her purse, and my eyes drifted to the hot pink packaging. I had no idea how long she'd been walking around with a pregnancy test in her dark floral-print bag, but I didn't care. The only thing that stood in my way was the traffic light in front of us that refused to turn green.

"Let's take a right up here," she instructed. "There's a Dairy Queen a few streets over."

My jaw went slack. "You want to find out if we are having a baby in a *Dairy Queen*?"

"It's a bathroom!" she protested, shoving the test back into her purse. "What difference does it make?"

I laughed. "But why Dairy Queen?"

Maci rolled her eyes, her bright blue gaze saying everything that she didn't need to. I knew exactly why she chose a Dairy Queen. It was where we first met. It was where everything we were began.

"Plus, I don't know how I'll feel about the result," she argued, her voice drifting into a whisper. "If it's a positive test, we'll get Cotton Candy. If it's negative, we'll get Oreo, deal?"

I stared back at her, reaching for her hand as I gently asked, "You want it to be positive?"

The small quirk of her lip gave me my answer. "What makes you say that?"

"The day I met you." I parked the car under the giant red sign and sat back in my seat. "You walked in for Cotton Candy. You only ordered Oreo because they were out."

She leaned over the gearshift and pulled my forehead to hers. "Let's go see if they're out?"

I chuckled, planting a soft kiss on her lips before we headed inside. As Maci closed the restroom door behind her, I paced around the tables in the dining room, looking like a madman forming figure eights on the floor. I created an unsteady beat with my hands against my legs, trying to find something to focus on other than what was happening on the other side of the wall.

What if it *were* positive? I'd be a father.

Would I be good at it? Of course, I'd be decent. I had the greatest man in the world raise me as his own. I had Alex and Connor, who would raise their own kids alongside me. I had Evelyn Hayes, who would drop everything to come and help us if we needed it. Her last three clear scans eliminated any doubts we had about her traveling, and it was the one argument I had no problem losing.

I had Maci, the only woman in the world I even saw this part of my life with. She'd handle the English homework, and I'd cook the lasagna. We'd talked about it. We'd had a plan.

We'd be okay.

Maci stepped out of the bathroom with her hands behind her back. With glossy eyes, she tried her best not to smile. I knew it was her nerves. She'd promised not to look. But as she crossed the room, my stomach began a never-ending cycle of somersaults. Regardless of what this test said, everything would change.

Maci held the test between us with a shaky hand. I pictured this moment—I tortured myself with it when I was living in California. This life that I almost gave up. This love that I tried to live without.

Even through my blurred vision, I knew what it said. I pulled Maci in for a hug, cradling her head in my chest as she pressed herself against me. When her tears subsided, I took her face in my hands. Until this moment, I was convinced that neither of us really knew what we wanted. We didn't have the words. But when Maci led me to the counter, I prepared myself to speak since I knew she couldn't.

Sometimes, it was the smallest moments that changed our lives the most. The impulsive decisions and the calls we almost didn't make. The sparks we fed and the chances we took.

Eight years ago, I ordered a Cotton Candy Blizzard. In one small moment, I offered the girl with blue eyes the lid of my ice cream, and she promised me a drink at the bar. I had no idea that I had just met my wife—that Maci Lawson would shift my entire world.

I ordered us two Cotton Candy Blizzards, and we ate in the Jeep. We laughed in between bites, both of us embracing the chaotic aftermath that came with processing the last thirty minutes. When she was done with her ice cream, Maci turned on her playlist, singing along as "Unwritten" by Natasha Bedingfield played through the speakers.

"Jared once told me that it's impossible to be sad while listening to this song," Maci insisted with a soft smile. Her face was free of tears, and it took me a second to realize that she was referring to me.

"I'm not sad, baby," I said, brushing my hands across my cheeks. "I'm just . . . fuck, I love you, Mace."

Maci squeezed my hand, waving her arms as the song broke into the chorus. We sang along to the lyrics, embracing the moment and another glimmering memory.

I met the girl. I fell in love. I made her mine.

It really was that simple.

Author's Note

Are you still with me?

You don't hate me for hitting you with a breakup?

I have to admit, I was BEYOND nervous for how this book would land with readers. From the moment that Maci and Jaxon met in that Dairy Queen, I knew that they were going to end with a phone call. It was the way I saw their story going from the beginning, and I could only hope that readers would be open to the concept of a second chance romance.

Life after college is messy and unpredictable. It is full of choices and mistakes, and then, even more mistakes after that. Once they all graduated, new relationships formed while others were lost. Unfortunately, the people we see in our futures don't always follow us there. Sometimes their chapter is cut short—not because of some dramatic falling out or conflict. It starts with one decision:

A breakup over the phone.

A new job.

A new city.

A marriage.

A decision to cut off everyone because you believe it's easier.

And then, if we're lucky enough and it's meant to be, they find their way back to us. Some love stories are linear—survive high school, choose a pathway, meet someone you want to do life with, and then, well, live it! Other love stories are filled with complications and surprises. Disappointments and mistakes. But that doesn't make them any less filled with love.

When Jaxon and Maci come together again in the end, it was important for me to emphasize how happy Jaxon is with his life in Chicago. It wasn't the massive house and lavish lifestyle that he thought he would provide for her. In the end, he chooses the life that Maci built for herself. He embraces a fixer-upper full of charm and character and remnants of an old friend.

There is a scene where Jaxon finds Maci grieving Jared. There are so many moments in romance stories and movies where this scene would've led to some form of physical intimacy. I'm not going to lie . . . I debated it! But then I remembered my own grieving process. How in the darkest times, when you feel so alone, that no one else could possibly understand or hold your hand through it. In that scene, Jaxon lets Maci be emotional. He lets her take off the mask, and *that* is arguably the most powerful form of intimacy we can give to someone.

There are meant to be some loose ends for our Bowling Green gang.

Do Connor and Katie end up having another child?

Do Bryson and Elle make it official?

Does Spencer do MORE signings at Brooks Books?!

Come on, I had to connect my college couples!! Lyla and Deacon being in Chicago was just too tempting *not* to have them all meet.

I think the dangerous part of writing a series is how you'll let it go in the end. I could write five more books about the lives of these characters, but something feels right about leaving it at three. Jaxon and Maci come full circle, and I find a lot of peace knowing that they are happy where I left them. If I'm being honest, I think that's why I went back and forth about writing the third and final book. Typing out this author note means I'm done with the characters that launched my author journey.

If you've made it this far, thank you for reading the final book of The Hookup Series. Thank you for giving these characters a chance, and thank you for following their story.

Thank you to my husband, Noel. You've always believed in me and my books, and I am so lucky to call you my endgame.

Thank you to my friends and family. Dad, I hope you never understand publishing timelines, and always ask me if my next book is available for you to buy before I've even found a cover artist.

Thank you to all of the incredible readers and authors who I have met through social media. You'll never know how much your comments, shares, and messages mean to me. I have found new friends and embraced a community that I feel accepted in, and there are no words to express how much that has done for me as a human, a writer, and a creative.

Thank you to Sadie at Dot The I Edit. I'll always appreciate your comments and your ability to find plot holes and character names I'll randomly drop into chapters. Without you, there would be a random female character in *The Hookup Type*, and Bryson would be known as Byron in a few scenes. Not only are you an amazing editor, but you're a fantastic human and friend.

And lastly, thank you to all of the amazing educators in the classroom. Here's to hoping that we have a change in the future, where our children and their educators can have a safe learning space without preparing for the worst. If you work in a school, my heart is with you. You deserve better. You deserve more. Teaching is one of the most demanding jobs in the world, and I am optimistic that one day we'll have decision makers who know what the fuck they are talking about.

It's the end of where I began, and it is bittersweet in the most delicious way.

Sometimes life goes exactly how we plan it. Other times, the roughest roads bring us back to our endgame.

Find your road. Embrace the journey. Fight for your endgame.

With love,
Brittany

About the Author

Brittany Wilson is an author who writes romantic comedies and contemporary romance. She graduated from Bowling Green State University with a degree in education and the college serves as the setting for many of her books! Brittany has always had a love for writing and a passion for telling stories. Her books are available on all platforms! Make sure to follow Brittany on social media to stay updated on her author journey!

TikTok and Instagram – @brittanywilsonauthor
http://www.brittanywilsonauthor.com

www.ingramcontent.com/pod-product-compliance
Lightning Source LLC
Chambersburg PA
CBHW031958150726
47990CB00005B/1764